JUST SAY YES

While she'd threatened quite a few, there was only one man on the face of the earth whom Rachel had ever contemplated joyfully shooting. And that man now stood in front of her. Elijah Trent.

"Hello, Rachel."

"Good-bye, you no-good piece of—" She tried to shut the door in his face, but he already had his foot in the opening.

There was only one possible reason Elijah was there. Dwight had sent him.

Realizing there was no way she was going to physically keep him out, Rachel released the door and stepped back from the opening. Instead of closing the door behind him, Elijah left it open.

She boldly returned his once-over. He looked good, she admitted. Damn good. Tall, dark, and devious.

BOOK YOUR PLACE ON OUR WEBSITE AND MAKE THE READING CONNECTION!

We've created a customized website just for our very special readers, where you can get the inside scoop on everything that's going on with Zebra, Pinnacle and Kensington books.

When you come online, you'll have the exciting opportunity to:

- View covers of upcoming books

- Read sample chapters

- Learn about our future publishing schedule (listed by publication month *and author*)

- Find out when your favorite authors will be visiting a city near you

- Search for and order backlist books from our online catalog

- Check out author bios and background information

- Send e-mail to your favorite authors

- Meet the Kensington staff online

- Join us in weekly chats with authors, readers and other guests

- Get writing guidelines

- AND MUCH MORE!

**Visit our website at
http://www.kensingtonbooks.com**

LAUREN BACH

PROJECT EVE

ZEBRA BOOKS
KENSINGTON PUBLISHING CORP.
www.kensingtonbooks.com

ZEBRA BOOKS are published by

Kensington Publishing Corp.
850 Third Avenue
New York, NY 10022

All Kensington titles, imprints and distributed lines are available at special quantity discounts for bulk purchases for sales promotion, premiums, fund-raising, educational, or institutional use.

Special book excerpts or customized printing can also be created to fit specific needs. For details, write or phone the office of the Kensington Special Sales Manager: Attn. Special Sales Department. Kensington Publishing Corp., 850 Third Avenue, New York, NY 10022. Phone: 1-800-221-2647.

Zebra and the Z logo Reg. U.S. Pat. & TM Off.

ISBN 0-8217-7632-0

First Printing: June 2005
10 9 8 7 6 5 4 3 2 1

Printed in the United States of America

To Special Friends

To Donna Kramer Wenke—
the memories from our childhood
grow sweeter with age.

And to the 99GHfinalists—
a phenomenal group of writers
who share an unusual bond of sisterhood.
You guys amaze me.

Acknowledgments

Special thanks to:

Karen Kearney—for reading and helping. And more.

Lori Harris—ditto, ditto, ditto. And more.

The Guy Who Can't Be Named—heartfelt appreciation.

PROLOGUE

Lampang, Thailand

The man rubbed himself through his trousers as he watched the video. Off camera, a whip cracked. Once. Twice.

A naked woman, her wrists manacled to a stone wall, writhed when the slender leather braid finally lashed her flesh. She moaned in what appeared to be ecstasy, head rolling gracefully to one side as she glanced over her delicate shoulder and begged for more. Working the camera.

He closed his eyes as she pleaded for more of the punishment being meted out. He stroked harder, perilously close to a climax that had nothing to do with the video. He'd seen movies like this so often he was immune to the violence, to the sex. To the marred beauty of the blond women who populated them.

A different perversion heated his blood: obscene wealth . . . and the influence it gave him over people. Over governments. His enemies had no idea what his true power even was.

He sucked air through clenched teeth, unwilling to allow himself release. It really was all about control.

On the video, the woman had been unchained. As he watched, she crawled across the floor, straight toward the camera, asking for the privilege of performing fellatio, in hopes her punisher would reward her with more of the torture she craved.

For a few seconds, her face filled the screen. It was the face of an angel. *An angel with shattered wings.* He drank in the sight of her dilated eyes, her trembling lips. Lips he knew well. She'd been one of the few he'd actually liked.

Abruptly, the man shut it off. He knew the ending. It wasn't happy. Of course, her death would be edited out. Saved for his growing private collection. This wasn't the first time his men had become carried away. Further proof the drugs had yet to be perfected.

Unfortunately, coming so quickly after the last *incident*, it had meant shutting down production until additional talent could be procured. Which meant another unscheduled delay. And time was money.

Picking up the phone, he punched out a string of numbers. The call was answered on the third ring.

"Do you know what time it is?" a sleep-graveled voice asked.

He didn't bother checking his watch, accustomed to having his desires met regardless of the time. Or the need, for that matter. "I require two replacements. Now."

There was silence as the man on the other end of the line figured out the events that precipitated the call. Then he started swearing.

The caller chose to ignore the tirade, waiting as the other man sorted through his infantile emotions.

"You promised to do better," the other man accused.

He held his temper. For a short time, he still had need for this partnership. And when he didn't . . .

"The men responsible have been rebuked," he said calmly.

"That's not good enough. I warned you that this would happen again if the protocols weren't followed exactly. Let's end it here. Do the best you can with whatever you've got on film."

"We will not end it here! You agreed to continue our arrangement for another sixty days. And I made certain commitments based upon that time frame. I expect you to live up to your word."

"It was also agreed that the stock on hand, and already in your possession, would be sufficient for the remainder of our contract."

In spite of his mood, the man smiled at the phrasing. While they were always careful to disguise their words—for even with precautions, one never knew who was listening—it was an accurate description of these women. Stock. Cattle. Chattel.

He narrowed his eyes and ran a finger back and forth tracing the scar at his temple. He could force compliance with a threat, but in this case it benefited him to prolong their affiliation amiably. So the other man would keep his defenses low.

With practiced ease, he kept his voice friendly.

"I regret that I underestimated the requirements. How soon can I expect another shipment?"

The sound of shuffled papers came over the line. "It will be at least two weeks."

"That's unacceptable."

"Take it or leave it. There are issues beyond my control here."

He cursed, unused to being denied.

A woman had entered as he'd been on the phone. He glared at her. She wasn't the one he'd wanted, but as a vessel for his anger, she'd do.

He snapped his fingers twice. As he watched, she stepped out of her robe and, dropping onto all fours, crawled toward him. As her lips closed around his erection, he shut his eyes.

"Two women, two weeks," he snarled and hung up.

ONE

Richmond, Virginia

"You have to take this job, Rach. *Pleeease.* For me!" Jimmy Parsell, Rachel Anderson's younger cousin, kept his voice whiney and low as he escorted her down a hall to the private office of U.S. Senator Thurston Benjamin IV.

Jimmy looked even more desperate than he sounded, his spiky hair poking out in twelve directions, its bright red color contrasting sharply with Rachel's fairer blond.

She grabbed his fidgeting hands. "I agreed to meet with him. For you. And until I know more, that's all I'll commit to."

It was a small lie. When Jimmy called yesterday, asking for this favor, Rachel had flat-out refused. Then his mom called. Jimmy, the little weasel, knew damn good and well Rachel couldn't say no to Aunt Laura.

Still, there was no way in hell she'd accept this case. She knew from experience that celebrities and public officials were pains in the ass to work for. Every move first had to be weighed for its impact on the client's image, then maximized for publicity.

Worse, if anyone came up with mud on their face, it was always the hired help. And the fact that a U.S. senator needed a private investigator—a discreet private investigator, Jimmy had emphasized—signaled a potential mudslide.

As a courtesy to her aunt, Rachel would listen to the senator, suggest a course of action, then recommend another firm. She planned to be back in Atlanta by ten tonight.

"Before this, the senator didn't even know I was one of his aides." Jimmy turned at the end of the hall. "Now he's hinting that I have a shot at a higher position after graduation. Do you know what a leg up that is?"

"I realize this means a lot, but don't pin your hopes of promotion on me."

"A lot? It means everything!" Jimmy wailed. "Look, the man's had a hellacious year. He lost his daughter and now his wife is seriously ill."

Rachel scowled. "Don't play the sympathy card, Jimmy. I'm not in the mood. I dropped everything to come here and—"

"Shh!" They had reached the senator's office and had to stop talking.

Giving her one last beseeching look, Jimmy straightened the lapels of her suit before adjusting his own tie.

"By the way, I told him you were a Republican," he hissed as he knocked.

If the door hadn't opened just then, Rachel would have decked her cousin. Instead, she gritted her teeth as Senator Benjamin greeted Jimmy enthusiastically.

A distinguished-looking man with piercing blue eyes, the senator was shorter than she expected. Perhaps only an inch taller than her own five-six. And he exuded a sense of energy that belied his age.

He held out a hand. "You must be Rachel. Jimmy's spoken highly of you."

"I could say the same. It's nice to meet you."

Smiling, the senator dismissed Jimmy with a curt nod. Rachel caught a brief glimpse of her cousin's crestfallen face as the door shut. Had he honestly expected to be included in their meeting? The kid had a lot to learn.

Benjamin motioned Rachel toward his desk, an oversized mahogany barge. The matching credenza was loaded with expensive Steuben glass sculptures. One piece, a crystal eagle poised for flight, was spotlighted from above, a fitting symbol of devotion to country.

Rachel recalled what she knew about the man. In his early fifties, Benjamin was in the midst of his fifth term in office. His marriage to an oil heiress made him the second wealthiest member of the Senate. And the second most powerful.

Coincidence? Hardly. Money and power went hand in hand, especially in the Capitol.

"I appreciate your coming on such short notice," the senator said.

"Jimmy mentioned you were preparing to leave with an overseas delegation." While still pissed about the Republican thing, Rachel tried to make certain her cousin got some of the credit.

"The timing for this trip isn't ideal, but it's not

every day we get invited to China to discuss international banking security issues."

Rachel took a chair in front of the desk.

"Coffee? Or perhaps something a bit stronger?" the senator offered.

She settled back. "Not for me."

"I'm afraid caffeine is one of my true vices."

Rachel raised a brow as he turned away. The fact that he needed a discreet investigator suggested it wasn't the only one.

Having poured a cup, Benjamin started to take a seat behind the desk, but at the last minute took the chair across from hers. She recognized the maneuver for what it was—an attempt to lower barriers between them. Which made hers rise.

The whole time, he continued making small talk. Small talk with a point. "Jimmy's a fine young man. He has a bright future here."

"That's good to hear. Of course, I'm prejudiced since we're related."

"Which brings up a delicate point." The senator reached across the desk and slid a single sheet of paper toward her. "Do you mind signing a confidentiality agreement? The matters we'll be discussing are highly personal. None of my staff here or in DC are aware of these issues and I want to keep it that way."

"I have no objection to signing one, though I always treat any disclosures by prospective clients as confidential."

"So I've heard. Your firm's name in the field is sterling."

As confidentiality agreements went, this one was straightforward and blessedly short.

It wasn't the first time Rachel had been asked to

sign one, and as always, it piqued her curiosity. Particularly the subject line: Cindy Benjamin. After scribbling her name, Rachel pushed the sheet and pen back.

The senator looked relieved. "I'll get right to the point. You're aware my stepdaughter, Cindy, died in an automobile accident seven months ago?"

Rachel nodded. The tragic story had garnered headlines. It had been Christmas Eve and Cindy had been on her way home from college when her car plunged down an embankment after being struck by a hit-and-run driver. Twenty-two hours later, she was found. She was estimated to have been alive for ten of those hours.

Was that what this meeting was about? Did Senator Benjamin want what the Virginia Highway Patrol hadn't been able to give him? The person responsible for his stepdaughter's death?

She relaxed slightly, beginning to see the man in a different light. What father wouldn't want justice for his child? She understood the need for answers, for without them, closure was incomplete.

But why the secrecy? Unless there was more to the accident. Something he didn't want publicized. God knew politicians were notoriously paranoid when it came to the press.

"If I remember correctly, the other driver was never found," Rachel said. "Is that what you're seeking?"

"No." The senator glanced away as if gathering his thoughts. "The police have exhausted all leads. It was snowing and dark the night of the accident. Witnesses saw only the taillights of a speeding vehicle. Road conditions were so slippery it wouldn't have taken much to trigger the accident. So it may not even have been a hit-and-run. The other car could have simply passed Cindy, causing her to swerve and lose control. At least that's what the police are now suggesting."

Uncertain what to say, Rachel nodded again and waited for him to continue.

"You're also aware my wife has been diagnosed with leukemia." He cleared his throat. "While we've tried to keep the news releases about her illness positive, the truth is . . ." He glanced down at the cup he held, his mouth tightening. "Well, the truth is she hasn't responded well to treatment."

"I'm sorry," Rachel offered, feeling guilty that she'd misread the senator's actions at the beginning. Perhaps his decision to sit opposite her instead of behind the desk hadn't been calculated.

Looking up, Benjamin nodded and took a sip of coffee. "My wife's doctors have expressed serious concern over her will to live. On top of everything else, she's suffering with deep depression. We, ah, got her diagnosis just two days after Cindy's funeral. Not many people know that at the time of the accident, my wife and I were estranged from Cindy. We hadn't seen her in nearly eighteen months. So her coming home—what we assumed was to be the first step in mending our differences—was a total surprise to us. And it made her loss that much more difficult."

Several questions about why they had been on bad terms came to mind, but Rachel stopped herself from voicing them. No matter how sorry she was for the senator's loss, she wasn't changing her mind. "I can't imagine how difficult that must have been."

The senator grimaced. "Yes, well, in hopes of finding proof that Cindy had indeed had a change of heart, I did something I probably shouldn't have."

He stood, crossed to warm his coffee. "Shortly after her death, I received some of her belongings. The college had done as I asked with her clothes and furniture, donating them to charity, but they had boxed up some of what they viewed as more personal items. I went through them last week for the first time and found a diary. Much of it was what I expected to find. An outpouring of frustration with us. With her professors. With her classmates."

He looked at Rachel. "Even as a child, Cindy was incapable of accepting love. As she grew older, she became more so. Nothing her mother or I did seemed to help. I suppose my chosen life path, the demands of public office played a part."

Rachel sensed he was stalling, mentally justifying his behavior in violating his stepdaughter's privacy. "What else did you find?" she pressed. "In Cindy's journal?"

"That she claimed to be pregnant."

"Claimed?" The senator's choice of words struck her as odd.

"Unfortunately, Cindy occasionally . . ." He paused as if considering his words again. "Let's just say it wouldn't be the first time she'd played with the truth."

"But certainly a pregnancy would have shown up in the autopsy."

He rubbed his forehead. "I'm sorry. I guess I wasn't making myself clear. The entry was made back in February of last year and on the final page of the diary." Frustration cracked his voice. "If she began a new diary after that one, it wasn't in what was sent to us."

Rachel's middle tightened as she recognized the direction the conversation was taking. Given her firm's reputation for finding missing children, she now knew why the senator had wanted her to take the job. "So you want to know if she was pregnant? And, if she was, what became of the baby?"

"If Lenore thought she had a grandchild out there . . ." Again his voice faded. "Well, I think it's about the only thing that will make her continue with treatment." He looked Rachel in the eye. "To be completely truthful, it's not the child that matters so much to me as my wife. I'll do just about anything to keep Lenore alive."

He glanced down at his cup again. "And that's hard for me to admit because if there is a child, the press will have a damn free-for-all with the story. It won't exactly end my career, but it certainly won't put me in the White House either."

As he spoke, Rachel had found herself leaning toward him, but with the last she sat back. For a moment, she had actually started to warm to the man. Until he had revealed his true motive.

Bottom line, the reason he'd chosen Rachel—an outsider on the DC scene—was because he was concerned about his damn political image. Her skill in the field had nothing to do with it.

He was afraid the scandal of having a stepdaughter who had become pregnant out of wedlock and given up the child, before then getting herself killed, might keep his name out of the presidential hat come next election. Which made him just another self-serving politician.

Rachel was suddenly anxious to end the interview, but recognized that because of Jimmy—or rather, her aunt—she needed to be tactful. She'd ask a few more questions and tell him she needed to think over the case. In the morning she'd make a call to the senator, declining.

"You're convinced, solely on this diary entry, that Cindy had a child?" Rachel asked.

"Coupled with the fact we hadn't seen her in so long, yes. And while the diary entry rambled, Cindy mentioned being counseled against abortion, though she seemed to consider adoption an alternative. She was also worried her mother would disown her—which Lenore would never do. My wife would be crushed to know that. In spite of their ups and downs, Lenore truly loved Cindy."

"Have you checked with her boyfriend?"

"She, ah . . . wasn't dating anyone that we know of." His tone held mild censure.

"How about her other friends at college? Do you know who counseled her? And what about her medical records?"

The senator drew a deep breath and briefly held it. "I've done what I could, but there are extenuating circumstances you should be aware of. Cindy had a troubled past that we've worked hard to hide. She had been treated for drug abuse, alcohol, and sexual promiscuity. There were also a couple of incidents where she falsely accused young men of date rape, causing one psychologist to label her a pathological liar. As much as I want to believe for my wife's sake that Cindy might have had a child, I have to remember the entry could have been fabricated."

Rachel gave herself a moment to process all

he'd just said. It was evident Cindy had been a troubled young woman. Their estrangement made more sense now.

"Still, her giving birth should be easy to ascertain. Cindy would have had to deliver somewhere. There are computerized records that can be inconspicuously searched." She stopped herself from saying *hacked*.

Shaking his head, the senator stood and paced toward a window. "Believe me, I thought of that. But searching the records of Shepherd's Cross College is impossible from outside the campus. I don't know if you've heard of it, but Shepherd's Cross is a small divinity college in rural West Virginia, and they brag about how they're Internet free. I understand their parent church had an incident where their database was stolen. Afterward, both the church and campus simply disconnected from the Internet—formed their own network or something. Sounds rather rash to me, but darn if they haven't put a remarkable spin on it. Several other campuses are considering doing the same thing."

Rachel was aware of the incident, as it had made the cover of *Newsweek*. While the college was small and obscure, the church was anything but. Thousands of credit-card holders, mostly elderly, who had ordered videos, CDs, tapes, and books had been ripped off for hundreds of thousands. And the church had reimbursed every dollar.

Subsequently, Shepherd's Cross had for all intents and purposes disconnected from the Internet, allowing a third party to handle Web-site sales. None of their data mainframes had modems, making it a hack-proof system.

Overreaction? Yes. But with their trademark

positive-thinking flair, the college instead boasted that their private intranet was a model of brilliance. Well, brilliant or not, it meant someone had to physically go to the campus to snoop their database.

"Have you considered a back-door approach, contacting someone from the church instead of the college?" she asked.

"I looked into that, but grew even more concerned after hearing about intrachurch adoptions. Apparently couples seeking to adopt have joined Shepherd's Cross Church, made sizeable donations, and been able to adopt shortly thereafter. Of course, the church's legal staff handles everything. For both parties."

The implication chilled Rachel. "Are you saying the church is running a black-market adoption scam?"

The senator vigorously shook his head. "I'm trying very hard not to say that. Are you familiar with the church's founder, William Hanson?"

"I've seen his books, though I haven't read any." Rachel knew William Hanson was a prolific author whose books dominated both the religious and secular best-seller lists. "And who hasn't seen his church on television?"

Everyone with cable had seen Shepherd's Cross's elaborate wall-to-wall-people-filled church at some point in their channel-surfing life. The soaring, pink granite edifice, with its three carillon towers, was enormous and beautiful.

A recent poll had listed the church as the third most recognizable structure in North America. Only the White House and Cinderella's castle had managed to outrank it. Even the Washington Monument had come in a distant fourth.

"Actually," the senator said, "I was referring to Hanson's political connections. The man's been spiritual advisor to three of the last five presidents and has probably baptized half the Republicans on Capitol Hill."

It was Rachel's turn to read between the lines. Obviously, William Hanson was widely revered in DC, as much an icon as his church. Meaning his political clout was probably stronger than Benjamin's.

The senator moved back toward her and sat on the edge of his desk. "I wouldn't dream of accusing Hanson's church without solid proof. Which brings me to the reason I want to hire you, Rachel. I need to know if the diary entry was the truth or a lie, and I need to have it done discreetly."

He clasped his hands in front of him before continuing. "The college virtually shuts down during the summer, while the students volunteer at their missions, but fall classes begin in less than two weeks. I need someone who can pass as a student and enroll at Shepherd's Cross College. A female who will be able to get close to Cindy's girlfriends and teachers without arousing suspicions. Someone skilled at getting into the woodwork, without leaving a trace. It goes without saying that money's no object."

Rachel decided to level with him, end it here and now. "Unfortunately, I have several ongoing cases that I can't ignore. I can, however, put you in touch with another investigator who would be perfect for the job. She's trustworthy and could pass as a student." The woman wasn't as adept as Rachel at getting into computer systems—few PIs were—but she'd manage.

The senator leaned forward slightly. "Jimmy warned me that you're booked solid. So let me add I'm prepared to offer a special bonus."

Frowning, she shook her head. "Money doesn't enter the equation. My word is everything, and I always meet my professional commitments to clients."

"Your brother died in Afghanistan several years ago, didn't he? While working for the CIA?" Silence stretched, grew brittle as the senator walked around his desk and sat. "Jimmy told me his body was not recovered and that the family was never given a satisfactory explanation for his death."

Her pulse became ragged with a mixture of dread and hope as she squeezed the wooden arms of her chair. By *the family*, he meant Rachel. "What are you suggesting?"

"I have some contacts with the State Department. If you take this case, I'll make sure you get the answers you've been looking for."

Intentionally or not, the senator had touched a raw nerve. Rachel's brother had died five years ago while overseas. All they'd found was a tiny bone fragment that matched his DNA. Had blabbermouth Jimmy also told the senator she'd buried an empty coffin because even that precious fragment had been lost?

To this day she had no idea of how her brother died. Oh, she'd heard whispered conjectures, which the Company neither denied nor confirmed. And the little they had told her, she had reason to doubt. All of which simply prolonged her grief.

Now to have a chance to learn what actually happened . . .

"You can access CIA data?" she asked.

"Me? No. But I have well-placed friends who

owe me favors. I can't promise the exact results; however, it would, of course, be in addition to your normal fees."

Rachel swallowed against a swell of bitter disappointment as she forced herself to focus on three words: *I can't promise.* With that, Benjamin had effectively presented a blueprint for failure, a ready excuse. Been there; done that.

But what if it was true? What if he could get answers? Any answers. How could she not take this job, not take the chance?

The senator smiled, as if certain they'd struck a deal. "At least think it over. Thoroughly." He handed her a calling card. "That has my personal cell phone as well as my private home number. Let's talk in the morning."

Rachel took the card and slid it into her pocket without a glance. Whatever she had expected when she'd entered Benjamin's office, it hadn't been this. The senator had, with Jimmy's help, come up with the only thing that might make her consider taking his case.

Benjamin escorted her to the door, then held out his hand. "In some ways we're very much in the same boat."

"How's that?" she asked as they shook hands.

"We both lost people we love. You a brother. Me a daughter and maybe even a grandchild. You of all people must understand just how important it is to have resolution."

She nodded, then realized her hand was still held in the senator's. She withdrew it and raised her chin. "I'll give it some thought."

"That's all I'm asking." He pulled the door open behind her. "We'll discuss it again tomorrow."

Rachel left the senator's office and was escorted back to the lobby by his secretary. Jimmy had left a message that he was tied up in a meeting and would call later.

She crumpled the note. It was probably just as well she didn't see her cousin right now. She'd scalp the little twit.

When she reached her rental car, she peeled off her suit jacket and turned the air conditioner on high. The late-July weather had heat indexes registering above one-ten. The interior of the car felt twenty degrees higher. And still it felt cooler than the inside of her skull as the low throb of headache spiked with the heat.

Damn it, she didn't like being pressured. Into anything.

Pulling onto the expressway, Rachel headed toward her downtown hotel. Since her flight back to Atlanta wasn't until evening, she had arranged a late checkout, which meant she had several hours to kill.

Time to think about the carrot the senator had dangled. Time to repack her emotional baggage. And time for a reality check.

As much as she wanted to believe Senator Benjamin could furnish answers, he was a politician. By definition, that meant he was highly skilled in the art of promising the undeliverable.

Rachel would do almost anything to learn more about how her brother had died. Her mentor and good friend, Chase Scoggs, had suggested that was because Nick's remains had never been recovered and that subconsciously, she hoped her brother was still alive.

She knew better. She'd spent years as a preteen

furtively hoping her parents would turn up alive.
That the bodies found in a tragic motel-room fire
hadn't belonged to them. That their perfect, happy
family hadn't been forever shattered.

But Nick had forced her to accept reality. Their
parents were dead. Just as Nick was.

Some days, the knowledge that she was the only
person left in her family was unbearable. Sure, she
had extended family, but aunts, uncles, and cousins
weren't the same.

As traffic grew heavier, Rachel slowed, her mind
already weighing and discarding ways to get answers for the senator without having it interfere
with her current obligations. And without having
to go to West Virginia and enroll in classes.

She glanced at her reflection. Though she was
twenty-nine, she could still pass herself off as a student on most college campuses. But a divinity college? Where there were probably more virgins per
capita than dishonest politicians in Washington?

The thought made her wince. Chase Scoggs's
cynicism was rubbing off on her, a sure sign she
needed a life.

Rachel's eyes flicked back to the rearview mirror. Two cars behind hers, a black Ford changed
lanes. For the second time. She checked the side
mirrors, unable to get a better view.

She mentally ticked off recent cases. Two perps
came to mind, the most likely one the son of a
mobster. But following her to Richmond didn't
make sense. If he wanted to pay her a visit, he
could do so in Atlanta.

And since she wasn't working here, there was no
reason for her to have picked up a local tail.
Unless the senator was having her followed.

But for what reason?

She changed lanes again, and after several seconds the other car did the same. As it did, another, even less appealing scenario presented itself.

Perhaps the senator hadn't hired whoever was following her. Perhaps the senator himself was under surveillance; whether by friend or foe didn't matter. By default, she had gotten involved. A situation she knew just how to rectify.

As soon as she exited to downtown, she turned right without a signal, then sped ahead and turned right again, brakes squealing as the car in front of her stopped short at a traffic light.

She watched her mirrors as the Ford barreled around the corner and slid to a stop, having no choice but to pull up directly behind her.

Neither the driver nor the man riding shotgun looked like anyone she'd seen before. And given Rachel's near-photographic memory, she'd remember. She made eye contact in the rearview with the driver, letting him know she'd made him.

Rachel knew he'd break off the tail now, which part of her didn't want. At least, not until she knew who they were and why they were following her.

The driver used his cell phone, trying to act nonchalant. Just as nonchalant, Rachel reached over and opened the glove box. She'd stashed her weapon before meeting with the senator.

These days, going anywhere armed was a hassle, but at times like this, it was worth it. She placed her holstered handgun on the seat next to her thigh and loosened the strap.

When the light turned green, she accelerated slowly, hoping the tail car would pass so she could get a tag number. If the man turned off at the corner, she'd double back and try to catch him.

Instead, the Ford went even slower than she did, allowing another car to slip between them.

Rachel circled away from her hotel. Finally she caught a light and sped off ahead of them. But instead of continuing to floor it, she pulled into the closest parking garage in plain view of the Ford. "Come on, boys."

Inside the multilevel garage, she took the first empty slot. She was out of the car almost as soon as the wheels stopped, dashing toward a white Escalade three cars away.

She ducked behind the left rear fender and dropped into a crouch to wait, holding her breath against the exhaust fumes and smog.

A red Miata raced up the incline, windows open and radio blaring. A white van followed, tailed closely by a Corvette. Over a course of minutes, four more cars passed by, none of them the black Ford.

Whoever the tail was, she seemed to have lost them, which made them pretty inept. Maybe they were just media types looking for a story on the senator. Had someone already learned about Cindy? Rachel climbed back into the rental and immediately flicked on the air conditioner.

As she turned the ignition key, she noticed the Corvette and the white van coming back down. *Upper floors must be full.*

"Hurry up," she muttered, dropping the car into reverse, her foot on the brake.

The Corvette sped off, but at the last second, the van's driver gunned the engine and pulled in behind, blocking her car. Shit! Two men jumped out. They were too well dressed for street thugs and moving too fast for press vultures.

As the first man approached, Rachel wrapped her left hand around the door handle, her right reaching for her weapon.

When he leaned down to window level to look at her, she smiled, waiting half a beat before she threw all her weight against the door.

Surprised by the maneuver, the man grunted in pain as he fell to the ground. She leaped over him, keeping both men in her sights.

The second man took one look at her Walther PPK and froze.

"Smart move," Rachel said. She glanced at the first man aware that, though he was down at the moment, he still posed a very real threat. "Keep your hands where I can see them. Who are you and why the hell are you following me?"

The man on the ground groaned and rolled up enough to prop himself against the rear tire. "Tell her."

"Dwight Davis sent us," the second man said.

Rachel didn't know whether to laugh or scream. Dwight Davis was CIA. They'd clashed on several occasions, mostly over her attempts to gain information on her brother. Small, small world.

While they'd had no contact in years, she'd heard Davis had pole-vaulted up the ranks at the Company, but he must have really been up there to pull a stunt like this.

"Tell Dwight he can kiss my ass."

"Tell him yourself." Still rubbing his shoulder, the first man started to reach inside his jacket. Rachel swung her gun toward him.

He paused midmotion. "Just going for my cell phone."

She gave a sharp nod and watched as he pulled the phone out. The guy was decent looking. Clean cut, like most domestic Company guys. She should have known.

He nodded to her gun. "We both know you're not going to shoot, so why don't you put that away before another car comes by. The last thing either of us wants is cops asking questions."

She waited a few seconds before dropping her hand to her side. He was right. Few cops were understanding about civilians brandishing handguns, but why would these two worry about that? Unless Dwight told them not to attract attention.

The man punched in a few numbers, then handed her the phone.

She barely pressed it to her ear before a man answered.

"Davis."

"Your men suggested I tell you personally to go to hell."

"Rachel. Welcome to Richmond. We need to talk."

She glanced at the two men. "So call my office and book an appointment."

"Like I could get past that bulldog you call a secretary."

Rachel made a mental note to give Sheila a raise. "We have nothing to discuss, Dwight. Goodbye."

"Wait! I can help you find information on Cindy Benjamin."

She tightened her grip on the phone. There was

only one way Dwight could know about that. "You've got the senator's office bugged."

"Like I said, we need to talk."

"No, we don't. I'm not taking the senator's job." Her mind hadn't been made up until now.

"Look, I know what the senator promised you. Info on Nick. Trust me, nothing he can get will come close to what I can access."

Irritation climbed Rachel's spine. Dwight was playing games. "Replay your tapes, Einstein. Benjamin promised nothing. He said he'd try. Even Yoda wouldn't accept *try*."

"I can do better."

"Right. That's pretty much what you told me five years ago. I might have believed you then, but even I learn from my mistakes." She glanced at the man on the ground and offered an insincere smile. "So I guess this is good-bye. Hopefully, for the last time."

"I know you have every reason to doubt me, Rachel—"

"Finally. Something we can agree on. Now if you'll just admit what a sleaze you are, we'll have made real progress."

Dwight exhaled noisily into the phone. The fact he had remained on the line while she insulted him was revealing.

"Tell Franklin to give you the envelope," Dwight said.

Exasperated, Rachel looked at the two men, not even sure why she was still standing there. Except that, no matter how much she wanted to tell Dwight to fuck off, she wanted answers about Nick more.

"Which one of you is Franklin?" she snapped.

The one on the ground half raised his right hand.

"It seems you have an envelope for me."

He pulled it from his pocket and held it up.

Rachel took it, pausing to slip her weapon back into the holster on the seat before opening the envelope.

Inside was a black-and-white photograph. The shot was so fuzzy she couldn't make out any features. It was a crowd shot that had been cropped until only one face stood out.

Nick?

She cleared her throat before pressing the phone back to her ear. "The photo is blurred."

"But I've got others that aren't. Now get in the van with my men."

TWO

The cell phone went dead. Rachel tossed it back to Franklin. Both men stared at her as if uncertain what to do next. She knew they couldn't force her to go along. Dwight wasn't *that* stupid.

No, Dwight's style was simply to land a blow, usually below the belt, then retreat. Unfortunately, he'd managed to punch the exact same spot the senator had. Worse, he'd done it on purpose.

And it bothered her that Dwight knew how vulnerable she was, that she'd do almost anything to learn more about her brother's death.

But likewise, it was a clue to just how desperate he was. Which was worrisome, too. Why drag a civilian—particularly *her*—into Company business?

Her cousin had only approached her yesterday morning, so her appearance today at the senator's office had likely come as a surprise to Dwight.

Which meant he was flying by the seat of his pants right now. That explained the sloppy tail. Dwight had no doubt hastily dispatched these men without giving clear instructions.

"Where is Dwight?" she asked the men.

They glanced at each other. Obviously their directive hadn't included what to do if their subject started asking questions.

Franklin, who was back on his feet, shook his head. "I am not at liberty to disclose—"

"Forget it." She moved toward her vehicle.

Without warning, Franklin grasped her shoulder. Rachel reacted instantly, grabbing and pinning him against the car before leveling her gaze with his. She knew the second agent had gone for his pistol, but she ignored him, her eyes locked on Franklin's.

Franklin's pupils enlarged. *Good.* At least now she had his attention—though she knew it had nothing to do with the expression on her face and everything to do with the sensation of having his nuts held firmly in her fist.

"Nice handful, Franklin. If you want to keep them, I suggest you get your hand off my shoulder. Now."

"He's at the Tower Hotel. Suite 1209," Franklin offered as he lowered his arm. When she loosened her hold, he stepped back.

The Tower was a brand-new hotel near the airport, only a short distance north. Knowing they weren't meeting at an out-of-the-way safe house made her relax slightly. "I'll meet you there."

"It would be better if we arrived together."

Rachel couldn't hide a smirk. It made her feel better that they knew she'd lose them. More likely they were only concerned that if they didn't show up together, they'd have a lot of explaining to do. Not that Dwight would be surprised by his men's inability to control her, seeing as he'd never had much success.

She opened her car door with an exaggerated sigh. "Appears chivalry really is dead, isn't it?" Sliding inside, she closed the door. But instead of cranking the engine, she lowered her window and flashed a smile.

"So which one of you wants to catch a ride with me? Save some face?"

After tossing the keys to his partner, Franklin started to drop into the passenger seat.

Rachel shifted into reverse, but kept her foot on the brake. "Leave the hardware with your friend, too."

Franklin hesitated for the briefest of moments, then handed his weapon over as well. The move surprised her. *Damn, Dwight must really want me bad.*

As soon as Franklin was back inside the car, Rachel came down hard on the accelerator. Two seconds later, they emerged from the parking structure and onto a crowded downtown street.

"Christ, lady!" Franklin shook his head. "I bet chivalry took one ride with you and committed suicide."

Sparing him only the briefest of glances, Rachel lowered the sun visor and focused her thoughts on meeting with Dwight, a man she not only loathed, but also didn't trust.

It hadn't always been that way.

When her brother Nick had first joined the Company, she'd been away at college, but on several of her trips home, she'd met some of his friends. Dwight was one of them. While Nick had rarely divulged details of his work, she knew that in the early days, he and Dwight had worked in the field together. *Spies like us.*

And while Dwight had never been as close to Nick as Elijah—

She cut off any thoughts of Nick's closest friend. No. Not *friend*. Friends took care of each other. Watched each others' backs. Elijah had done neither.

Checking the rearview, Rachel noticed she had lost the white van. She could tell from Franklin's expression that he wasn't too comfortable with the idea that, in essence, he was now the prisoner.

The trip to the Tower took less than ten minutes because Rachel managed to catch every traffic light. "Relax," she said, slowing in front of the hotel. "Gotcha home safe and sound."

"Just valet the car," Franklin suggested.

She shook her head. No way was she going to turn her keys and her car over to an attendant. If things got unpleasant upstairs, she wanted the ability to disappear in a hurry.

Rachel found a parking spot one block west of the hotel. She followed Franklin in through a side entrance, just steps away from a bank of elevators.

The man used his cell phone briefly. "We're coming up now."

"I would have preferred to show up alone and unannounced."

Franklin closed his phone. "So I was told."

The elevator ride was intensely quiet, both of them staring at the changing floor number. Rachel wondered what Dwight had told his men about her, about their past, about his connection to her dead brother.

Probably nothing. Or at least nothing accurate.

Franklin rapped on door number 1209. It opened immediately, revealing another agent who could have been Franklin's clone.

The man stepped aside and waved her in. "Ladies first."

"That's no lady," Franklin warned.

Rachel knew the agent had said it loud enough for her to hear. She opened her mouth to respond, then quickly closed it as Dwight Davis strode into view.

In the nearly five years since she'd last seen him, Dwight had put on twenty pounds. He looked more like fifty-two than forty-two. A result of moving out of the field and into a desk job, no doubt.

His sandy-colored hair was thinner and grayer, his cheeks ruddier. Some women would still consider him handsome. She didn't.

Dwight looked at Franklin. "Is she armed?"

Rachel snorted. "Of course. Afraid I'll shoot you?"

She shifted to get a clear view of the door that led into the bedroom as her eyes swept the spacious room. How many audio and video devices were planted?

Dwight smiled, the action making him appear younger. But also more dangerous and cold. Calculating. He shrugged. "No sense tempting fate."

"Sorry, sport, but you're not worth jail time." She nodded toward Franklin. "Besides, I'd never shoot you in front of witnesses."

Dwight chuckled and seemed to loosen up a bit. "God, I'd forgotten how feisty you were. You look great, Rachel. Really great. Of course, you always did."

"Cut the flattery."

"Sure. How about a drink, then?"

"No."

"Worried I'll poison you?"

She realized his question was a parody of hers and in that brief moment, she recognized that she was almost enjoying herself. In some ways, hatred was like loving. It made you feel very alive. Something she hadn't felt in a long time.

"You can raid the minibar if that feels safer," Dwight said. He popped the top of a cola can and moved to one of the sofas. "I hear you've opened a second office in L.A. Business must be good."

"It's good enough I can pick and choose the clientele." Rachel helped herself to a soda from the small refrigerator, taking a can from the back. "We don't, by the way, do government contract work."

"I bet Chase Scoggs taught you that line. How is that old coot anyway?"

"Peachy."

Chase had owned the Red Dog Detective Agency before Rachel bought him out three years ago. What started as a part-time filing job when she was seventeen became an all-consuming passion. After helping Chase with a couple of cases, she'd dumped her plans to go to law school, but ended up a criminal justice major after her brother threatened to kick her ass if she didn't finish college.

Everything she'd learned about being a successful private investigator came from Chase. Through all her personal ups and downs, he'd been a good friend as well. In many ways he was more family than some of her blood relatives.

"Look, I've got to catch a flight soon," Rachel

continued. "Why don't you just blurt out whatever it is that you brought me all the way across town to hear."

"Lighten up. Your flight doesn't leave until eight tonight. And since we're bypassing social niceties, I'll get straight to the point: I'd like you to accept the senator's case. Help him find his missing grandchild."

Whatever explanation she'd expected Dwight to offer, that hadn't been it. "You said you had information on Cindy. Is that true?"

Dwight put a hand to his heart, as if feigning pain. It looked more like he had gas. "You always expect the worst from me, don't you?"

"When have you ever failed to disappoint?"

Her remark seemed to hit a nerve. Granted, when Nick had been alive, Dwight had been different. He'd even flirted with her when her brother wasn't looking. But Nick's death had changed everything.

"I understand Cindy went to an off-campus clinic," Dwight said. "Under an assumed name. I'm trying to verify it as we speak."

That was one of the first things Rachel had considered. An alias not only prevented Cindy from being recognized, it also made it difficult to trace a child placed for adoption. Especially a private adoption where all parties were anxious for it to appear as if nothing had happened.

She paced away, pretending to admire the fresh floral arrangement on the side table. Franklin still stood near the front door. She winked at him.

"And why would the CIA care if the senator finds his grandchild?" She looked over her shoulder at Dwight. "I know the senator has some friends in high places, but getting involved in what is obviously a very personal matter seems a bit beyond the Company's usual scope. Nor does it explain the bugs planted in the senator's private office."

"I suppose you want the truth?"

Facing him, Rachel rolled her eyes. "I realize that's a tough concept, so feel free to lie. I'll do my best to translate."

Dwight ignored the jibe and sipped his drink. "You already know the senator's stepdaughter attended Shepherd's Cross College. The church, in conjunction with the college, maintains a number of overseas missions. We're interested in a certain financial transaction that occurred between one of the missions and a foreign organization that's been known to support terrorism."

"And you think the senator ties in somehow?"

She knew there was more, something that Dwight didn't want to divulge outright. He was trying to get her to play ball, without giving up anything he didn't absolutely have to. But one financial transaction? Did he honestly think he could sway her onto their team with that little information?

Meeting his gaze, she realized he did. Of course. He'd used the T-word. And fighting terrorism was synonymous with patriotism. The tactic might work with someone else, but not her. And Dwight knew better than to question her loyalty to country.

So what was he really after?

Curious, she decided to play along. "What you're saying makes little sense. The senator—who is admittedly a power monger—nearly has his name on the next presidential ballot. He's not going to allow himself to be linked to even a hint of terrorist activity. Not in today's political environment. I also find it hard to believe, if what you're telling me is even true, that your overseas office can't trace this alleged transaction."

Dwight leaned forward. "Tracing it wasn't the problem. There's an electronic trail showing the deposit hitting one of the mission's bank accounts before it was immediately reversed. The overseas bank claimed it was a simple data-entry error they found and corrected."

"It happens. The bank gave me an extra ten grand a few months ago. Some teller transposed two digits of the account number. They didn't let me keep it, either."

"But I bet that bank teller wasn't found with two bullets in the back of the head."

Two bullets. A professional hit. Rachel sobered. "What's the church's explanation for the deposit?"

"We haven't asked."

Rachel weighed Dwight's words. "That still doesn't explain the senator's involvement."

"We tried to initiate a tax audit so we could look at the church's overseas bank accounts. Senator Benjamin quashed the audit."

She knew the senator had considerable clout with the Treasury Department. "And you think he may have done it because he's covering up?"

"Or protecting someone."

"Maybe he's just doing someone a favor. Politicians do that. Surely you have other means of triggering an audit."

"Absolutely. However, until we know for certain, we don't want to force an examination and show our hand."

Suddenly she knew why the CIA was trying to

enlist her help. They wanted an inside track on both the senator *and* the church; a mole who wouldn't raise suspicions. Dwight probably figured she could explore Cindy's past while simultaneously keeping an eye out for anything that might interest the Company. The man was a slime ball.

But what about Senator Benjamin? What was his excuse? And why torpedo an IRS audit?

Unless the church's founder asked for a favor. She recalled the senator specifically mentioning Reverend William Hanson with a tone of awe and envy.

"Pulling strings doesn't necessarily spell conspiracy," she pointed out. "Maybe Benjamin did it in hopes of getting information on his stepdaughter. The old scratch-my-back routine."

Dwight tilted his chin. "I need you to scratch my back, Rachel, and accept the senator's case."

"Why haven't you already planted your own agent on campus?"

He took another swig of soda. "No time. This twist just surfaced. Besides, I don't have anyone available at this time with the right skill set to play the part. Which means I'd have to hire a contract agent anyway. The senator's suggestion that you enroll as a student is perfect. You'd be just right. I'll send you in with one of my operatives who can work with you behind the scenes. And while you search for information on the senator's stepdaughter, my agent will check their accounting records. We both win."

Once again, she ignored the remark, knowing he was fishing for a confirmation. "I'm not convinced I actually have to go to the campus in order to get answers for the senator."

"Trust me, you do." Dwight's look said he'd tried. "I'll pay your full rate, plus all expenses. That will be in addition to whatever you charge the senator, by the way."

Rachel set her drink aside. "Let's get one thing straight. The only thing the senator said that even remotely interested me was his offer to get information on Nick. You alluded to the same." She dug out the blurred photo she'd been given and tossed it onto the table. "This means nothing."

"It was meant to entice, a token of potential."

"Potential means zip. I want cold, hard facts. Facts I can corroborate, not more of the bullshit you gave me before."

Dwight had the grace to look guilty. "Corroboration is tricky."

"Then there's no deal." Rachel headed for the door.

She had told herself coming in that she wasn't going to trust Dwight, and she didn't. But what she hadn't counted on was the hard knot in her gut. A knot put there by the fear that she might be walking away from the very answers she'd been waiting five years to get. Hope was a mind game, and Dwight played it well, the son of a bitch.

When Rachel got within arm's reach of the door, Franklin quickly stepped out of her way. As their gazes met, his pupils expanded. She suspected his balls drew up tight, too. Nice to know she hadn't lost her touch.

"Shit, Rachel! Wait!" Dwight called out. "I didn't say it was impossible, I said it was tricky."

She released the doorknob and turned back, saw that he had followed. She waited for him to go on.

Frowning, Dwight checked his watch. "I'm due in another meeting in five minutes."

"And I'm due back in Atlanta." Exasperated, Rachel reached for the doorknob again.

"Don't leave town," he said. "I'll send a package to your hotel. It might help you make up your mind."

"Don't kid yourself, Dwight. My mind was made up when I walked through this door. And you've done nothing to change it."

When she arrived back at her hotel, Rachel stopped at the front desk.

The clerk looked up from what she was doing and smiled. "May I help you?"

"I need to stay another night."

"No problem. Which room are you in?"

"I'd like to switch rooms. To something on a higher floor, with a better view."

Rachel fully expected Dwight to have sent someone by to plant a few listening devices while she was out. With any luck, her current room would end up occupied by some snoring slob with intestinal problems.

Twenty minutes later, she was settled into a new room. She mulled over just what remaining in town really meant. That she had been kidding herself. That for all her assurances that she had finally managed to let go of Nick, she hadn't. The questions resurfaced just as desolate and rash as when she'd buried them. Damn it! If there was even the smallest of chances to get answers, she couldn't walk away. Wouldn't walk away.

But was there truly any chance? Or was Dwight just setting her up for another fall?

Rachel jerked open the drapes and looked down at the street below. Earlier, she'd planned to go shopping. But she wouldn't now. Now she'd wait. For Dwight's package.

She turned back and surveyed the room with its ultramodern sparseness. The tables were stainless steel and frosted glass, the chairs chrome and black leather. An operating room would be warmer.

Determined to do something productive, she picked up her briefcase. Whenever she took on a new job, she always wrote up an investigative approach that included all known details and the ultimate goal of the investigation. She'd found by staying firmly focused on the latter, she normally managed to deliver what the client was after.

This time, however, the goal was personal.

She fired up her laptop and began inputting what she knew. It quickly became evident the whole investigation was overloaded with pitfalls. She looked at the list of players with a skeptic's eye.

In light of his wife's illness, Rachel believed that the senator wanted to locate Cindy's child—if it existed. At the same time, she knew he wasn't being completely forthright about the reason for his search. He really wanted control. Politically speaking, he'd want to spin the child's existence favorably to the media himself. Having that type of news leaked by another could spell disaster.

Next there was Dwight. His track record with her pretty much guaranteed that most of what he'd told her so far was crap with a coating of truth. The man would lie to God if he thought it would get him somewhere. Add to that the fact the CIA had invented the term *hidden agenda.*

She suspected at least part of the reason the Company wanted one of their operatives to accompany her to Shepherd's Cross was so they could plant more sophisticated electronic devices on the premises.

More than that, though, she also suspected they planned to use her to breach the computer systems. It was no secret the Company's technical people were stretched thin right now. They'd stick her with a low-level bean counter and expect her to do all the real legwork on the case.

Which might work to her favor. If Rachel could find whatever Dwight was after before his agent did, she could force Dwight to give her everything he had. And then some. Yes, it was a little underhanded, but he deserved no less.

Rachel recalled the bleak months following Nick's death when it had seemed an abyss had swallowed her. She'd clung to memories of a big brother who had seemed so invincible, who had cared for her, who had protected her. But most of all, who had loved her.

Nick had sworn he'd *always* be there for her, that he'd never leave. And while, as an adult, she'd understood it was the one promise no one could keep, as a child, that promise had kept the darkness at bay.

Dwight had visited her three times after delivering the news of Nick's death. Each time he'd fawned over her, answering all her questions, patiently explaining over and over that Nick had basically died in a random act of violence. A car bomb.

Rachel had argued the notion. Nick simply would not have let that happen.

That's when Dwight admitted the incident had happened near the U.S. embassy. They believed nearby guards were the targets.

Rachel checked and found the time consistent with published reports of a car bombing in Afghanistan. And until the Company identified Nick's DNA in a single bone fragment, she'd held out foolish hope. But with that irrefutable evidence she'd been forced to face reality. Though she had no body to bury, she had lost her brother forever.

Then she got a phone call from Belinda Nunez.

Belinda had been trying to reach Nick. She'd found his name and number among her late husband's personal belongings. He had been a CIA agent, too, and the story Belinda told of her husband's death had been nearly identical to Nick's. Right down to the recovered bone fragment and the man responsible for delivering the explanation: Dwight Davis.

Like Belinda, Rachel had never been told another agent had died with Nick.

When Rachel confronted Dwight and demanded he hand over the bone fragment, everything changed. No more info was forthcoming. *National security concerns.*

And when the bone fragment suddenly came up missing, Rachel began to believe that her brother hadn't died as Dwight said, that something else had happened to her brother, that perhaps he'd been on a mission the government wanted to keep quiet.

In the end, the laboratory produced slides, but admitted losing the bone specimen, leaving the only proof of her brother's death a four-page lab report. Ink and paper. Words on a page.

When Rachel tried to contact Belinda again, she seemed to have dropped off the face of the earth. Rachel then tried contacting other agents she'd known had worked with Nick most recently. But she either couldn't find them or they dodged her.

Except one: Howie Stevens.

She'd worked Howie over, plying him with alcohol and tears, until he broke down and admitted what he'd heard through the grapevine. That Nick had been on an assignment with three other agents when their camp was bombed. Only one agent had escaped alive, a man who had left the camp to rendezvous with a local.

Elijah Trent.

The news that her brother had been working with Elijah again stunned Rachel. Swallowing her pride, she attempted to contact Elijah. Which promptly earned her another visit from Dwight. And a threat.

Dwight denied everything Howie said. "It's bullshit with a purpose. So let it drop. Or risk being silenced."

"You wouldn't dare!"

"The hell I wouldn't. You have no idea what's at stake here."

It had been Chase Scoggs who called in a few favors and ferreted out the news that Elijah had actually been captured and imprisoned overseas. Chase had also surmised that until the issue died down, Dwight couldn't arrange Elijah's release.

"Back off," Chase had advised. "You've lost your objectivity and you're letting your emotions rule. And none of it will bring Nick back."

For all of ten seconds, Rachel had hated Chase . . . for being right.

Ultimately, she had forced herself to make peace with it. Until today. Seeing that blurred photo of Nick made her realize how fragile that peace was.

Blinking, she refocused on the computer screen, at the list she'd made. All things considered, when Rachel got to the bottom line, she was the only person who she knew was being honest.

"That should make for a real interesting investigation."

As she did anytime she was stumped, she picked up the phone, intending to call Chase, but stopped. While she felt confident her room wasn't bugged, there was no guarantee about the hotel phone. And other electronic devices could pick up her cell.

It was probably just as well she didn't talk to Chase right now. She knew full well that he'd tell her not to take the case. And her mind was made up. She was going to take it. Quite simply, she could not turn her back on the chance to learn more about her brother.

Impatient, Rachel turned back to her laptop and flipped over to e-mail, then waited for it to download. There were fifty-three unread messages. Probably three-quarters were spam. She clicked the Delete key repetitively, getting rid of every name she didn't recognize. Except one.

Message from Dwight, the subject line read. There was a file attached.

Before she could open it, a knock landed on her door. She frowned, checking the time. She wasn't expecting anyone, but her cousin knew where she was staying. Meaning the senator would know. And of course Dwight . . .

The knocking repeated more loudly. "This better be good." Eager to get rid of whoever it was and download Dwight's message, she stalked to the door and flung it open.

Rachel's heart stopped. And for five long seconds she didn't think it would ever beat again.

The knot in her stomach hardened, as did her heart. While she'd threatened quite a few, there was only one man on the face of the earth whom she had ever contemplated joyfully shooting. And that man now stood in front of her. Elijah Trent.

"Hello, Rachel."

"Good-bye, you no-good piece of—" She tried to shut the door in his face, but he already had his foot in the opening.

There was only one possible reason Elijah was there. Dwight had sent him.

Realizing there was no way she was going to physically keep him out, Rachel released the door and stepped back from the opening. Instead of closing the door behind him, Elijah left it open.

She boldly returned his once-over. He looked good, she admitted. Damn good. Tall, dark, and devious. The slightly shaggy hair and a two-day beard only made him look that much more dangerous. Desirable. As if he'd just climbed out of bed after a night of . . .

Rachel inhaled sharply as she turned away. How could she hate a man so damn much with her brain and her heart, while the rest of her body couldn't seem to forget what they'd done together? Never mind that he'd done it with the rest of the world.

Moving back to her computer, she exited out of her e-mail program. Obviously, Elijah's timing was a bit off. No doubt he was supposed to arrive after whatever Dwight sent had softened her up.

"You can tell Dwight he made a big mistake. No matter what's in his e-mail, I wouldn't work with you if you were the last—"

"Dwight doesn't know I'm here."

She faced him slowly. "And I would believe that . . . why?" She held up a hand when he would have answered. "It doesn't matter. It doesn't change my position."

"Just hear me out, okay?"

A door opened across the hall and a concerned-looking woman stuck her head out. Their raised voices were attracting attention. Rachel forced a smile and waved, then frowned at Elijah. "Five minutes," she hissed.

As soon as Elijah closed the door, the room seemed to shrink. She moved toward the window. Damn him. He had her retreating. Not a good sign.

To feign disregard at this point was stupid, so she opted for controlled impatience as she waited for him to speak.

"You look fantastic," Elijah began.

The compliment was gratifying. If she were in the mood to be honest, she would have said the same about him.

"You look like hell, actually," she said instead. "Whose bed did you crawl out of this time?"

Women had always clamored after Elijah. Rachel had learned too late what a liability that was. Nick had warned her. Dwight, too. She hadn't listened.

Instead of answering, Elijah stood mutely just inside the door, studying her with eyes as dark as the coal that naughty boys got at Christmas. She recalled how when they were together she knew the moment he entered a room. How she would *feel* him even before she saw him, her body responding to his invisible force, making ready.

As much as she wanted to be able to say this man held no ability to affect her, she couldn't. Which made him still very hazardous.

Rachel glanced at the Walther sitting next to her computer, then at Elijah. As she looked down, he had moved toward her, so silently that she hadn't heard him.

This time she found it impossible to control the urge to retreat. "So if Dwight didn't send you, why are you here? We both know it's not a social call."

"Your help on this job could cut through months of red tape—"

"Oh, please! That's a crock and you know it. What are you really after here? Is there something about the senator's involvement Dwight's not telling me?"

"The senator is nothing. His desperation to find his grandchild—as tragic as that is—is simply an opportunity Dwight's piggybacking in on. It's a long shot at best, but we've been grabbing at straws all along." Elijah jammed his hands in his pockets. "The financial transaction Dwight told you about ties to some of the biggest terrorist funding we've uncovered. Up until now the source has been impossible to trace. And that source is a major moneyman, Rachel. Cut him out of the picture and the others scatter. But if we don't act fast, the trail will be useless. This guy changes banks every few months."

She pursed her lips. "Tell Dwight I'll only consider doing it if you're not involved."

"And would that be because of what happened in Venice? Or because of the bullshit Howie Stevens told you?"

"Take your pick."

Elijah ran a hand across the back of his neck. "As much as you don't want to believe it, this isn't personal, Rachel. Dwight didn't pick me because of our past. I've been trailing this source since right after September 11. The bottom line is about saving lives. Protecting our country. The woman I knew wouldn't let anything keep her from doing the right thing."

"Don't you dare question my patriotism or call on the woman you knew." She crossed her arms. The weight of hurts and losses between them was substantial. For her at least. "You lost that right six years ago."

Elijah shook his head. For a moment she didn't think he'd respond. Then he shrugged. "Obviously, you've changed more than I'd realized."

With that he turned and left.

For several seconds Rachel just stared at the closed door. Even if she hadn't seen him leave, she would have known he was gone. It was as if he'd taken all the air with him, leaving her in a vacuum.

And suddenly she realized that was where she'd been living for the past few years. A vacuum. Where she existed. Where she performed her job. Where she pretended to have a life.

Rachel sank into the chair in front of the desk. Unbidden, the memories of her relationship with Elijah spilled forth. *Venice.*

Nick had called from Italy. Their three-day R&R had been unplanned and left no time to fly home. She had wheedled, cajoled, begged until her brother had given her their location. Then she'd sworn him to secrecy.

"This might be a mistake," Nick had warned. "Wait until he calls."

No. She and Elijah had had a fierce argument the last time he had called. One of the many pitfalls of a long-distance love affair. She knew the argument had been her fault and wanted to make up for it in person.

The overseas flight had been long. Costly, booked at the last minute. She had arrived in the middle of the night and then wheedled, cajoled, begged the Venetian desk clerk for Elijah's room number, wanting to surprise him.

He had answered the door shirtless, his eyes widening with shock. Then feminine laughter—not hers—filled the air as a hand, nails long and red, had snaked possessively around his abdomen.

Rachel had fled, making it all the way back to the airport before realizing he hadn't come after her.

She shook her head and turned her laptop back on. *I won't let him get to me again,* she vowed.

After double-clicking the e-mail icon, she waited. Dwight's message was already highlighted. She wished she had the strength to delete it. To walk away.

Instead she opened it. The text was short:

There's more where this came from.

She scanned the attachment for viruses before downloading it. With Dwight, the term *spyware* had new meaning.

The file took a full minute to download. When it finished, her screen blinked, fading to black before flashing back to white. A virus?

"Shit!" That quickly, her hand sought the power key. She'd shut down before letting one of Dwight's malicious programs run.

At that moment a segment of a photograph came into view, making her pause. It was black-and-white, very similar to the one she'd been given earlier.

And instead of being blurred, it was crystal clear. It was a crowd shot, the sea of faces once again cropped, eliminating identifying landmarks.

But it was the face in the center that held her.

"Nick."

Throat tightening, she touched the screen. In the photo, her brother had long hair and a full beard. His face was thinner than she remembered, accentuating his high cheekbones. His eyes were clear and piercing as he looked directly at the camera.

In real life those eyes had been bright aquamarine, just like hers, though he frequently wore dark contact lenses to disguise them.

She hadn't seen Nick for almost a year before he died. As was his way, he called periodically and wrote even more sporadically, but she rarely knew where he'd been or what he was doing until after the fact.

Such was the existence of a CIA operative. She had accepted that. Just as she accepted he was gone now.

What everyone got wrong about her queries wasn't the fact she questioned her brother's death. She knew it was unfair, but that came with the territory. That came with the life he'd chosen.

Yes, she wanted the truth about how he had died, but mostly Rachel had simply wanted to know what Nick's life had been like in that year before he died.

Had he seen any interesting places? Dated anyone? What had made him smile? They'd always told each other everything.

Even pictures, like the one on the screen, filled in the blanks. Nick hadn't been sentimental and kept few photographs, particularly of himself.

Talk to me, Nick.

The screen blinked and the photo disappeared. "No!"

Once again the background faded, but in place of the picture was another message from Dwight.

Do we have a deal?

Frantic, Rachel checked her mailbox, wanting to retrieve the photograph. But only the text was there.

"You bastard."

THREE

Shepherd's Cross, West Virginia

Ten days later, on a rain-soaked morning, Rachel left Atlanta and drove eight hours north to the travelogue-perfect community of Shepherd's Cross.

After the fiasco with Dwight's disappearing photograph, Rachel had made a few demands of her own. First, she had refused to even negotiate until a hard copy of the picture was delivered. Next, she had insisted all the information on her brother be handed over up front.

Dwight had, of course, refused. "Look, I know you're pissed that I didn't tell you about Elijah, and I know the guy broke your heart once. But what you're asking for isn't even reasonable."

"Broken hearts mend. Especially when you're young and stupid," she had replied. "But losing my only brother . . . Reasonable doesn't play into that."

"Elijah's not responsible for—"

"So I've heard, though I haven't seen any hard proof."

Dwight had sighed. "You know what the real problem is? You blame him for surviving when Nick didn't."

She tried to deny it. Couldn't. Instead she changed the subject.

In the end, she and Dwight had achieved a compromise—that she'd receive information as they went.

Which meant if Dwight didn't deliver, Rachel wouldn't.

And after their predawn meeting this morning, she would lay odds that Dwight was even more desperate for answers than she was. His tension had been tangible, more so than the Senate investigations and budget hearings he blamed it on.

She hadn't set eyes on Elijah since that afternoon in her hotel room, but he had often entered her mind and unfortunately, her dreams. They were bizarre dreams, almost Picasso-like. Disjointed. Seemingly disconnected. And always sensual.

They were a stark reminder that she wasn't invulnerable when it came to Elijah. Meaning she had to stay on her toes, limit her exposure where he was concerned.

Rachel tried to focus on her real mission: to investigate the possibility that Cindy Benjamin had left behind a child. The assignment would be short. She planned to be in and out of Shepherd's Cross in less than a week. If that wasn't adequate time for Elijah, too bad.

After doing her own legwork, Rachel was beginning to find Dwight's and Elijah's theory of a possible link between the prominent senator and either

Shepherd's Cross or a terrorist to be unlikely. Which once again left her wondering exactly what it was the two men were after and if she had been given the whole story. Or even the real one.

Same with the information Dwight had claimed to have that Cindy used an alias. When Rachel had pressed him, he admitted it hadn't been Cindy.

Rachel realized it might have been a lie to get her interest. Or it might have been the truth. She knew too well the hundreds of false leads that had to be followed up just to get one correct answer.

In the end, she decided that what the CIA was after didn't matter so long as she got the promised information on Nick.

When she reached the city limits of Shepherd's Cross, Rachel checked her speed. Dwight had furnished the car, a brand-new BMW convertible, along with fake IDs and transcripts. As of today she was Rachel *Ives*, a pampered junior who last attended Florida State University in Tallahassee.

She actually had attended FSU—just not anytime recently. It was always better to stick as close as possible to the truth when creating a new identity. Less chance of getting tripped up at the wrong moment.

The fact she was portraying a well-to-do socialite was enough of a stretch. Her family tree was deeply, lovingly rooted in middle-class America. And she'd gone through puberty and adolescence with Nick as a role model. Consequently, she could fight and swear with the best of them. But tea and manicures . . .

Rachel circled the town square, taking in its quaint, mostly brick architecture. The brick roads and elaborate wrought-iron streetlamps, coupled with the town's rural location, made it feel more like a village.

It had surprised her to learn that over half of the town's fifteen thousand residents were retired church members, many from outside the country. Consequently, the town had an above-average number of nursing homes and assisted-living facilities.

Rachel glanced at the sprawling cemetery on her right. Just ahead was a hospital. It seemed that Shepherd's Cross was prepared to take care of its citizens from birth to salvation to death.

Slowing, she studied the six-story hospital. If Cindy Benjamin had given birth, chances were she'd done so here. Which meant Rachel needed to come up with a reason to go to the hospital. What was it going to be this time? Sprained ankle or cramps? She'd toss a coin when the time came.

Next, she passed the church's corporate compound, a deceptive hive of buildings that served the needs of the world's largest congregation. Without a doubt, William Hanson had been a genius when it came to pioneering broadcast religion into the mainstream. While others came and went, he grew more popular.

Traffic picked up as she passed a shopping mall. A greenway adjacent to the college campus was crowded with students.

Eager to escape the car, Rachel parked near the administration building and hurried toward the housing office.

The line was short since the majority of students had already returned from a summer spent overseas and had kept their dorm rooms.

She eavesdropped on an enlightening conversation the receptionist was having. Apparently, a software glitch had the computer system down right now—a problem the school hoped to have fixed before classes started tomorrow.

Great. Rachel needed to access the college's computer network to review Cindy's school records. She eyed the banks of file cabinets along the far wall, guessing they only held current information. The church and college had contracted with a digital-imaging company three years ago to establish a paperless archive.

As she waited, she surreptitiously observed some of the other students milling about. Someone at the Company had nailed the demographics of this affluent crowd.

At first, Rachel had felt Dwight had gone too far when he'd even suggested how she dress and wear her hair. Just for spite, she'd been tempted to do the opposite. He had commented that her blond hair was perfect; hence, she'd been tempted to darken it. He'd told her to dress like a debutante, complete with pearls and heels; she'd considered gothic-punk.

As it turned out, he did know what he was talking about, right down to cutting a few wispy bangs. They softened her face and made her look ridiculously younger. Rachel typically wore her shoulder-length hair in a practical French braid or ponytail. Today it was loose, curling softly on the ends.

She grudgingly gave Dwight credit. No one seemed to question her cover.

Before getting her dorm keys, she had to sit through a boring campus orientation video. Twice she caught herself dozing, something she'd have to guard against since virtually every class on campus utilized multimedia.

When she finally reached her dormitory, she lugged in boxes, grateful she was on the ground floor. It took five trips, the majority of it clothing she'd borrowed from her secretary, Sheila's, clothes-horse, fashion-plate daughter. While Rachel didn't plan to stay long, she had to make it look as if she intended to be here all semester.

Out of habit, she swept the room for bugs and found none.

She gave the dorm's built-in study niche with its sleek monitor and keyboard a jaundiced glare.

The monitor was dual purpose, acting as both television and computer screen. The TV offered one network and one local station. The other channels were either student offerings, campus news, or twenty-fours of Hanson's taped sermons and rallies.

As a computer, the system was useless. It had no CPU and only allowed access to the student net-work, which ran on a separate server. What Rachel needed to find was a terminal connected to the larger administrative system.

She quickly unpacked. Her room was spacious, more like a small studio apartment, complete with a tiny patio that overlooked a wooded area.

Like everything on campus, the building was fairly new and totally different from what she'd experienced at Florida State. Which made sense. Most of Shepherd's Cross's students were from wealthy families that expected more than a mildewed, crowded dorm room for their offspring.

While Shepherd's Cross College was minuscule compared to most others, Rachel knew they had aggressive plans for growth. They had a well-funded scholarship program—the rich liked free rides as much as anyone—and regularly trolled for students at other private campuses across the country.

Accusations abounded that they skimmed the cream off the top. The academic cream, Rachel wondered, or the financial? As if the church needed more money. They were clearly rolling in dough.

She checked the time, wanting to call her office before it closed. Once Rachel had agreed to take on this job, her life had gone crazy. The ever-efficient Sheila had cleared Rachel's schedule, either rearranging jobs or, if they were of a time-sensitive nature, referring them on to an agency that they often used when the case log became more of a logjam.

Still, Rachel had had to work double time to wrap up several open cases. She had also met with the senator again, quizzing him on Cindy's friends and habits. He had given her a couple of photographs of Cindy. One included Lenore Benjamin. Mother and daughter looked alike with their dark hair and dark eyes, but even on film their distance was, sadly, evident.

The photographs weren't current, but the senator said Cindy hadn't changed a great deal. And it wasn't as if Rachel intended to go around flashing a picture before asking, "Have you seen this girl?"

Rachel had requested a copy of the complete diary, hoping that it might give some insight into the senator's dead stepdaughter, but she'd been given only the single entry that mentioned the pregnancy. The senator claimed there was no other mention of it.

His unwillingness to share the whole diary made Rachel wonder what it was that he hadn't wanted her to see. Had it had been a real diatribe, with an unflattering behind-the-scenes look into their home life? If so, the senator might have wanted to limit the number of copies in existence, to avoid any possibility of the media getting their hands on it.

Still, Rachel wondered if there might have been something in another entry that would have helped her to pinpoint a possible due date for Cindy's baby. A complaint of not feeling well, perhaps. Or weight gain.

Being able to narrow the time down to a two-month window would have helped. As it was, given the date of the diary entry and the fact that Cindy hadn't been pregnant at the time of her death, nor had there been any mention of a recent pregnancy on the autopsy report, Rachel's investigation had to cover a period of at least a year.

She had run the usual background check on Cindy Benjamin. Nothing helpful came up. Her driving record was clean except for an unpaid parking ticket that was two years old. Her car title and credit cards had been in her mother's name, which meant no credit history. In fact, other than a birth announcement and an obituary, Cindy had left little behind. Except possibly a baby.

Rachel dialed her office. "It's me."

"All moved in?" Sheila asked.

"I just unpacked the last box. How are things there?"

"The big news is Gerry found the McElroy kids. He traced the father through a forger who was prepping fake passports. Another few days and they'd have been out of the country."

Which would have made them almost impossible to track. The McElroy case had been particularly difficult. The father, who'd been jailed for abuse, had picked the children up from school in spite of a court order banning unsupervised contact. It had been one of the cases Rachel had found difficult to turn over to anyone, even Gerry.

"Tell Gerry congratulations. I'll want to hear the full story as soon as I'm back," Rachel said. "Any luck with the court records?"

Sheila was attempting to search adoption records that had been filed by the church's law firm over the past year. It was a tedious process.

"I'm halfway through and already I've come up with eighteen," Sheila said.

Rachel scribbled notes. "At that rate, the total could exceed thirty couples. Where in the hell are they finding that many babies?"

"I knew you'd ask, so I'm also tracking down all the pregnancy counseling services within the area. There's a number of smaller ones, but so far it appears Shepherd's Cross runs the largest."

"Gee, what a coincidence."

Had Cindy Benjamin been counseled at Shepherd's Cross and been advised to place her child for adoption with the church? Maybe. But if she had, it would have been under her own name. There would have been no way for Cindy to have used a fake name. Which would make it easier to get to answers.

"What about the list of area medical clinics?" Rachel asked.

"Got it. There's more than I would have thought, considering how rural the region is. Should I e-mail these to Elijah?"

Rachel frowned. "I'm not sure."

The dorm phone jacks had been disconnected since all students carried cell phones. And by limiting the local cell phone service to analog, the church had effectively eliminated e-mail by cell phones or other handheld devices. Besides sucking battery power, analog reception was rarely clear enough to establish a connection to an ISP in the first place.

The fact that the church, or its members, owned all the surrounding property prevented anyone from erecting a digital tower nearby. Clever devils.

Since Internet access from campus was nearly nonexistent, Rachel would have to depend on Elijah to receive and send e-mails, which she didn't like.

"I take it you haven't heard from him yet." Sheila was the only one at her firm who knew the full down-and-dirty story about Rachel and Elijah.

"Not yet." Rachel tried to conceal her irritation over Elijah's lack of communication.

He had her cell phone number, but she didn't have his. When he finally got around to calling her, he wasn't going to like what she had to say.

If he wanted her cooperation and assistance, it was going to have to be a two-way street. She wasn't going to be treated like some rookie investigator, given only the info he deemed necessary. If they were going to work together, it was damn well going to be as full partners.

No sooner had Rachel hung up from Sheila then someone knocked on her door. Straightening her clothes, she answered it.

Rachel recognized the pretty blonde even before she introduced herself. Emily Jarrett had been a friend of Cindy Benjamin's; they'd been roommates their first semester. Rachel's curiosity danced. Had Cindy confided in Emily that she was pregnant?

"This is to welcome you to Shepherd's Cross." Emily held out a small fern. "I checked the student roster to see who was moving in. I'm right next door, by the way."

Rachel wiped her hands on her khaki slacks, suddenly feeling self-conscious. Emily looked like she'd just left a garden party. "Excuse the mess. I've been unpacking."

She accepted the fern, but nearly dropped it. As a general rule, she avoided the plant kingdom. Except at mealtimes. Sheila, who talked to the office plants as she cared for them, referred to Rachel as Dr. Death.

"Don't apologize," Emily soothed. "I was here last semester, so this part is easy for me. I wanted to remind you that there's a social to welcome everyone, tonight at the gym. If you like, we could go together."

It was Rachel's turn to smile. Attending the social with Emily was a good way to break the ice and cultivate a friendship—an important step in gaining the other girl's confidence.

While meeting Emily seemed a good starting point for Rachel's investigation, part of her couldn't help but wonder, of all the students enrolled at Shepherd's Cross, how she'd ended up next door to Emily. Was it Dwight's doing? Or sheer luck?

"That sounds great." Rachel offered her hand. "Why don't you just knock on my door when you're ready to walk over."

As she closed the door, the delicate fern wilted slightly, as if sensing its imminent demise. A bad omen?

Rachel set the plant on the counter, then moved it nearer a window. The fern shuddered. She glared at it. "Oh, buck up. It's only for a week."

Rachel and Emily walked the short distance to the social hall near the center of the campus, which gave Rachel an opportunity to learn more about the other girl.

It was a surprise to discover how closely Emily's background paralleled the story Dwight had concocted for Rachel.

An only child of well-off parents, Emily had lost her mother when she was eight. Her father had succumbed to cancer three years ago, leaving her virtually alone in the world. She had been at Shepherd's Cross for two years after transferring from another private college.

"I can't believe how much we have in common," Emily said.

When mapping out Rachel's cover, Dwight had made her a wealthy only child, too, with parents who had supposedly died while she was an infant, leaving an aunt to raise her. While the similarities had the intended effect of making Emily more open, it also stirred Rachel's sympathy for the other girl.

Before they reached the hall, Emily stopped her.

"I'll warn you up front that you'll be heavily recruited for service clubs tonight. Including by me."

It took Rachel a moment to recall that instead of fraternities and sororities, the college had service clubs. Each centered around one of the church's charity organizations.

"Which one are you soliciting for?" Rachel asked.

"Eve's Circle."

Rachel blinked. You couldn't get any more biblical than that. "And what is Eve's Circle?"

"You'll love it. Reverend Wright is our sponsor. He administers the church's mission program, so naturally we support one of the overseas missions. I hope he'll be here tonight so you can meet him."

The inside of the large hall was crowded with students and faculty. Though not formal, the event was still a dressy get-together. The male dress code must have specified neckties as mandatory and sport jackets optional, while all the women wore cocktail dresses. Not flashy dresses intended to draw attention, but those decorous little black or navy numbers that were every worried mama's delight.

A Christian rock band played at one end of the room, but there was nothing jamming about the crowd. Rachel recalled her own college concert days. The throbbing percussion of instruments, the singer's voice nearly unintelligible above their sound. The constant jostling of other concertgoers, many of them inebriated.

If she had to guess, she'd have said few of the current occupants of the room had ever let anything alcoholic past their lips, and when someone mentioned *weed* they thought of dandelions and sedge.

"Come on." Emily reached for Rachel's hand, obviously intending to lead her through the crowd.

Rachel's natural instinct was to avoid the contact, but in the next instant she felt Emily's fingers close around hers. It was strange to think that she couldn't recall the last time she'd held hands with a woman. In any other crowd it would have raised eyebrows and whispers, but in this one it went unnoticed.

As they moved through the room, Rachel was inundated with pitches for different clubs and more than one flirtatious offer. That was something else she'd forgotten about college. The pheromones. The testosterone. And the glorious blooming of one's sexual power.

Not that anyone she'd fooled around with in college had come close to Elijah. The man had been . . .

Nothing.

She forced her thoughts back to the moment by concentrating on the noise, the chatter. The press of bodies.

Emily pulled her toward the far side of the room where buffet tables were set up. Rachel suddenly recalled she'd skipped lunch, and her eyes widened at the array of food.

Gourmet hors d'oevres were intermingled with exquisite desserts. Nothing healthy, low carb, or sensible on this spread. No classic student food like pizza, either. They catered to a well-heeled palate, offering lobster, crab-stuffed prawns, smoked salmon, and even caviar.

But it was the dark chocolate tortes, the decadent

caramel cheesecakes, the French pastries dusted with sugar that called to Rachel. Desserts outnumbered hors d'oevres four to one.

She had counted.

Bypassing all the food, Emily went straight to the punch bowl in the corner. She pressed a crystal cup into Rachel's hand.

Rachel stared at it in disbelief. The fruit punch was cold and frothy thanks to the scoop of sherbet dished into the cup, but it wasn't cheesecake. Or chocolate.

"It's low fat," Emily whispered. "Yet sweet."

"But I like fat," Rachel grumbled.

Emily lowered her cup and smiled. "You're so funny."

Rachel glanced toward the section of the buffet table where desserts reigned, trying to decide how many she could stuff in her purse without anyone noticing.

She fidgeted. It was going to be difficult to maintain her cover here. And it wasn't just her eating habits. The dress code would kill her. She could count on one hand the times she'd worn panty hose in the past year. Three baptisms and a funeral.

Two girls greeted Emily warmly, then turned to Rachel.

"I'm Carol." The petite brunette introduced herself. "And this is Megan. I'm sure Emily's already been plugging her Circle group, but I'd like to tell you about Hope's Sisters. We do volunteer work at one of the nursing homes in town."

Carol then launched into a monologue on what her group had accomplished in the past year.

"That sounds wonderful," Rachel said when she finished. "But Emily's got me very curious about Eve's Circle."

Emily's face lit up in a triumphant smile. "That calls for a toast. I'll get more punch."

As Emily walked away, a man and woman approached their group. The woman's heavy cologne greeted Rachel before she even held out her hand.

"You must be one of the new students. I'm Dr. Sarah Wetherington and this is my husband, Richard."

Rachel introduced herself, her interest piqued. Sarah Wetherington oversaw the student clinic on campus. More importantly, she worked at the town's private hospital and clinic. *In obstetrics and gynecology.* If Cindy Benjamin had been pregnant, there was a good chance Sarah knew the details.

But it wasn't as simple as pumping the woman for information. Her husband, Richard Wetherington, was chief legal counsel for Shepherd's Cross. Richard oversaw the phalanx of lawyers that handled everything from the church's nonprofit tax status to its members' legal affairs.

Including intrachurch adoptions. After what Sheila told her about the high adoption rate, Rachel couldn't help but wonder if there was any collusion going on.

Richard took her hand. "A pleasure to meet you, Rachel." A tall, good-looking man, he let his eyes sweep over her, lingering at her breasts.

He wasn't the first man to fail the I'm-up-here test, but the fact he ogled Rachel with his wife present was a new low.

Sarah seemed oblivious to her husband's wandering attention. How could the woman not notice? Rachel withdrew her hand, fought the urge to rub it on her dress.

Smiling even wider, Richard turned back to his wife.

"How do you like Shepherd's Cross?" Sarah asked.

"From what I've seen, it's beautiful. I just arrived this afternoon, though, so I haven't had a chance to explore."

"Hopefully, you'll find some free time before classes to just wander the campus a bit," Sarah said.

If you only knew, Rachel thought. "I plan to do that."

Richard Wetherington gave a sharp nod. "If you ladies will forgive me for rushing off, there's someone I need to speak with. We'll visit later."

Rachel watched him hurry toward a man who'd just entered a back door. Why the sudden sense of urgency?

Curious, Rachel eyed the newcomer. A handsome, hulking blond in a dark suit. Make that a hulking, *armed* blond.

She studied the slight bulge beneath the man's jacket. Either his shoulder holster was fitted improperly, or he was careless. PI? Cop?

He didn't strike her as being either, but who came armed to a church social? Unless Reverend William Hanson was making an appearance.

Rachel knew the minister had recently retained bodyguards after making enemies in several third-world countries. Apparently the ruling parties didn't always like Hanson's missionaries feeding and educating the people. Ignorant, starving masses were much easier to oppress.

As she continued watching, an older man stepped from behind the hulk. Sarah made a surprised noise.

"I knew William wouldn't miss this." Sarah waved, catching the minister's attention.

William Hanson made a beeline for their group, leaving Richard and his bodyguard to scramble behind, and greeted Sarah with a hug.

Rachel studied the church's founder. It was hard to believe this man had more influence in Washington than Senator Benjamin.

Rotund and balding, Hanson looked older than his seventy-something years. Obviously the photo on the back of his latest best-seller was dated. Or digitally enhanced.

Following brief introductions, Hanson monopolized the conversation, sharing anecdotes from his latest overseas book tour that had coincided with an old-fashioned tent crusade. He raised millions for his missions, probably did the same for his publisher.

After a few minutes of listening to the man talk, however, Rachel understood why his church had grown to its amazing proportions. Sincerity and charisma oozed from him.

He had a certain soothing cadence to his voice, a hypnotic way of making you feel like you stood in sunshine. Without even realizing it, she had shifted closer with the others to tighten the circle around the man.

When Reverend Hanson and Richard Wetherington shared a private moment, Rachel stepped back, mentally reaching for her cynicism. Did Hanson know that members of his church were possibly into black-market adoptions?

Granted, that was conjecture on her part, but so far it seemed logical. Her sixth sense, while not perfect, told her she was on the right track. She smelled cheese, knew the rats couldn't be far behind.

When Hanson finally left with the Wetheringtons in tow, Carol let out a sigh of mock relief. "I didn't think they'd ever leave. Hunk alert at three o'clock. Anyone know who he is?"

One by one, the girls swiveled their heads to see whom Carol was eyeing. When it was Rachel's turn, she found herself doing a double take.

Elijah.

She almost didn't recognize him. His long hair had been cut short, in a sleeker style, and he was clean shaven. He wore a sport jacket and tie, easily fitting in with the crowd.

But what the hell was he doing here? He was supposed to work behind the scenes.

She carefully checked his jacket for signs that he too was armed, but his bulges were purely physical. And in all the right places.

She lifted her eyes and found him checking her out every bit as intently, his dark eyes glittering with secrets. He was scowling. Christ, he always scowled.

Which meant few people realized he had sexy-as-hell dimples and a megawatt smile. She'd rarely seen either . . . outside of bed, that was.

When his eyes met hers, her stomach fluttered. Low.

She quickly turned away, cheeks burning. *Smooth move, Rach.*

"Dibs!" Carol bit her knuckles in an exaggerated fashion. "I think I'm in love."

Megan laughed. "Oh yeah? Well, Emily may have beat you to the punch again. Look. She's being introduced to him."

Rachel looked around and saw Emily speaking with Elijah and another man.

"That's Reverend Wright." Carol's lips formed a moue of mild irritation. "I'm sure Emily's gloating that she's signed you up for the Circle."

Rachel paused to recall who Wright was.

The Reverend Mason Wright was William Hanson's protégé. The second in command and considered to be the heir apparent, Wright oversaw the college's large media center, where thousands of Hanson's sermons were duplicated for mail order to an international audience. The income from the video sales alone could go a long way toward lowering the national debt.

As soon as Emily rejoined them, Carol pressed up next to her.

"So spill. Who's the doll you were just talking to?"

For a moment Emily looked as if she wasn't going to say. Then she grinned. "His name is Elijah Harris. He's a part-time teacher. Reverend Wright said he'd be teaching remedial computer classes."

Carol straightened and smoothed an imaginary stray hair with one hand while she gave the short jacket of her cocktail suit a firm tug that lowered the neckline, taking the suit from demure to suggestive. "Tomorrow morning, ladies, I'm changing my schedule."

"How much you want to bet you're not the only one?" Megan said. "Everyone's drooling."

"Except you, Rachel," Carol observed.

"He's not my type." Rachel lifted her shoulders. "The hulky blond, though . . ."

"Is gorgeous," Megan agreed. "With just a hint of mystery."

"Two down, a hundred to go," Carol quipped. "I can deal with those odds."

As Carol vowed to be the first at the office the next day, Rachel shifted her eyes toward Elijah one last time. *And so it starts.*

At least this time when women threw themselves at Elijah, she wouldn't be affected by it.

Elijah swept his eyes around the hall. He'd spotted Rachel the moment he'd walked in.

Even though he'd been prepared for it, the sharp kick of awareness left his solar plexus smarting. She was standing in one corner with a small group of girls. And try as he might, he couldn't stop sneaking looks.

Seeing her again brought the memories back. The delight, the hurt. Loving her had never been simple. Leaving her had damn near killed him. Yet they'd both moved on. Survived. It was what they did.

A glutton for punishment, he let his eyes drift over her yet again. The dress threw him. She rarely wore one. But when she did . . .

He narrowed his eyes, remembering. South Miami. Years ago. The party had been at a friend's beach house. Rachel had arrived late, with Nick, in a short, tight, red number that defied gravity as it slid off her shoulders and simply stopped.

Elijah had been taken aback when she showed

up. Things had been tense between them. And ass-hole that he was, he'd opened with a crack. "If that dress were any shorter, your panties would show."

She had shrugged. "Only if I were wearing any." Then she'd strutted toward the pool table and grabbed a cue stick. The room's collective blood flow dived south.

Long-buried hurt scratched at his lungs. Forcing himself to look away, Elijah briefly studied the other girls. From what he'd seen of the female student body at Shepherd's Cross, they were all beautiful.

Each was impeccably groomed and graceful. To a point they practically looked alike. Sure, they had different color hair, varying height, but basi-cally they all had that overeager ingénue look.

They watched not only him, but also every other male under forty. Husband hunting? One of the stats he'd read was that seventy-five percent of the alumni married fellow graduates, often before grad-uation.

He cast another glance at Rachel. She was, of course, the exception. And he wasn't the only one to notice her. Hell, even Reverend Wright had drawn a sharp breath when Emily had pointed to her.

What was it about Rachel that made her stand out from all the others?

What an expensive cocktail dress did for the other female occupants of the room, Rachel's body did tenfold for the simple black dress. On most women it would have merely looked nice, but Rachel's figure, her long athletic legs, her narrow waist and . . .

He couldn't think about the rest without imag-ining his hand gliding upward from her waist, capturing her fullness. He felt his body begin to respond. The next few weeks weren't the only thing that was going to be hard.

He'd known working with Rachel would be treacherous. They were too much alike. Strong. Confident. And hot tempered. Hell, nothing between them had ever been easy. Except sex.

Seeing her in Richmond two weeks ago had confirmed this job would require an unusual amount of endurance. She hadn't been happy to see him. No surprise there. In fact, he'd gone in expecting her anger.

What had blindsided him was his own rush of emotion. Seeing her again left him feeling weak in the knees. And his groin.

His chest tightened. After Richmond, he'd avoided her, mentally psyching himself to work with her. He honestly thought he'd been prepared for seeing her again.

But what Elijah hadn't counted on tonight was for Rachel to look almost as she had the first time he had ever seen her, seven years ago, walking down that airport terminal. Elijah had flown to Atlanta with his best friend to attend Nick's kid sister's college graduation.

Nick had given Elijah the same I'll-kick-your-ass-if-you-look-at-her-wrong speech that Nick gave everyone who went home with him. And Nick dragged everybody to his house.

But the physical attraction between Rachel and Elijah had been instantaneous and powerful. From the moment he'd locked on to her bright turquoise eyes, he'd been lost.

It had been lust at first sight. Love followed quickly.

Everyone envied him. Rachel was the ultimate fantasy girlfriend; great mind, great body. Independent as hell. She liked sports, fast cars, and faster motorcycles, and she was always ready for an adventure.

The woman had a mechanical aptitude and was as comfortable under a car hood as he was. And Christ, what they had done on that flat, wheeled floor dolly . . .

Nick hadn't been happy that they dated. And their friendship had never been the same—especially after Elijah and Rachel split up.

Once again, his gaze landed on her as she laughed at something the brunette said. Even from across the room Elijah recognized it as her practiced, controlled laugh. The Rachel he knew had a deep belly laugh that was infectious.

The Rachel he knew way back when.

He looked away. Had he honestly believed he could do this and feel nothing? Maybe Dwight was right. Maybe taking this job hadn't been such a great idea.

He hid a wince. In the last few months, Dwight had expressed concern several times that perhaps this assignment had become too personal for Elijah. On several levels.

It was difficult to deny.

It was no secret that where others wanted to see Kito Mzuzi—the moneyman—pay for his crimes in a court of law, Elijah wanted him dead. He had a lot of scores to settle with Kito.

First were the deaths of his friends. Second was the more personal hell that he himself had suffered.

Elijah had been within inches of catching Kito

too many times to count. Stepping aside to let someone else ensnare the man now was out of the question.

In the end, even Dwight had to acknowledge the simple truth that no one knew Kito as Elijah did. Plainly put, he was the best weapon in the Company's thinly spread arsenal.

And this time, Elijah vowed to get him. At any cost.

FOUR

All Emily talked about during their walk back to the dorms after the social was Rachel joining Eve's Circle. "I'm so sorry you didn't get a chance to meet Reverend Wright tonight, though."

Rachel hadn't minded. She'd exhausted her small-talk skills early on in the evening. "Reverend Hanson seemed to monopolize his time."

"Well, the good news is, when I spoke to him earlier, he agreed to meet with you tomorrow! And I've already put in a good word for you."

They had reached Rachel's door. She started to invite Emily in when her cell phone rang. She glanced at the caller ID, not recognizing the number. But she knew who it better be.

"I have to take this call. It's my aunt," Rachel offered. "I'll see you in the morning."

Once inside, she answered the phone.

It was Elijah. "We need to talk."

"Not we. You. *Professor Harris.*"

He breathed sharply into the phone. "The teaching thing came up last minute."

"Last minute? How long have you been here?"

"I arrived over the weekend. Dwight said he'd fill you in—"

Dwight, of course, hadn't said jack. "Oh, gee, that explains it all. I should have known better."

"From here on, I'll brief you myself. And while it damn sure wasn't my idea, it does have some advantages."

For him? Perhaps. But for her, if Elijah no longer needed her help, it meant she'd lost leverage with Dwight.

She kicked off her shoes and groped for a snappy comeback, not wanting either man to know how much she had emotionally invested in this. She'd lick her wounds in private.

"Actually, it makes it easier for me to wrap up and get back to Atlanta."

"I still need your help, Rachel. If anything, I need it even more than before." His voice lowered as if that admission was difficult. "Look, meet me behind the art center in thirty minutes. It's due east of the social hall. And watch out for campus security."

While the news that she still had a shot at information on Nick relieved her, the fact that Elijah disconnected before she could respond ticked her off. Damn the man.

They needed to establish ground rules. Number one: she wasn't a CIA flunky. He couldn't bark orders and expect her to jump.

After changing into dark jeans and a long-sleeve turtleneck, she strapped a small pistol to her ankle. The familiar weight was oddly calming. Bullets were a girl's best friend. If Elijah gave her too much grief, she'd just shoot him.

Before slipping out the back door, she studied
the campus map since she planned to take a different route to the social hall and art center.

The campus was eerily quiet, reminding her of a
note she'd read on the Web while doing research.
A former student had dubbed the college St.
Dullsville.

> The student center closes at eight-thirty. The
> mall at nine. Precisely thirty minutes later, the en-
> tire student body is either sound asleep or saying
> their bedtime prayers. No drinking. No smoking.
> No nookie. It's not normal. Run,

the poster had warned.

Seeing as the social had lasted until ten, Rachel
knew it was an exaggeration. But not by much. It
had also been the worst observation she'd found
posted on-line. The majority of the college's alumni
praised Shepherd's Cross.

Avoiding the sidewalks, Rachel crept across the
lawns, grateful for the abundance of trees. Since it
was only early-August, the trees still had their leaves,
though that would change in another month. Still,
the evening was cool, reminding her that here in
the mountains, summer would fade sooner.

When she drew close to the art center, she hun-
kered down beside a juniper and studied the building, watching for Elijah. The brief orange flare of a
match signaled his position. It also confirmed they
were alone. That he had spotted her first was no
surprise. The man had always had an uncanny
sense of night vision.

As Rachel drew close, she caught the heavy,

slightly sweet scent of cigar smoke. Her jaw tightened.

Her brother, who had disapproved when she had taken up cigarettes in college, had been fond of cigars. Particularly the fragrant Cubans that, while contraband here in the U.S., were readily available elsewhere.

Elijah took a final draw before stubbing his cigar out. "Let's move back to where you were. It's more private."

She cast a glance over her shoulder. "How big of a concern is security?"

"Negligible. They have two old men, both widowed retirees. Twice a night, at ten and two, they make rounds. Which consists of a door check. In between, they play cards at the student center. If you startled either of them, they'd go into cardiac arrest."

They were talking as they walked. Rachel tried to stay ahead of him, but he matched her pace.

"What about alarm systems?" she asked.

"On campus? None. Guess you haven't been here long enough to get the we-have-no-crime spiel."

"I probably slept through that part of the orientation film."

"A few buildings at the church compound have alarms, but nothing elaborate." Elijah stopped walking. "We can talk here. This is what I thought we'd do—"

Rachel cut him off. "What we need to *do* is set a few things straight." Drawing up to the balls of her feet to scrounge whatever height advantage she could, she jabbed him in the sternum. "I am not the low man on your totem pole. I expect to be treated as an equal and to be kept fully apprised of everything."

Wordlessly, Elijah snatched her finger and yanked her off balance. Rachel recovered quickly, but not without leaning into him, her hands catching against his chest. Strong arms encircled her.

Of their own accord, her fingers spread wide against his firm muscles. Memories shimmered, teased. The intimate contact weakened her knees. She forced herself to push away.

Except he wouldn't release her. He had his arms locked in a show of strength. She narrowed her eyes, refusing to back down. Elijah met her challenging gaze, silently reminding her she had drawn first blood.

If he expected an apology, he could go to hell. Instead of poking him in the chest, she now wished she had kicked him in the groin.

As if reading her thoughts, he straightened, forcing her to tip her head back to maintain eye contact. God, she hated tall men.

Without warning, he released her and stepped away. "There's a lot we need to set straight, Rachel. Personally as well as professionally."

She tucked her hair behind her ears. "My only concern is our professional relationship. Or lack of one."

If she and Elijah ever did set things straight personally—and she firmly believed that some sleeping dogs were not only best left alone, but should be euthanized—it would be on her terms. And her turf.

"I don't work with a partner these days, so my team etiquette is rusty. I'll work on it," he said. "I do view you as an equal, though, and there are not many people I'd say that about."

His capitulation surprised her. She had expected an argument. Hell, she wanted an argument. But where to begin? And where to end?

Her memories had their own crazy yin and yang. The bad harbored seeds of the good. Why couldn't she simply hate the guy and be done with it? It was a breeze to despise Dwight. Elijah should have been that much easier.

"Let's move on." Rachel cleared her throat and gathered her thoughts. "If you're on board here as staff, it should make computer access relatively uncomplicated."

"'Fraid not. I'm temporary, part-time help, which puts me just below plankton on the teacher food chain. I don't get any privileges."

"What about access to the computer network?"

"My password is barely a notch above the janitor's. I can enter grades and attendance, and that's about it."

She felt a moment's satisfaction over his admission that he wasn't savvy enough to bypass the software's security. "That's a start. What about building access?"

"I've got a key to the media center. Which I may have to turn back in. Evening classes require at least twelve students. As of this morning, I had one. I need you to sign up for my class, too."

Rachel didn't want to spend any more time with him than she had to. "Give it a day. I'm sure you'll make the minimum."

"Even if I do, I'm not certain I can come across as legit. The classes are video based, so I'm really not much more than a glorified movie projectionist. But the questions worry me. I can do basics, but beyond e-mail and spreadsheets, I'm out of my league."

"The class is remedial. I doubt you'll have more than one or two rocket scientists."

When his scowl deepened, Rachel realized he really was nervous. This man was a fish out of water behind a desk. Drop him in a jungle to extract prisoners, set him on a minaret with a sniper rifle—piece of cake.

"I'll think about it," she said.

His mouth relaxed. "Thanks. My class starts tomorrow night. As soon as it's over and things quiet down, we'll get to work."

"I'll need a little time to subvert the system. And don't forget, there's no guarantee we can even access the church's data from campus."

"Dwight told me the church and college shared the same network."

"They do. But they could still maintain their bookkeeping on a stand-alone computer. To give themselves another layer of security."

"How long before you can confirm that?"

Rachel shrugged. "Not long. Are you sure the network will be operational tomorrow?"

"At the teachers' briefing they said it should be up by morning."

"We'll need access to more than one terminal." While Elijah wanted to look at accounting records, Rachel needed to search Cindy's academic records. And she wasn't about to sit around waiting on him.

"Not a problem. There's an office adjacent to the one I use." Reaching in his pocket, Elijah withdrew a slip of paper. "Here's my cell phone number and address. I've rented a small apartment near the edge of campus, less than a mile from here. By the mall. Giving you a key is redundant. You were the only girl I ever dated who carried a pick set on her key ring."

"That's amazing, considering your statistics."

Rachel regretted the remark as soon as she made it. At best, it sounded catty. Worse, it hinted that she was still sore. *I'm not.*

But rather than apologize, she stuck the paper in her pocket and turned to leave. "I'll call you tomorrow."

His hand hooked her elbow, and for a moment she thought he'd tug her back into his arms.

"As I said, there's much we need to set straight. But this isn't the time or place. So we both have to be pros."

Pros. Right. "Agreed."

His hand dropped. "One last thing. You really fit the part, Rachel. You looked better than anyone else at the party tonight."

She avoided his eyes and resisted the compliment. She didn't want any warm fuzzies between her and Elijah.

"It's all part of the job. Don't forget I've got my own case here. My own priorities. And I made it clear to Dwight that I'm out of here as soon as I get my answers, by the way, even if you don't have yours."

Elijah gave a mock salute. "Then we need to make the most of our time."

After oversleeping and nearly missing her first class, Rachel met Emily for a late breakfast. Emily had offered to show her around campus before

Rachel's afternoon appointment with a guidance counselor.

The student cafeteria offered a buffet with everything from scrambled eggs to fresh fruit to Danish. Rachel loaded up on fats and protein. Out of guilt, she grabbed a bran muffin.

Noticeably missing from the lineup, though, was coffee.

"Not even decaf?" Rachel asked in disbelief.

"It's one of the health initiatives the students voted in last semester. We're caffeine free. They even replaced the soft-drink machines with ones that offer juice and spring water."

Rachel stared at the small mountain of crispy bacon piled on her plate. *Thank God they still allow cholesterol.* She made a mental note to pick up a jar of instant coffee. At least the dorms had microwaves.

"I bet Starbucks wasn't happy to hear about that initiative."

"Actually, there's one at the mall, if you feel the need to imbibe." Emily wrinkled her delicate nose, toying with the diamond-encrusted *E* that hung from a gold chain. "You really shouldn't drink that stuff, you know. Reverend Wright says it's an impure drink and unworthy of our temples."

That was at least the fourth time Emily had attributed a quote to Mason Wright. It was obvious the other girl was trying hard to sell Reverend Wright and Eve's Circle.

And while belonging to the same social club as Emily would accelerate their connection, Rachel really wasn't looking forward to kissing up to Mason Wright, who sounded increasingly self-righteous.

Three girls stopped by their table and reintroduced themselves. By the time they left, Rachel's head pounded. How could people talk that much? And be so blasted cheerful without coffee?

She dug in her purse for aspirin. The brand she used had caffeine.

Emily grew alarmed at the sight of the battered aspirin tin. "Are you okay?"

"Tension headache. I get them all the time." Rachel swallowed the tablets and winked. "Don't tell me the campus is aspirin free, too."

"We're not that bad," Emily grinned. "Yet."

After leaving the cafeteria, Emily insisted they start on the eastern side of the campus. Rachel hid her impatience in wanting to cut to the chase.

"This is what I wanted you to see." Emily pointed to a building. "You won't get the full effect today, but as the sun rises, the carved friezes at the top of each building seem to light up."

Shielding her eyes, Rachel looked upward. The carvings were, naturally, biblical scenes, each one beautifully rendered. "They're magnificent."

Emily beamed proudly, as if she herself had created them. "The rock that was used is loaded with crystals and quite rare."

"Quite costly, I imagine." It was clear that no expense had been spared in construction. And every building bore the name of a wealthy benefactor.

"This is the media center," Emily said.

Rachel squinted at the building, the largest one on campus. "Is this where they make copies of Reverend Hanson's sermons?"

"Most of those operations have been transitioned overseas, to the church's sister media center."

"So this building is empty?"

"Except for one or two classrooms, yes. The rest is being remodeled. They're planning to produce original television programming beginning in the spring."

"Remodeling? But the building doesn't even look that old."

"Nothing here is, really, considering the college has only been operating six years. This is phase two," Emily explained. "After all five phases are completed, the campus will be one of the largest private colleges in the country."

Rachel let her gaze sweep across the deep green lawn. One of the features she admired most about the campus was its vast amount of open space. Small, parklike vistas were everywhere, the undeveloped stretches dotted by majestic trees.

But with the college's expansion plans, that would likely change. "Sounds rather grandiose."

Emily hooked her arm in Rachel's and leaned close. "That's what they said when this was just a mountain. No city. No campus. Those same naysayers now call it brilliant. Visionary. It's another one of Reverend Wright's brainchildren. And it's exceeded everyone's expectations. There's even a waiting list of patrons." She tugged her along. "Let's go into the library."

Inside, Emily pointed to the row of computers. None were being used. "They're really unnecessary since the library catalog is now on the student network. Everyone accesses it from their dorm."

Rachel trailed her fingers along a keyboard. "So how do you access the Internet when you need to?"

"The short answer is, we don't need to. The college has its own state-of-the-art, private intranet."

State of the art, my foot. "What about e-mail? And research?" Rachel found it difficult to believe that someone hadn't found a way to circumvent the no-Internet policy. It was un-American.

Emily shrugged. "Everything needed to support our studies is already here. Teachers and students can e-mail each other on the system, but communication with family and friends off campus is done via traditional methods—telephone, mail, or personal visits—which builds core values."

Core values was a Hansonism for the church's fundamental beliefs. God, family, church. The graphic representation showed a triangle, with God on the top and family and church on equal ground below.

Falling out beneath those were other, smaller triangles. The husband at the top, the wife and children beneath. Under the guise of espousing family values, the church held that the man was the master of his home.

To Rachel this implied that the woman was the servant. Subservient. Not for the first time, she reminded herself she wasn't here to believe. Or to criticize their doctrine.

Well, except for the Internet piece. That sounded like a giant technological step backward. For better or worse, the World Wide Web was entrenched in everyday life.

"What about downtime?" Rachel persisted. "You know—just surfing the 'net for fun?"

"Reverend Wright calls that the Great Waste of Time. And we have fun without it. It takes a little getting used to, but trust me, you won't miss it." Emily glanced at her watch. "Yikes! You were due at the guidance office ten minutes ago. And I'm late for class!"

Rachel met with a saccharine-voiced academic counselor, who reviewed her schedule. Undergraduates had a prescribed program that varied only by class time.

"I understand you also have a remedial computer course. In the evening," Rachel said.

"I believe it's almost filled." The counselor swiveled her chair toward her computer. "If demand stays this high, I'll have to speak to the dean about offering a second class."

Rachel resisted the urge to roll her eyes, wondering how many girls, like Carol, were taking the class merely to ogle the instructor.

"You're in luck. There's one spot left."

The phone rang just as Rachel was leaving. The counselor held up a hand. "Wait. That was Reverend Wright's secretary. She said he'll see you now. His office is at the other end of the building. Just follow that hall to a small lobby."

Forcing a smile, Rachel swallowed a groan. The last thing she wanted to do right now was visit with Reverend Wright. She was hungry again, which fueled her headache.

And her cheeks, her face, actually hurt. *From smiling.* Which proved the crap she'd always heard about how it took more muscles to frown than to smile was bogus.

Reverend Wright's secretary greeted her with an enthusiastic hug. "Welcome to Shepherd's Cross, Rachel. We're glad to have you join us."

"Yes, we are," a male voice said.

Rachel turned as Mason Wright strode through an adjacent doorway. At last night's social, he'd worn a dark suit. Today he looked more pastoral with a long, black tunic over trousers.

"I'm Reverend Wright. And you must be Rachel Ives."

She braced for another hug, but when he instead extended his hand, she accepted it with relief. A firm handshake. She liked that. Mason turned away to get the file his secretary held out.

Rachel took advantage of the moment to study the man. He was tall, nearly six feet. And while she knew he was approaching fifty, he looked much younger. The gray at his temples looked too precise, as if he'd applied it to give a more mature look. He was an attractive man, not drop dead, buff city like . . .

She quickly squashed the thought.

"Come in." Mason motioned for her to follow.

His office was cavernous, with odd-shaped walls that seemed to break the room up. It had floor-to-ceiling bookcases, with built-in cabinets and shelves setting off a fireplace.

The space had been divided into two areas, a desk and chairs for business, a couch and love seat for more casual visits. Lush oil paintings, mostly landscapes, gave the room warmth. Classical music played softly in the background, the speakers hidden.

Mason held a straight-back chair for her, then took a seat behind his desk.

Rachel looked at the mortar and pestle filled with lemon drops that rested on the corner. Her stomach rumbled at the sight, embarrassing her. "That's an unusual candy dish."

"Please help yourself."

Unable to resist, she took a piece. It practically melted in her mouth, making her wish she could grab a handful.

Mason popped a piece of candy into his mouth. "The mortar belonged to my father. He was a pharmacologist, obsessed with the dream of inventing the perfect pill. I keep it there to remind me that only God has the perfect solution."

He winked playfully, not flirtatiously, making her feel more at ease and suggesting that perhaps he wasn't quite as starched at the collar as the rest of the faculty.

Opening her file, he scanned the top sheet. "So, tell me your first impressions of Shepherd's Cross."

"From what I've seen, it's beautiful. Peaceful."

It was the truth. The campus was immaculate inside and out. Every desk Rachel had seen gleamed with polish and there was virtually no desktop clutter, no visible paper.

"That's the first thing everyone notices," Mason agreed. "Our founder, William Hanson—you probably met him last night—believes that cleanliness, beauty, and order are the core values of godliness. When I first came to his church twenty years ago I thought it was a little idealistic. But this town, our campus, is a shining example of that truth."

Steepling his fingers, Mason tilted his head slightly to one side, seeming to study her intently. "Emily tells me you have an interest in joining our little group. Has she explained what Eve's Circle is?"

"She mentioned they support one of the overseas missions. I believe it was one of the ones they visited this summer. She sounded eager to return."

It was a minor fib. Emily had talked about their summer trip so much that Rachel had tuned out most of what she said.

"We did eight countries in six weeks," he said. "It was exhausting, but exhilarating. There were even a few who decided they couldn't wait until next year to return and stayed behind. It happens every summer. Did your church in Tallahassee do any mission work?"

"None that I participated in." Rachel was prepared for the question, giving the name of one of the larger Tallahassee churches, where a transient student body was typical. "My class load prohibited volunteer time."

Mason made a *tsk* noise. "That's a common story. And it's why we consider our summer program vital. It allows us to introduce students to the various mission ministries without interfering with their education. While a high percentage of our students choose to serve a year overseas after graduation, the summer program helps them decide whether it's right."

"It must take a very special person to dedicate themselves to that type of work."

The remark seemed to please him. "I spent ten years at a mission before coming here. It's an experience I treasure. Now, let me tell you more about the Circle. We're a very small group and therefore considered exclusive. As a general rule, we don't recruit new members like the others do. It's basically by invitation only. Let me say, however, Emily's recommendation says a lot."

That she might not be allowed into the group hadn't occurred to Rachel. Straightening, she re-crossed her ankles and leaned forward slightly. "Perhaps if you described your criteria, I could explain why I'd be an ideal candidate."

"That's a commendable attitude." Mason smiled. "But in truth it's more of an esoteric process. Once I've interviewed all the candidates, I pray for divine guidance in choosing prospective members. Those selected come in as initiates, and are required to do three months of in-depth counseling before acquiring full membership."

"It sounds interesting," Rachel lied again. It sounded awful, especially the counseling.

After scribbling a note in her file, Mason stood. Motioning her to stay put, he then moved around to the front of his desk and leaned his hips back against it casually. "I'd like to close with a prayer, Rachel, that God will guide you in your choices while here at Shepherd's Cross."

She shifted. "Sure."

To her surprise, Mason dropped to his knees and took her hands, looking briefly like a man getting ready to propose.

She panicked, uncertain whether she should kneel or remain sitting. He folded both her hands in his and leaned forward, his elbows on either side of her hips, effectively pinning her in place.

Feeling increasingly uncomfortable, Rachel closed her eyes. Thankfully, it was a brief prayer.

"And may we all reach the Kingdom together." Mason stood, pulling her to her feet. He squeezed her hands briefly before releasing them and stepping away.

"I think God has a very special plan for you,

Rachel. In fact, I get the feeing you were led to Shepherd's Cross for a divine purpose."

She cast her eyes suspiciously toward the ceiling. "And what purpose is that?"

Mason burst into laughter. "I don't know. He didn't tell me that part. But I trust He'll show both of us if we're simply open to His grace. I'll meditate on it further in prayer. As should you."

Nodding, Rachel followed him back toward the door. On the wall behind it hung an oil painting she hadn't noticed earlier.

The framed portrait was done in a style reminiscent of an old master and showed only a woman's head and shoulders. The woman was breathtaking, her profiled face seeming to reflect elation.

There was no mistaking the fact that she'd been painted through the eyes of love. Light glistened in her blond hair as if the paint itself had been flecked with gold.

A masculine hand, only partially visible, cupped the woman's chin, tilting her gaze up. To whom did she look? The artist? The slender line of her bare throat sloped down to a hint of generous bosom that was left unpainted. Behind her shoulders were swirls of . . .

Rachel cocked her head to one side. "Are those wings?"

Mason clapped his hands. "You obviously have an eye for detail."

"It's stunning. But I'm afraid I don't recognize the artist."

"Few would. Vito Palini was a fourteenth-century Italian. The man was a visionary who claimed his paintings were divinely ordered, that God whispered in his ear as He guided his hand."

Without thought, Rachel stretched out her fingers. Drawn. "That's quite a claim."

"In this case it was also a curse. Palini was the darling of the Vatican. Until this painting. After Rome pronounced it blasphemy, a group of zealots kidnapped him. He was burned upon a stake, his beloved paintings feeding the very flames that consumed his flesh."

Rachel sucked in air and withdrew her hand. "That's barbaric!"

Mason grimaced and nodded as if it also pained him to imagine dying in such manner. "I find it ironic that the very painting responsible for his death is the only one to have survived."

"I don't understand. What's blasphemous about this?"

Bending slightly, Mason brushed a bit of dust from the frame. "Palini claimed this painting wasn't ordered by God, but by His Son. That she was His one perfect angel, His one frailty. She was also the one thing His Father would not allow. Hence she was made mortal and sent to earth."

Turning toward her, Mason spread his hands and smiled. "The painting was entitled *Original Eve.* I like to think that if the story is indeed true, then part of her lives on in her offspring. And by that, the Son ultimately granted her immortality."

Blinking rapidly, Rachel turned away. For a moment she'd been hypnotized by the painting, by Mason's deep voice telling the story of a woman so perfect that heaven couldn't hold her. It was a fairy tale.

It also reminded her that great art moved the soul, sometimes in delight, sometimes in sadness. Pain and beauty were two sides of the same coin.

Clearing his throat, Mason opened the door, blocking her view of the painting.

But in that last flash, Rachel could have sworn the woman in the portrait looked just like Emily.

FIVE

When Rachel arrived for Elijah's class, the room was packed. How could she be late?

She checked her watch. Seven P.M. She was right on time. Everyone else had arrived early. To get bird's-eye seats, no doubt.

Elijah stood behind his desk, talking with a student. She took in his tie and button-down shirt, the cuffs folded back and tucked under.

This was twice in two days she'd seen him in a tie. In the two years they'd dated, he'd worn a tie ... never.

Same with the khaki trousers. The man wore jeans. *Wore* them. Like a second skin. And the rattier the pair, the better he looked.

He turned, nodding imperceptibly as their eyes met. She looked away, ignoring the twinge in her stomach. *I'm getting an ulcer.* Or so she hoped. Butterflies were unacceptable.

She worked her way to an open spot in the back, between the only two male students, and slouched in her seat. Both looked at her appreciatively before introducing themselves.

Their attention soothed her ego. After a fast phone call to Sheila's daughter, Rachel had combined a pair of embroidered jeans with a hot pink sweater and a suede blazer. If it wasn't black or white, she was out of her element. She had wanted subdued—sexy and chic, which she thought would be fine for an evening class.

But compared to the others, Rachel felt underdressed. Their dresses and skirts showed a lot of shapely leg. Maybe even more from Elijah's viewpoint at the front.

The next hour and a half passed at a lame tortoise's pace. After introducing himself, Elijah passed around an outline and started a video.

Then he moved to the back of the room. While she couldn't see him, Rachel was aware that he stood directly behind her, making her ulcer act up.

The video was painfully rudimentary. *How to Turn On a Computer 101.* That it even evoked a question in anyone's mind amazed her, yet they spent over thirty minutes on Q and A. Elijah held his own, which wasn't saying much. A distracted preschooler could have fielded these queries.

As soon as class ended, Rachel darted for the door. Since they had agreed to meet at eleven, she didn't need to stay.

Carol blocked the exit. "Stand here and talk to me for a few minutes." When the room finally cleared, Carol winked. "Thanks!"

But before Rachel could escape, Elijah called out, "Miss Ives."

Forcing her shoulders to relax, she turned. He had glasses on again, for effect. On most guys the dark frame would have looked geeky.

"If you could stick around." He motioned to Carol, indicating he needed to finish with her first. "I have a question on your prerequisites."

Right. The only prerequisite for this class was no brain activity. Rachel took a seat and watched Carol breathlessly describe a problem using terms like "thingy" and "doodad."

"Defrag your hard drive and see if that takes care of it," Elijah advised. "We'll talk next week."

When Carol left, he tossed the glasses onto his desk. Unrolling his sleeves, he crossed to shut the door. "How terrible was I?"

Rachel shrugged. "That was a half-decent answer. A defrag shouldn't hurt anything."

"I meant the class." He piled into the chair next to her and stuck a finger in the knot of his tie to loosen it. The two buttons he opened exposed a smooth vee of tanned skin and a tantalizing hint of dark hair. "You frowned the entire time."

"After today, my smile is permanently broken."

"That bad?"

She shook her head. "Actually, I'm envious. I wish I had the stamina to be as happy as these people. Maybe I need to rethink organized religion."

"Let me know if you find one that allows vices. Preferably smoking, drinking, and swearing."

"That's all?"

The remark hung awkwardly, and while she really hadn't meant anything by it, the ensuing silence grew uncomfortable.

"So—" They both spoke at once.

"Go ahead," Rachel said.

"The office I'm using is adjacent to another with a computer. There are only a few interior offices not affected by the remodeling, but we should be able to work undetected."

"How complex is your password?"

"Four alpha, four numeric. Case sensitive. Any problem?"

"I'll need my laptop." Rachel had several password-busting programs that would get them into the system.

"That reminds me." He pulled a disc from his shirt pocket. "Your secretary sent you an e-mail. I downloaded it onto this."

"After reading it?"

"Of course. You'd have done the same."

She snatched the disc and stood. The plastic was still warm from his body heat. "I need to go."

Elijah flexed his arm to look at his watch. "I'll meet you outside at eleven. Back entrance."

Rachel's eyes widened with recognition. Was that the watch she'd given him years ago? Nodding good-bye, she took off.

The watch meant nothing, she reminded herself. It hadn't even been a gift. She had bought it to replace the one she'd somehow managed to step on and smash.

It had been expensive and he'd insisted she return it. Which she couldn't do, because she'd had the back engraved. *Until the end of time—Love, R.*

He'd probably had the back replaced.

She would have . . .

Elijah watched Rachel set up her laptop. They were working with red-lensed flashlights, both to minimize ambient light and to protect their night vision.

He adjusted the tiny but annoying receiver in his ear. It was tuned to the sensors he'd stuck on the exterior doors. If anyone came in, he'd get a signal.

She bent over the desk to fiddle with the ports on the back of the college's computer terminal. He heard the words *cluster fuck* and smiled.

"Need help?" he offered.

"Nope."

Good. He leaned back to get a better view of her ass. The jeans she wore rode low on her hips—not as bad as some he'd seen, but effective all the same. Especially now.

Her butt lifted as she bent and twisted, sending the waistband lower in the back, exposing bare skin and a hint of crevice. A narrow strip of pink ribbon poked up on one side. A thong? Shit! It was a sure bet she wore a matching pink bra. D-cup, front hook.

Sexy underwear had been one of her guilty pleasures. He'd dropped a small fortune on lingerie. Damn stuff wasn't near as durable as boxers, not that he cared. When he'd wanted her naked, all that mattered was getting her clothes off. With her, he had no patience.

Rachel stretched, sending the jeans lower while offering a few more centimeters of pure temptation. And . . . *no tan lines.*

Elijah swallowed and felt himself harden. Sunbathing nude had been another of her guilty pleasures.

He remembered the time he'd flown in unexpectedly to surprise her. She had been staying at her brother's house. When she didn't answer the door, he let himself in and discovered her poolside wearing nothing but headphones and the sheen of SPF 15.

While part of him wanted to stand there forever and look, another part wanted to throttle her for being out in the open naked. Some weeks Nick's house was like Grand Central. Everybody had keys to the place.

And as Elijah's primal, possessive needs had warred with reason, she had sat up.

Her shocked expression had given way to excitement as she gracefully climbed to her feet. She had walked toward him, slowly, confidently, her full breasts gleaming with sweat and oil. Rooted in place, he'd watched them sway.

The bouquet of roses he held in one hand fell to the ground, followed quickly by his pants. They'd made love standing up. Fast and furious.

"That should do it." Rachel straightened, tugging her sweater down before adjusting her jeans.

He straightened, needing to adjust his jeans, too. When he moved closer, she looked at him accusingly then moved sideways, in front of her laptop, blocking his view as she activated a screen saver.

"I'm sure the software I use is similar to what the Company uses," she said. "Still, my methods are proprietary."

Elijah forced a smile. While his intent had only been to get nearer to her, he doubted her statement about her software. Knowing her—and that geeky little dweeb she was still friends with—he'd lay odds she had programs only God was beta testing.

Rachel was a damn good PI. The best. Though her firm handled a little bit of everything, she specialized in the cases most police departments didn't have the time or manpower for: kids abducted by a noncustodial parent or relative. Her recovery rate was remarkable.

And while she didn't advertise it, a large part of her success rate was attributable to her computer-hacking skills. The woman had microprocessors embedded in her DNA. Small wonder Senator Benjamin had enlisted her.

Rachel's laptop beeped, drawing her attention. Turning away, she closed it, then moved to sit in front of the other computer.

Elijah watched her fingers fly over the keyboard. "We're in?"

"Yes. Give me one sec." Rachel flipped through several screens that made no sense to him. Then she frowned. "There's good news and bad news."

"Let's hear the bad."

"The system automatically shuts down at two-thirty for backup and self-maintenance. I can override it, but my guess is the system administrator checks his backup tape first thing every morning."

"Then we'll plan to be out of here by two."

"The good news is you can access both the college's and the church's accounting records with the password I have." Climbing to her feet, she shoved the chair toward him. "How much hand-holding are you going to need?"

He caught the chair with one hand. "I'm not that bad."

Her eyes showed her doubt. "It's in read-only mode, so you can't mess anything up."

"That's fine for tonight. But eventually I will need to print and copy."

She slid her laptop into her bag. "I'll be next door. By the way, if the keyboard or mouse is inactive for more than fifteen minutes, it will lock you out."

"So what's the password to get back in?"

Rachel looked at him. "My deal with Dwight was to get you into the system, not give you free rein."

Touché, Elijah thought. He knew about the deal she had negotiated with Dwight for information on Nick. He also knew that the declassified stuff Dwight would pass along would not answer her questions.

The two men had discussed the issue at length. Dwight had bluntly pointed out his concern that Rachel would use her feminine wiles against Elijah to get information.

Fat chance. Cherry trees would bloom in hell before he ever got a sample of her wiles again.

Rachel hadn't moved, and Elijah realized she expected an argument over the password. *Choose your battles.*

"I'll take it up with Dwight," he said.

"You do that."

Within minutes, Rachel was logged on to a second computer in the adjacent office. She knew Elijah wasn't pleased with her efforts to control his access. And him contacting Dwight was exactly what she wanted.

For a price—more information on Nick—she'd give them a password. In the meantime, withholding it bought her time to figure out exactly what Elijah was searching for.

To that end, she had attached a keystroke

recorder to the back of his terminal. The tiny-but-clever device would log every page. Once she downloaded the recorder's contents, she would retrace Elijah's steps, which meant deducing what he was looking for. It might be like looking for a needle in a needle factory.

"For now, I need to concentrate on Cindy," she muttered. Perusing the archive, Rachel located Cindy Benjamin's academic records. They held little of interest. Cindy's grades had been slightly above average and didn't seem to waver. There were very few absences, none of them consecutive.

Instructor comments ranged from benign to positive, with many referring to Cindy as a quiet student. Since the *quiet* notation popped up consistently, Rachel dismissed it as a clue that could be attributed to worry over an unplanned pregnancy.

Rachel had two of the same instructors that Cindy had and made notes of the rest. Approaching them would be trickier than approaching the students.

Cindy's housing record confirmed that Cindy and Emily had been roommates during their first semester at Shepherd's Cross, before each girl then moved to private quarters.

Under social activities, Rachel noted that Cindy had also been a member of Eve's Circle. That was interesting. Had she and Emily joined at the same time? That was two solid links she'd discovered between Cindy and Emily now.

Curious, Rachel opened Emily's academic records.

Emily's grades were near perfect, as was her attendance. Instructor remarks were generous. Emily was described as bright, energetic, cheerful, lovely . . . *a pure pleasure to teach*. There were also notations by Mason Wright, commending Emily's leadership role with the Circle.

Flipping back through the software indexes, Rachel opened the membership roster for Eve's Circle. The current semester was blank, but she looked through the prior one. The only names that rang bells were Cindy and Emily.

Exactly seven members were listed each semester, which struck Rachel as odd even though Mason warned it was a small group. She tried to recall the biblical meaning for the number seven. The perfect number?

Retrieving her notebook, Rachel looked up three other students that Senator Benjamin had mentioned were friends of Cindy's. None had been Circle members, and all had either graduated or left the college for another reason. Rachel scribbled down their last known addresses and phone numbers.

A noise at the door alerted her she had company. Elijah leaned against the doorjamb. He had his hands stuffed in his front pockets, which drew her gaze *there.*

She turned back to the screen, feigning disinterest.

"It's almost two," he said. "We should call it a night."

"Give me a minute to erase our activity from the log."

Elijah straightened. "I meant to tell you earlier that I've got dial-up access through the phone at my apartment. It's slow, but if you need to check e-mail, you can come by my place."

Come by my place.

Her cheeks grew warm. Obviously, he didn't remember that had been one of their little code phrases, something they'd say when others were within earshot; verbal shorthand for *I'm dying to have sex.*

Which, back then, had been all the time. Or at least every second that Elijah was home. Like Nick's, Elijah's job frequently required him to disappear, sometimes for months. Incommunicado.

Then he'd sweep into town, usually without notice, expecting her to drop everything and live in his bed. Fool that she was . . .

"Maybe tomorrow," she said. "I'm pretty tired tonight."

Sick and tired, she corrected. Of recalling only the blissful times. She needed to remember the hell this man had put her through. Because of him, she'd sworn to never trust another man with her heart.

The next day, Rachel barely made her early class again. Four hours of sleep, combined with the fact she still hadn't picked up any coffee for her dorm room, spelled disaster.

One of Chase Scoggs's lines came to mind. *On days like this, I could go rogue. Be a professional hit man. Knocking off two people before breakfast sounds relaxing.*

Yes, it did.

As soon as class ended, Rachel cut across campus and hit the mall. When she arrived back at her dorm an hour later, she was smiling. That extra shot of espresso in her latte had done what aspirin couldn't.

She looked at the poor, wilted fern Emily had given her. Grabbing a spoon, she opened the jar of instant coffee she'd just bought and sprinkled some granules atop the dirt, then watered it. "Trust me, it helps."

Tucking the coffee in a cabinet, she left the box of herbal tea on the counter. She had left a message earlier on Emily's phone, inviting the other girl over for tea that evening. Tea and questions.

Opening her laptop, she reviewed the list Sheila had sent and began making notes. Twenty-eight couples had adopted children within the targeted time frame. The number certainly raised Rachel's eyebrows and seemed to corroborate Senator Benjamin's claim that the church had an abnormally high incidence of adoption.

What she wanted to know now was when had the adopting parents joined the church? And were they still members? That information would be available from the church's records, which she could access later that night on the network.

She also wanted to visit the student clinic. While the senator had furnished copies of Cindy's autopsy report, he hadn't included any medical records.

And if there was time, she would hit the campus counseling center as well. Sheila promised to send the names of other nearby pregnancy counseling agencies, too, though Rachel wasn't certain how she'd access their data. Perhaps she'd start by visiting as a potential client.

Her cell phone rang. She expected it to be Emily, but instead it was Mason Wright's secretary.

"Reverend Wright would like to see you again. Are you free?"

She checked the time. "I have class in an hour."

"Then I'll tell him you'll be here in fifteen minutes. He said it wouldn't take long."

Rachel hoped it meant Mason had made a decision on her Eve's Circle membership. A positive one. The thought that she might not be selected had ruffled her feathers.

Wanting to make a favorable impression, Rachel changed into a demure summer dress before leaving her dorm.

Mason Wright's secretary ushered her straight into his office. He was writing notes but dropped his pen and stood when she walked in.

"Rachel, thank you for coming on such short notice. Please sit. I have fresh juice." He moved to a nearby refreshment tray and picked up a carafe of orange juice, then pressed a glass into her hand. "I'm sure you're wondering why I called you here."

"Yes."

He returned to his chair and leaned forward on his desk. "Remember I said that I knew God had a special purpose for you?"

Rachel resisted the urge to squirm. She had an uneasy relationship with the Almighty, which was a graceful way of saying she was still pissed over losing both of her parents and her brother. "I remember."

Mason offered a reassuring smile. "I had a vision this morning. About you. And the reason you were sent here. The message was quite clear: you're to join Eve's Circle, Rachel. It's obvious someone," he pointed to the ceiling, "has big plans for you."

The news relieved her more than it should have. "Thank you. I feel flattered."

"And you should, my dear. Only a few are chosen, so it's an honor and a privilege." Mason stood. "I'll get back with you this evening to set up our counseling sessions."

"This evening?" she asked.

"Yes. Tonight is our first group gathering of the new semester. Emily can bring you to the meeting and fill you in."

It was after five when Rachel's class ended. Her cell phone beeped, indicating she had messages. Elijah had called to confirm their meeting that night at eleven. And Emily would pick her up at six-thirty for their Circle meeting.

Detouring past the cafeteria, Rachel picked up a sandwich and devoured it on the way back to her room.

She climbed into the shower. Clueless what to wear, she chose a deep purple skirt and top she could dress up or down once she saw Emily. In the past two days, it felt as if she'd changed clothes fourteen times. Fashion was exhausting.

When Emily arrived, she greeted Rachel with a small squeal. The same small squeal that Rachel now realized always preceded a hug. "I had hoped you'd be chosen!"

Rachel nodded and grabbed a necklace and heels. Belonging to a group, the feeling of sisterhood, would make it easier to ask questions. "Me too. But I'm still not even sure what Eve's Circle is all about."

"You'll love it. It's fun," Emily said as she followed Rachel out the door. "The social groups have meeting rooms in the administration building. A few groups are so large they have to use the conference room, but we have plenty of space. We meet once a month with Reverend Wright to study and discuss our group goals. And of course he works individually with us, as his schedule allows."

"Have I met anyone else who's a member of the Circle?"

"You met most at the social. But you may not have realized they were members." Emily ticked off names.

None were familiar. While Rachel was good with names and faces, the social had been an overload.

The Circle's meeting room was retro-Barbie with walls painted pale pink and deep rose. A floral border formed a halo just below the ceiling. Chintz-covered sofas and chairs circled a coffee table. An epidemic of silk flowers and throw pillows completed the look.

Rachel drifted toward a display of photographs. The pictures were black and white, semiformal shots, each matted with a small plaque listing seven names.

"Those are prior year members," Emily said.

Rachel quickly scanned the names, finding the plaque that listed both Emily and Cindy Benjamin. But it took her a minute to spot Cindy. The girls in the photograph had light hair. The pictures from Senator Benjamin had showed Cindy as a brunette.

It was sad to think their estrangement had left the Benjamins without current photographs. Rachel knew the value of a picture all too well.

Emily moved in beside her. Rachel pointed to the photograph. "Look at you!"

Sticking out her tongue, Emily made a face. "That was two years ago, when I first arrived. Look how fat I was."

Fat? Hardly. Rachel ran her finger along the line of girls. "I don't recognize any of them, except you. And . . ." She squinted and pointed to Cindy. "She looks familiar. Isn't that the senator's daughter who died recently? I just read something about his wife being sick."

Emily nodded. "Her name was Cindy Benjamin. And we were all pretty shocked to hear about her accident."

"You were close?"

"Cindy and I roomed together our first year and formed a special bond. After that we drifted apart a little bit." Emily's voice tapered off. "I felt like I let her down."

Rachel placed her hand lightly on the other girl's shoulder. "Let her down how?"

"By being too busy. I let myself get too caught up in school to notice she was having problems."

Problems? Rachel tilted her head. Had Emily known about Cindy's pregnancy? "I'm sure you did all you could. Had this problem come up while you were still roommates?"

The door opened, distracting Emily and shattering the moment.

"We'll talk later," Emily whispered. "Let me introduce you to everyone."

Rachel cast a last glance at the photograph, sensing she was making progress. *Finally*. Emily's remarks were telling, and being left open ended, the subject would be easy to pick up again.

Turning to greet the others, Rachel immediately did a double take. Five girls had arrived. All of them were blond. Fair eyed. Like Emily. Like Rachel. And like Cindy Benjamin.

Even their heights were within an inch or two of

each other. Goosebumps chased up her spine. What the hell was this? Stepford students?

Rachel slid her eyes back to the pictures on the wall beside her. Because the photographs were black and white, it hadn't been as apparent at first. And she'd initially been focused on the names. But now that she looked at the individuals, it jumped out at her.

Everyone was blond. And while a few of these girls were naturally fair haired, Rachel didn't believe they were trying to copy each other.

No, they were trying to mimic the painting that hung in Mason's office. The one perfect angel. Original Eve . . . Eve's Circle.

She realized they were all waiting for her to speak. "I feel like I'm seeing double."

"At least you didn't make a blonde joke," one girl quipped. "I'm Alisa Avery. And trust me, we've heard them all."

Rachel recognized Alisa's name now. She too had been a member back when Cindy had been at Shepherd's Cross.

"Let's move over to the couches," Emily said. "So we can tell Rachel and Tara more about us and our group."

Apparently Rachel and Tara were the only two new members.

"I'll start," Alisa volunteered. "Our Circle supports the mission in Thailand. Visiting it this summer made it personal for me."

"How do you support the mission?" Rachel asked.

"We do a fund-raising project each semester," Emily said. "Last semester, we furnished books for the children's library."

"Besides our mission-related activities, we also do in-depth studies with Reverend Wright," Alisa said. "So we better understand foreign cultures."

"Which sets us apart from the other groups," another girl added. "In fact, Reverend Wright frequently refers to us as an honors group."

Rachel's nose wanted to wrinkle. More studying? On what? How not to have fun?

From outside, footsteps shuffled. All heads turned expectantly toward the door as Mason Wright entered. He stood in the doorway and smiled.

"Sorry I'm late." His gaze landed on Rachel, then shifted. "Has everyone met Tara and Rachel?" At their nods, he clapped. "Excellent. Let's get started."

He took a seat in the Queen Anne armchair. In unison, the girls grabbed pillows from the sofas and sat in a semicircle at his feet.

"We're a little informal here," he explained to Rachel and Tara. "Make yourselves comfortable."

Sitting near the edge of the group, Rachel watched as Mason gave each girl his undivided attention for a minute or two, laughing at their exaggerated complaints of too-busy schedules.

"You're just readjusting after summer," he said. "If I remember correctly, these are the exact same remarks I heard last year at this time."

The girls grew more animated, wiggling like a knot of hungry kittens around a milk dish.

For a moment Rachel understood why men like Mason—William Hanson, too—never married. Why be tied down to one person when there were so many vying for notice?

Tara asked a question about their overseas trip. Everyone tried to answer, interrupting each other.

After a moment, Mason took over and segued from talk of the missions to a discussion of the Kingdom. As if by magic, the group quieted when he spoke.

From what Rachel gathered, the Kingdom seemed to be an analogy for Heaven. Live right, and you prospered in the Kingdom. Mason referred several times to the rules on living right, but didn't elaborate. Since even Tara seemed to know what he meant, Rachel nodded along with the others.

Once again, she reminded herself that while she was there to do a job, these people had a deep and abiding faith. They believed the church's teachings, and she needed to respect that.

The one thing Rachel couldn't fake, however, was the shining admiration she saw in most of the other girls' eyes. Especially Emily's.

While the other girls shifted at Mason's feet, Emily had gradually moved to his side and held his notebook as he talked. The look on her face hovered close to worship. Awe. And something else. Did Emily have a crush on Mason?

The meeting was quite benign and fairly short. Where Rachel had expected a lot of Bible thumping, there'd been none.

Mason closed with a prayer. "Tara, I'd like to meet with you in the morning at nine. Rachel, can you make four o'clock?" At their nods, he stood. "I'll leave you ladies to your . . . devices."

Something about the way he said it made Rachel glance at Emily, who smiled mysteriously.

As soon as Mason left, the others formed a circle with Rachel and Tara in the center.

"He knows, doesn't he?" Alisa whispered.

"Knows what?" Rachel asked.

"Of course he knows. He knows everything."

Emily spread her arms wide. "This is your initiation. Everyone goes through it their first night."

Tara seemed excited. Rachel pasted on a smile. "Initiation?"

"Don't worry. It's nothing bad," Emily assured. "Just girl stuff."

Great. Rachel was freakin' doomed.

Having been raised by her brother, she had failed miserably at *girl stuff* in junior high. Her closest friend had been Wendell, the penultimate computer nerd who suffered chronic nosebleeds and walked around with tissue crammed up his nose. Still did.

And while other girls her age had been actively defining *girl stuff* beneath the bleachers at the Friday night football games, Wendell had taught Rachel how to hack computer systems.

"You both need to kneel," Emily said. "And repeat after me."

Tara and Rachel vowed to never divulge the secrets of the Circle and to only discuss Circle activities with other members.

"And Reverend Wright," Emily added.

Next, the other five lit votive candles and set them around Rachel and Tara. When the overhead light was shut off, the room twinkled, shadows flickering.

A chalicelike goblet filled with a dark liquid was pressed into Rachel's hands. She sniffed it and suspected it was a cheap red wine.

"It's okay," Emily urged. "Take a sip."

Aware that everyone watched, Rachel took a small taste. It was awful wine, too sweet, too acidic.

Tara took the goblet next, sipped, then passed it around the circle.

Alisa drained the cup, then held it upside down. "Now we've all sinned," she giggled. "We could all be punished."

"Punished?" Tara drew back slightly. "As in divine retribution?"

Emily gave Alisa a withering stare. "Alcohol is forbidden on campus. We use it in our initiation to give us a bond and shared secret—one that could have us dismissed from school."

One sip of wine? Rachel rubbed her head, fighting a headache. Again.

Emily's face softened with sympathy. "It will pass. If you're not used to alcohol, even a little can make you woozy. But you're safe here."

Woozy? A half dozen shots of tequila did not make Rachel feel *woozy*. She glanced around the circle. All the girls were smiling—some almost looked giddy. Did they really believe one sip could make them drunk?

"Did Reverent Wright tell you that?" she asked.

Emily nodded.

The power of suggestion. Rachel felt her temper shorten. "So what are the secrets we've just sworn to keep?"

"It's the sacred knowledge of Eve," Alisa said. "How to be perfect women."

"Perfect women?" Rachel repeated. "You can't be serious!"

"She means perfect mates for our future husbands," Emily corrected. "Which complements the core values and suits our roles as women."

Their roles? Rachel bit her tongue to keep from blurting out that the term was archaic and sexist. Of course, most of what she'd heard about *core values* fit that same description.

"Perfect by whose standard?" Rachel pressed.

"Why, the Kingdom's. Who else's?" Emily's tone held a mild rebuke.

Rachel lowered her eyes and backed down. Speaking against the church's teachings would only raise suspicion. Which she didn't need right now.

But once she had her answers . . .

"Of course," Rachel said. "The wine has me confused."

"That will pass. And trust me, once you know the truth—" Emily winked. "Your life will never be the same."

SIX

Damp grass squeaked beneath the soles of Rachel's shoes as she jogged across the dark greenway that separated the campus from the town.

It was barely ten-forty-five, yet like the previous night, the campus was deserted. The occasional student she spotted remained on the walkway, oblivious to Rachel slipping along the wooded perimeter.

Once the main hub of extracurricular activity, the mall, closed at nine, most students returned to their dorms for study, prayer, and sleep.

Rachel doubted weekends were much different. Over half the students lived within six hours of home, which meant a mass exodus on Friday afternoons. Or as mass as such a minuscule college could muster.

One of the campus's basic tenets was that an ideal learning environment produced an ideal student. On the surface it appeared they were correct.

Students at Shepherd's Cross were far more diligent about their studies and sleep habits. No late-night parties, no surfing the 'net until four. No sneaking boys or beer into the dorm. They were so freakin' functional it was eerie.

Their religious beliefs undoubtedly played a part. But Rachel wondered how much was environmental. What else was there to do when so few temptations existed? No Internet. No alcohol. No caffeine. Even the late show at the cinema was over by nine.

When she looked at the campus as a whole, the girls in Eve's Circle didn't seem quite as strange. After all, bizarre religious beliefs were everywhere. Compared to the self-flagellating *Opus Dei* or the zealots who reenacted the crucifixion—including being nailed to a wooden cross—the quest to be a perfect blond woman seemed tame.

And where initially Rachel had thought the girls were too submissive, too eager to please, she'd sensed an underlying competitiveness as they vied for Mason's attention. Beneath the meek exteriors lurked more than one cutthroat. They weren't that different.

Except Emily . . . She was simply too sweet, too kind.

Rachel had hoped to discuss Cindy Benjamin again after the initiation, but Emily had to rush off to another meeting. They agreed to meet for breakfast in the morning.

Shifting her backpack, Rachel paused to check her surroundings. Earlier in the evening it had rained as a cold front passed through, leaving the air crisp.

She glanced at the cloudless sky, at the brilliant sparkling lights that seemed to have been tossed so chaotically into the night. Her brother had told her once that stars were the soul lights of their loved ones who'd passed away. That the star's twinkling was a form of communication, a sort of Morse code between souls.

As a kid, Rachel had spent many a night perched contentedly on the garage roof, delighting in every shooting star. After losing Nick, however, she had taken a very long time to again find wonder in the night sky.

Despite her earlier resolve, Rachel found herself thinking more and more about asking Elijah outright about his last assignment with Nick. And about the time Elijah had spent in captivity.

Unfortunately, everything to do with Elijah was embroiled in a maze of emotionally complex booby traps. It wasn't possible to discuss Nick without opening the Pandora's box of her and Elijah's failed relationship. At least for now, dealing with Dwight was more straightforward.

Darkness enshrouded most of the quadplex where Elijah lived. Rachel studied the building, then approached the end unit and tapped lightly at the back door. The small patio had a grill and a lone lawn chair. A single eight-foot section of privacy fence offered a slight barrier from the neighboring apartment.

He opened the door. "Come in."

Elijah's apartment was twice the size of hers, which simply meant he had a separate bedroom and a shoebox kitchen. "Do I smell coffee?" she asked.

"I just made it. Still drink it black?"

Nodding, she drifted toward the built-in dining table. A speakerphone dangled haphazardly atop a stack of files, its cord snarled into a large ball. Untangled, it would reach any room in the apartment.

She shoved the phone into a safer position, scanning the file tabs as she did. They were unlabeled. An open laptop sat next to a small printer, but unfortunately, the screen saver prevented her from seeing what he was doing.

"Here." Elijah moved up behind her, violating her personal space.

The need to bolt, to flee, flared, then just as quickly guttered out like a candle in a strong wind, leaving her chilled.

Turning, she accepted the mug of coffee. His fingers brushed hers, sparking a physical awareness. A familiar ache. She stepped away from the muddle of memories. The bad outweighed the good, yet still she had to endure recollections of both.

Rachel gulped coffee, burning her mouth as Elijah moved to gather the files and put them in a box on the floor. She pointed to his computer. "What are you working on?"

He shrugged, noncommittal. "Weeding through e-mail. Sheila sent you another file, by the way. Want to look at it?"

Without waiting for a response, he typed in a password. She caught the last four digits—1124— and tried to analyze them. If it was a significant date, Rachel didn't recognize it. Which didn't mean anything. It could be random. Or even the birthday of his latest girlfriend.

Which doesn't matter. She read the e-mail.

Sheila had sent a list of pregnancy counseling centers in the area. Rachel printed the list and tucked it into her backpack. "Do you mind if I plug in my own laptop to check my office e-mail?"

"Help yourself."

Working quickly, she downloaded her mail to read off-line later. Then she sent precomposed messages to Dwight and Sheila. The whole process took less than three minutes. Dial-up was outrageously slow.

"How was your club meeting tonight?" Elijah asked as she closed her laptop and repacked it.

"A little strange. They have some unconventional beliefs." Not wanting to discuss the concept of a perfect woman with him, she moved away. "I keep reminding myself that since Cindy Benjamin was a member of the same group, I have to play along. Ready to go?"

Setting his coffee aside, Elijah grabbed his own black backpack.

"I only have a few things to pull off the network," she said as they took off. "Then I need to visit the student clinic. I'll be back at the media center by two, though."

"The clinic has a service door in the back, on the west side, with no outside light. Don't forget the guards patrol around two."

Rachel looked at him suspiciously. She knew exactly why he'd been in the clinic. "Why bug the clinic offices?"

"Just covering all bases."

She frowned, uncertain if she believed that, yet unwilling to press for a better response. What the CIA was doing on campus didn't involve her.

Inside the media center, Rachel checked that the keystroke recorder was still in place, then she logged Elijah on to the same computer he'd used the night before. Later, she'd swap the recorder with another and download this one.

She spent time searching the church's membership directory. Of the twenty-eight couples Sheila had dug up, twenty-three were no longer active members and lived out of state. Had one of them adopted Cindy Benjamin's baby?

Continuing to dig, Rachel found that most couples joined the church three months prior to the adoption. Likewise, they dropped out approximately three months afterward.

Contribution records showed each couple made a sizeable lump-sum donation in the beginning, with smaller ones following. It appeared they were basically buying their way to an adoption.

Which still left the question of where all these babies were coming from. Based on what Rachel knew of the church's doctrine, premarital sex was taboo. However, the core values of family meant that even an illegitimate child would be cared for and loved, so she doubted the infants were coming from the legitimate membership.

After she left the media center, she headed for the student clinic, where she found the back door Elijah had described.

Chase Scoggs had taught Rachel to pick locks and then had made her practice for hours. "It's gotta be second nature, kid," he had said. "You have to stroll up to a door like you own it and be able to pick it and go through in no more time then it should take a person with a key."

Inside the clinic, she avoided the computers in the reception area, where any ambient light would be visible through the lobby windows. When she found a more private computer, she set up her laptop. Within minutes, her software delivered a password.

Logging on to the system, she scanned the choices on the main menu. PATIENT DIRECTORY. She typed in *Benjamin, C.*

CYNTHIA BENJAMIN popped up. RECORDS Y/N?

"Hell yes," Rachel whispered.

The cursor blinked as the computer retrieved data. PATIENT DECEASED—FILES ARCHIVED. It took Rachel a few minutes to locate the archive. The cursor blinked slowly as the system searched for Cindy's files.

Rachel checked the time. It was almost one. "Come on." Finally, Cindy Benjamin's records appeared. There were a total of fifteen pages.

Beginning with page one, she skimmed the vital statistics, noting Cindy's weight and the date of her last period. Nothing unusual. While Cindy took prescription medications for asthma, no birth-control method was noted. That explained a lot.

Cindy's first visit to the clinic was two weeks after she arrived on campus. The flu. After that she visited the clinic twice to get refills for her asthma meds, but Rachel noted no fluctuation to her weight. And the date of last period never exceeded four weeks.

Until February, a year ago.

Rachel leaned forward as she read the report. REASON FOR VISIT: *Possible pregnancy.* Blood tests were ordered. Skipping ahead to the next page, she searched for lab results. There were none. Had the tests been performed?

She looked again at the date. It coincided with Cindy's diary entry. Rachel reread the doctor's notes. In addition to ordering blood tests, Sarah Wetherington had referred Cindy for counseling for *sexual aberration.*

Rachel's stomach tightened. How embarrassing that must have been for Cindy. Or was it part of the overall plan? Make the poor girl feel even guiltier, then suggest she place the child for adoption?

The rest of Cindy's file yielded little. There was another refill of asthma meds, but no follow-up on the pregnancy test.

Rachel tried a few wild-card searches in hopes of finding the missing lab report, but came up empty-handed.

Next she searched for counseling records, which weren't on-line. That meant a trip to the counseling center. Unfortunately, it was too late tonight. She was already running behind.

She hurried back at the media center. Elijah met her at the door. "I was just getting ready to call. You're late!"

His tone had her bristling. Never mind that he had a valid point. "So sue me."

He started to say something, then stopped. "I'll retrieve the door alarms."

While he did that, she erased the log and switched the keystroke recorder. She'd have to wait until the next night to decipher it though.

When Elijah returned, neither of them spoke, but the strain rattled the air. Outside, she scanned the campus as he locked the door. A flash of light caught her eye. Twin flashlight beams.

"Security," she whispered.

"Shit! This way."

Before she could respond, Elijah grabbed her

wrist, tugging her over the small retaining wall and into the landscaping that flanked the building.

He shoved her ahead. "Get all the way down."

The bushes were so thick there wasn't enough room to crouch. Rachel pushed her backpack away, then dropped to her hands and knees. She tunneled beneath the branches, lying on her stomach.

To her astonishment, Elijah dove in next to her. She rolled up onto her side, flattening herself against the building, to let him squeeze past. But instead of moving away, he pressed against her, their bodies touching.

Claustrophobia engulfed her. She'd never been fond of tight spaces, but this . . .

She put her hands against his chest to push away, struggling for distance. Elijah's arms encircled her, twin steel bands that trapped her as they stilled her movements.

"Shh." His lips brushed her ear as he breathed the word softly.

The guards' voices grew louder as footsteps shuffled up the stairs.

"Cool weather's got my arthritis acting up."

"Take a break and rest that hip, Charlie. You never did tell me what your doctor said."

Rachel swallowed a groan as she realized the two guards were sitting on the wall just above them. And judging by their conversation, they were in no hurry to leave.

Elijah shifted closer, causing her to panic anew until she realized her fingernails were digging into his chest. Unable to lower her arms, she straightened her fingers, forcing them to relax.

Beneath her palm, she could feel his heartbeat.

Ta-da, ta-da. Her agitated senses were hyperaware of everything. She was breathing too fast, her breasts crushed against his chest.

And lower, his muscled thighs were pressed firmly against hers, making it impossible to ignore his erection. It was long and excruciatingly hard. Utter temptation.

She remembered the last time he'd held her this tightly. He'd had a hard-on then, too. But he'd been gloriously naked. She'd been free to touch, to tease. To taste. To run her hand up and down. And to graze her lips against his size and heat.

Suddenly, she felt feverish with want, remembering what it was to crave him. What it had been like to live on the edge of responsiveness, always on, always ready. Never satisfied.

Her awareness shifted to where his knee pressed lightly between hers. She released her thighs, opening them slightly.

He pushed in, eliminating the hair's breadth that had separated them. The move left her dizzy. The press of his body shattered her defenses and destroyed her determination not to be affected. Desire swamped her. Shifting imperceptibly, she hunched against his knee.

She felt the rasp of his chin as his lips brushed close to her ear once again. The scent of his after-shave mingled with the earthy mulch. His tongue traced the curve of her ear, just before his teeth nipped the lobe. Sensation shot straight to her pelvis. She bucked her hips.

Elijah's hands shifted to cup the sides of her head, his fingers splaying against her scalp, as he held her immobile. Time stopped. Then finally, he took her mouth.

Rachel accepted the onslaught, surrendering. His hands dropped away as hers came up to fist in his hair, holding him in place as his tongue swept deep.

Her hips undulated again, but not against his knee. Against his erection. His grasp slid down to her waist, tipping her pelvis slightly upward before maximizing sensation by pressing impossibly closer. She shuddered.

Then his hands slid beneath her shirt, invading her bra to tease her nipples. She tried to press fully against his hands, craving his touch, wanting *more.*

He caught her bottom lip lightly between his teeth. The erotic nip overloaded her senses. She jerked, cracking her head back against the brick foundation.

She welcomed the pain as reality crashed over her.

Elijah pulled back, his breathing just as ragged as hers. The guards were drifting away, leaving them alone. She didn't want to think about what she'd been ready to do.

"Let me up!" Rachel shoved against him. "Now!"

He caught her hands. "It's okay. Let me back out first."

She closed her eyes and ordered her breathing to calm as she straightened her clothes. Shimmying free, she sprang to her feet and quickly brushed away the dried leaves and mulch clinging to her.

Elijah grasped her arm. "I'm sorry."

She flinched and jerked back. Once upon a time, she would have given anything to have heard him say those two words. Now . . .

"I think it's best if we both pretend that never

happened." The lump in her throat threatened to choke her. She snatched her backpack and stepped away. "Good night."

After tossing and turning, Rachel awoke as she'd gone to bed: on the verge of an orgasm. Under any other circumstance she'd have simply masturbated and been done with it. But to do so knowing she'd gotten this way because of Elijah was unacceptable.

It was just one more reason she needed to get this job wrapped. How could she face him after their little fiasco under the bushes?

There was no denying she had desired him. If the bricks hadn't knocked some sense into her, she would have taken what he freely offered. Which was the last thing she wanted to happen.

Unfortunately, her regret was a double-edged sword. Elijah had been a magnificent lover, his sexuality unmatched. Women literally fawned over him, even when Rachel was with him. And when she wasn't . . . Doubt had eaten at her.

In retrospect, she realized they'd been doomed from the start. Nick had warned her about Elijah's reputation. Howie and Dwight, too. She hadn't listened.

And recalling her pain did little to make the memory of Elijah as a lover less potent. Frustrated, she dressed and walked next door a few minutes early.

Emily answered, clearly flustered. "I'm sorry! I seem to be running in slow motion this morning."

"That's fine. I'll come back."

"No. Just let me grab my purse."

When she turned away, Rachel noticed she limped. "What's wrong?"

Emily straightened. "I slipped in the shower. Graceful, huh? I feel like a clumsy old lady."

"You're lucky you didn't break your neck."

As they walked out the door, Rachel watched the other girl's gait. While Emily seemed to move more easily, she was obviously sore.

"Are you sure you're okay?"

Emily smiled, then winked. "I'm fine. Really. And I'm setting a poor example of the church's teachings. We should offer our discomfort as proof we're worthy to enter the Kingdom."

The remark made Rachel frown. "You're plenty worthy. So if it continues to bother you, go to the clinic."

"You're a good friend, Rachel." Emily hugged her. "I've missed that."

The embrace left her feeling like a heel. While Rachel had cultivated the friendship solely to get information, Emily believed they were friends. And maybe they were, on one level. It was impossible not to like the other girl.

"You mentioned last night that you and Cindy Benjamin had been pretty close friends. It must have been hard to lose her."

"It was. But I know it was much harder on her mother." Emily gazed into the distance. "I went to the funeral and there was simply no consoling Mrs. Benjamin. Then to get the awful news that she was sick herself. For all her troubles, I don't think Cindy would have wished that on her mother."

"I take it Cindy had problems. Did she let you help?"

They walked in silence for a few minutes before Emily spoke again. It was plain that the topic was a sensitive one.

"I listened, then I urged her to confront her parents. I believe that's what she was going to do when the accident occurred. In some ways I feel it's my fault she's dead."

"You are not responsible," Rachel interrupted. "Perhaps Cindy's troubles were deeper than she let on. Or maybe she and her boyfriend had had a fight?"

"She didn't date. When she first arrived here, she was painfully shy. She bloomed as a Circle girl, but she never seemed really comfortable with guys."

The statement perplexed Rachel, particularly in light of the senator mentioning the false incidents of date rape. Cindy must have dated at some point in her life. Becoming pregnant required a partner.

Perhaps Emily wasn't aware Cindy was seeing someone. Or maybe it had been a one-night stand.

Rachel tried a different tack. "Well, if Cindy didn't date, then at least she wasn't going home to tell her parents she was pregnant or something earth-shattering like that." She watched the other girl closely for reaction.

To her surprise, Emily's eyes flashed in anger. "I can assure you that wasn't the problem! That goes against our core values."

"Of course," Rachel soothed. "I didn't mean to imply anything."

She let Emily change the subject, eager to get back on level ground. One thing was sure: if Cindy was pregnant, Emily didn't know.

Inside the cafeteria, the other girl seemed to relax. "I haven't even asked if you had any questions about your initiation," Emily said as they sat down. "There's a sixty-day probation period, which basically means you can't vote for our fund-raising project. Same with Tara. But we'll welcome your suggestions on the topic."

Rachel tore a piece off her bagel. "I guess the one thing I'm confused about is who defines what a perfect woman is? I haven't found a reference to it in the church's teachings."

"That usually throws everyone, but it's part of the process you'll work through with Reverend Wright." Emily dropped her head. "But I'll give you a clue. There is no one definition. It's different for everyone."

It was after two before Rachel had the chance to read through the e-mail she had downloaded at Elijah's. Then she called her office.

"I've got something for you," Sheila said.

"What?" Last night, Rachel had e-mailed a demand for payment to Dwight. Had he sent info to her office?

"You know that list of area clinics I sent? I checked to see if any complaints had been filed with the business license office."

"Anything?"

"Nothing too unusual. Except that Sarah Wetherington does volunteer work at all of them. A half day per week. That could explain where they're finding all the babies."

The news was unexpected and intriguing. "Great work! That also means it's unlikely Cindy went to one of the other clinics under an assumed name."

Rachel talked with Sheila about other cases until it was time to head to Mason Wright's office for her four o'clock appointment.

When she arrived, Mason greeted her warmly. "You look none the worse for initiation. Of course, I'm sure what they do here is nothing compared to what you've seen in Tallahassee."

"Nothing at this campus compares to Tallahassee," she agreed.

"Let's sit over here." Mason motioned toward the sofas.

A refreshment tray sat on the table. He poured a glass of orange juice and handed it to her before taking a seat opposite.

"I suppose you're wondering what kind of counseling we do here." Mason tugged a tea bag from his coffee mug.

Rachel lowered her juice, glad that he'd brought the topic up. "I don't feel like I have any particular problems."

"That's why the term is a bit of a misnomer. We're looking for your strengths, to help you achieve your personal best. To that end, we'll first explore any traumas you've suffered. I've reviewed your files and I know you lost your parents, Rachel. That can be devastating at any age, but with you being so young it can create an imbalance that makes you either overcompensate and seek the wrong relationships or undercompensate and avoid attachments altogether."

"Honestly, I don't feel I do either." Rachel set her empty glass aside.

Mason offered an indulgent smile. "Everyone I talk with has that same initial reaction. Then when they break through, they're stunned."

"Break through?"

"To joy. Many describe it as breaking free."

"Free of what?"

"The barriers of the life you've created. You have to step beyond what's false to find the truth."

I simply want to find the truth about Cindy Benjamin, Rachel thought. Which meant playing along with his lame answers. "That doesn't sound too bad."

"Shall we start?" Moving to the end table beside her, Mason removed a portable CD player and headphones. "Have you ever been hypnotized, Rachel?"

"No." That was mostly true. She had tried it once in college to quit smoking. It didn't work. The hypnotist had explained she couldn't be hypnotized against her will and apparently she'd taken it quite literally.

"It's a simple process. Put these on. I have a video you watch with it, which will help you get into a light trance. Then we'll talk and I'll make some suggestions to help you. Sound good?"

Rachel nodded and prepared to bluff. She put the headphones on and sat back.

"Slip off your shoes and lie on the couch so you can see the screen." Mason had opened a cabinet above the fireplace, where a flat-panel television was hidden. "I'm going to step outside to speak to my secretary while you listen to this first part. But I'll be right back."

Feeling awkward, Rachel did as he instructed. The CD began with the sound of waves crashing against the shore. A seagull called, the sound echoing and melting back into the waves.

On the screen was a deserted, crescent-shaped stretch of beach. Sparkling sand stretched for miles, the water cerulean. The perfect Caribbean island.

Not bad, she thought, rolling her shoulders gently.

Then Mason's voice seeped in over the sound of the waves. "Take a deep breath. Feel your arms and legs relax. Feel the warmth of sunshine on your skin."

Rachel closed her eyes, felt the delicious kiss of the sun. A sigh escaped her lips.

"That's right," Mason's voice crooned. "Relax and go deeper. Trust that all is good . . ."

It felt as if Rachel were being pulled through a fluffy cumulus cloud. On a moonbeam. Over the ocean.

A hand gently squeezed her shoulder.

"Wake up, Rachel."

She stretched, resisting the compulsion to open her eyes. It was so peaceful here. So pleasant.

"Come on, now."

She recognized Mason's voice and turned toward it, like a flower seeks sunlight. He was crouched beside the couch, not too close, not too far. Smiling.

Unable to resist, she smiled back, suddenly struck anew by how handsome he was. And caring. Giving. Small wonder everyone liked him so much. She liked him.

The urge to stretch her body again was strong. "Oh no! Did I fall asleep?"

"You did indeed. I got called away longer than I realized, too. How do you feel?"

"Luxurious." The word came out of nowhere. But it was accurate. She'd had little sleep of late.

Mason moved back to the other sofa as she sat up. "Tell me what you remember."

"Water. I was swimming. On my own private island. It was divine." Once again the words flowed without much thought. "I feel . . ."

"Wonderful? Not a care in the world?" He scribbled a note.

She nodded, wide-eyed. "How did you know?"

"I've done this a lot. Remember?"

She felt mildly disappointed by his remark. Out of nowhere came an urge to convince him that her experience had been unique.

"Let's meet again Friday." He stood. "My secretary will call you."

"Friday?" As Mason walked her to the door, Rachel realized she didn't want to leave.

In the reception area, he grabbed a bulky envelope from the corner of his secretary's desk. "Here's an extra player and disc for you to use at your dorm, if you like. Listening as you fall asleep will help you go into a trance easier the next time we meet."

Rachel took the package eagerly. If using this at night made her feel this good . . . "Thank you."

Outside, the sun had dropped below the trees, making her feel disoriented. She checked the time and found she had been there nearly three hours.

God, she must have really fallen into a deep, deep sleep while Mason was gone. She also had no recollection of how the session went.

Since Rachel knew she didn't talk in her sleep, she wasn't worried about giving anything away. But it was weird to know she'd slept so soundly with another person in the room.

"All the more reason I have to get decent rest at night," she muttered.

Last time she saw Elijah, he sure hadn't looked sleep deprived. Of course, he wasn't having to maintain the façade of a student. He probably slept all day, damn him.

By the time she reached her dorm, the bliss she'd felt at Mason's had worn off, due in no small part to the fact she still hadn't decided what to say to Elijah about their kiss. The scene in the bushes was embarrassing.

In the end, Rachel decided to ignore it. And if he brought the subject up, she'd simply assure him it wouldn't happen again.

SEVEN

As it turned out, Elijah didn't mention the night before. When they met at the media center later, he was aloof, but polite, same as she was.

On certain occasions, sticking your head in the sand was the lesser of all evils. Sure, it meant something could fly right up your ass—as Chase was fond of saying—but in this case the alternative was unacceptable.

Rachel didn't want to discuss kissing Elijah. She didn't want to be reminded of what she'd been ready to do. Those thoughts, those feelings, were best left where she'd found them. *In the dirt.*

For now, minimizing contact was good. And after tomorrow, it might be moot. If she didn't get something from Dwight by noon, she wasn't helping Elijah anymore. She'd left Dwight a phone message to that effect. Not that he'd called back. Jerk.

As soon as Rachel got Elijah's computer set up, she took off for the student counseling center. Breaking in was a breeze, but when she finally located Cindy Benjamin's file, it was empty. A sign-out sheet indicated that the contents had been transferred to Mason Wright.

Had Mason requested it in conjunction with the counseling he did for the Eve's Circle members? And if so, did he still have it in his office?

Rachel checked her watch. She had little more than an hour and a half before she had to return to the media center. And she would make damn sure she was on time tonight.

Careful to leave no trace of her presence at the counseling center, she made her way back to the center of the campus. Getting inside the administration building was a little trickier since all the doors were well lit. She studied the shadows, then picked her target.

Inside, Rachel gave her eyes a minute to adjust, then headed straight for Mason's office. As always, his desktop was spotless. Using her trusty red-lensed flashlight, she searched his desk, but found little.

She turned to the file drawer in his credenza, but it held nothing on Cindy. Moving to the far side of the credenza, she swung open a door. Fitted behind it was a locked file cabinet.

"Bingo."

A faint noise caught her ear. A slight vibration and shift in the air. *The front door.* Closing the cabinet, she darted from Mason's office and ducked behind his secretary's desk in the anteroom.

Muffled footsteps approached. She held her breath. Whoever it was, was being just as sneaky as she had been. They were also headed this way.

Was it Elijah? Since Rachel had told him she was going to the counseling center, he wouldn't expect her to be here.

The person was now in the same room. She tensed, uncertain. Then the door to Mason's office was pushed open. She peeked around the desk, catching sight of a man's back as he disappeared inside and closed the door.

She recognized the man. *William Hanson's bodyguard.* What the hell was he doing sneaking around?

The answer was painful. He worked for Dwight. She should have known the CIA would have more than one operative on campus.

She debated confronting the man but doubted she'd get anything useful from him. He was obviously a rookie, meaning they wouldn't tell him much. Better to confront Elijah or Dwight.

And since Elijah was closer, she'd start there. Keeping an eye on Mason's door, she slipped away and left the building. Outside, she took off jogging toward the media center. Because of the sensors Elijah had at the doors, she called him to say she was returning.

"You're early," Elijah said. Then he narrowed his eyes. "What's wrong?"

"How many men do you have working here? Five? Six?"

"What are you talking about?"

"I just caught your guy breaking into Mason Wright's office."

Elijah stood, fists clenched at his sides. "What guy? There is no one here besides me, Rachel. Does that mean you've been made?"

"Hell no!" She scowled, confused. If Hanson's bodyguard wasn't working for the Company what was he doing? Had someone gotten wind of the senator's secret?

"What did he look like?" he pressed. "And is he still there?"

"He was there five minutes ago. And I know who it was, though I don't know his name. It was William Hanson's bodyguard. He was at the social."

Elijah grabbed his own backpack. "Let's get out of here."

Rachel quickly shut down the computer, then followed him outside.

"You lead," he whispered.

They raced across campus. The administration building was dark. Without going in, it was impossible to tell if the man was still here.

"I'll cover the back, you watch these doors," Elijah said. "If he comes out, we can buzz each other's cell phone."

"What then?"

"We'll follow. See where he goes. I don't want to confront him."

Crouching low, Rachel watched the building, scanning windows for movement. After twenty minutes, one of the doors opened and the man slipped out.

She punched Elijah's number. They both had their phones set to vibrate. "He's headed your way."

"Got him."

Dropping back, she tailed the man, but he didn't go far before climbing into a dark sedan and driving off without headlights.

Her phone vibrated.

"I got the tag number," Elijah said. "Where are you?"

"A hundred yards due east of the building."

"I'll be right there."

Rachel stepped out of the shadows when he drew close. "What do you make of it?"

"I'm not sure. I'll get a rundown on the tag ASAP. I suggest we call it a night. Tomorrow we can—"

She held up a hand. "Tell Dwight I'm finished until he pays up."

Elijah swore, but she ignored it, remaining stone faced as tension crackled between them, straining the edges of their civility.

He nodded. "Fine. I'll see that he gets the message."

"Fine. Call me tomorrow."

When she got back to her room, Rachel couldn't sleep, so she used the relaxation CD Mason had given her.

Almost immediately, she fell into a deep sleep. Too deep.

Without warning, the pleasant sensations gave way to gruesome images of violence, leaving her feeling trapped. A captive of darkness. She struggled to find the peace, the bliss.

A low noise broke through. *The phone.*

With a jolt, Rachel sat straight up. It was almost seven and she'd overslept again. She snatched her phone and snapped "hello."

Senator Benjamin's voice came across the line. "Sorry to call so early."

She grimaced. "That's okay, I have a class soon."

"I'm leaving town again this morning. I take it you're settled in?"

"Yes." While Rachel knew he was eager for a

progress report—all clients were—she was hesitant to disclose much. Mentioning the pregnancy test she'd seen in Cindy's medical records before she knew the results could build false hopes. "Unfortunately, I haven't found anything conclusive yet."

"I realize you haven't been there long," the senator said. "But I wanted to let you know about something new that came up. It may be nothing, but I'd feel better if you checked it out."

"Certainly." She hoped it was a solid clue. "What is it?"

"Cindy's laptop was one of the personal items returned to us. The case had been damaged in shipping and it wouldn't even power up." The senator sighed. "I don't know why I even kept it, really, except at the time it was simply easier to seal the box and pack it all away."

"That's understandable."

"Yes, well, it just dawned on me that perhaps a computer whiz could retrieve some of her e-mails. You know, maybe she'd sent a note to a friend or something."

Or even the baby's father? Rachel climbed from bed. "I have people who do that type of work."

"Actually, I had my personal computer guru look at it. But he was only able to retrieve fragments. There was a file labeled *maternity*. Inside was a list of baby names. And a video."

"What was on the video?"

"He couldn't retrieve it. File corruption or something. This all goes over my head, you know." Exasperation tinged the senator's voice. "The file was named 0913.MPG. He did find a second reference in the antivirus software that indicated the file had been downloaded in October of last year."

Disappointed, she ran a hand through her hair. "If it was something Cindy downloaded off the Internet, I can't trace it without more data."

"But she was at school last October, so it had to come from their private server, right? I mean, they have no Internet there."

"If Cindy left campus on the weekends, she could access the Internet anywhere," Rachel pointed out.

"We were told she rarely left."

She recognized the desperation in his voice. "I can search the databases here for a file with that name, but I wouldn't get your hopes up."

The senator made a relieved noise. "That's all I ask. I'm plagued with the thought the file could be a sonogram. Or perhaps even video of the child before she gave it up."

The thought gave Rachel chills, but still she tempered her response with caution. "Don't forget, we don't even know for certain Cindy was pregnant."

And while the fact the video name came from a file labeled *maternity* was indeed suspicious, it could have been anything from a child-birthing film to postpartum exercises. Which meant it was more unlikely Rachel would find the file on campus.

"At this point." The senator's voice broke. "I'm sorry. The latest test results on my wife are not good. If I don't get something soon . . ."

Guilt and pity washed over her. "Let me assure you, senator, that if a file with that name exists on campus, I'll find it."

"And when you do, just make a copy and I'll view it personally to see if it has relevance. Jimmy said I could count on you."

Rachel frowned. *Tell the little brown-noser I said hi.* "I'll be in touch."

Hanging up, she glanced at the clock and headed straight for the shower. As soon as she was dressed she moved toward the microwave to heat water for coffee.

That's when she noticed the brown envelope shoved under her door. She picked it up. The outside contained no markings, no *to* or *from*, and the edge was sealed with tape. While it was large, it wasn't thick.

Grabbing a knife, she slit the tape and cautiously peered inside. It was an eight-by-ten photograph. She slipped it out, letting the envelope fall to the floor. It was a contact sheet, created from strips of film negatives. There were twenty-four images, all small. She quickly scanned them.

Nick!

The shots were sequential, of her brother on a busy street. The poses didn't change much from frame to frame, but in the last one, she made out a traffic signal and realized he was crossing a street. A busy street.

She brought the sheet up closer, zeroing in on Nick. The cropped photo she'd been given in Richmond had been taken from this roll.

In some shots, Nick was looking off to the side. Left, then right. Was he watching someone in the crowd, or was he scoping out a site? For that matter, where was he?

The photographs were too small to see detail. She needed the magnifying glass from her bag.

But as she set the sheet down, she noticed the edges were beginning to curl. Before her eyes, the paper darkened. She knew what Dwight had done.

"No!"

She tried to stuff the sheet back inside the envelope, even though she knew it was too late. The photo had been printed on paper that disintegrated after exposure to air. The inside of the envelope would have been treated with a retardant that would be useless once the degradation process began.

Helpless, she watched the centermost image of her brother melt away. And when the sheet was completely black, she screamed.

Dwight Davis was a dead man.

Elijah slept till noon. His rest had been fitful, once again plagued with memories of Rachel. And Nick. Of happier times.

Nick had been the brother he'd never had. Even Elijah's parents and sisters had adopted Nick, welcoming him into their home whenever Elijah dragged him in. Which wasn't often enough. And then once Elijah and Rachel started dating . . . well, he'd practically abandoned his family.

Frustrated by his thoughts, Elijah climbed in the shower. He spent most of the afternoon scrutinizing the Company intelligence reports delivered the night before. Per usual, he gleaned nothing.

Likewise, he'd found little of interest so far on Shepherd's Cross's computer. Of course, there was still a lot to go through. And not just the records he was searching on the computer network.

After he left the media center each night, he went to the church's accounting office and pored over the data CDs the missions sent monthly. Those he could read on his laptop without Rachel's help. Unfortunately, there were hundreds of them.

Going through them was a painstaking process, like sifting dirt from sand, but he knew from experience that something usually popped just when he felt ready to throw in the towel. And his current dry spell was the equivalent of a seven-year drought. That meant he was overdue for a break.

It also meant he was dangerously close to being reassigned. These days, the brass were focused on the bottom line. Resources and manpower were stretched to the snapping point.

Elijah understood that investigations like this one didn't rank high on the priority scale. Particularly when no solid evidence was forthcoming.

Had it not been for Dwight's intervention, the case would have been shit-canned long ago. In spite of their differences—and despite denials that he cared—Dwight had a personal interest in this case.

Nick and the other two agents who'd died with him had been working for Dwight. Elijah, too. If Dwight hadn't *cared*, Elijah might still be rotting in a Syrian prison while everyone thought he was being held in Afghanistan.

He'd spent thirty months in captivity; thirty months in hell. And as horrific as that had been, he'd do it all again if it would bring his friends back.

Standing, he stretched, then padded barefoot into the kitchen for coffee before refocusing on the background information he'd just received on William Hanson's bodyguard, Nigel Kowicki.

The car Kowicki had driven was a rental, making it easy for someone at the Company to harvest his driver's license and personal data. But the man had no record. Mr. Goodie Two Shoes. So, if Kowicki was that blasted good, what the hell was he doing in Mason Wright's office? Some internal spying for William Hanson, perhaps? Hanson reportedly trusted the man explicitly.

And what if Kowicki had discovered Rachel there last night? If he was indeed faithful to Hanson, he would have turned her in, blowing her cover and possibly Elijah's case as well.

On the other hand, and far more likely, what if Kowicki was up to no good? To what lengths would he have gone to silence her? The thought turned Elijah's stomach to mush.

Sure, she could have protected herself. Rachel was one of the few women he knew who could. Which didn't take away his urge to protect her. Or his worry.

It never had.

Elijah would always remember the time he and Nick were in Russia. Nick's Aunt Laura had sent a letter with a news clipping about Rachel that detailed how she'd negotiated a trade, offering herself as a hostage in exchange for a terrified twelve-year-old.

One news photo showed the distraught perpetrator holding a gun to Rachel's temple as he shouted demands to police. A subsequent photo showed the man on the ground, Rachel cuffing his hands.

Elijah knew exactly what the man had done: he'd taken one look at Rachel and thought with his dick. Knowing her, she had probably encouraged his underestimation . . . until the perp let his guard down.

Then she'd nailed him.

Elijah had been proud of her. Nick, too. Yet Elijah could never get the picture of a gun being held to her out of his head. He understood what she did was dangerous, but he loved her. In his book, that changed everything.

His cell phone rang. It was Rachel. The fact he'd just been thinking about her—"What's up?"

"Can you get in touch with Dwight directly?"

Her tone had his grip tightening on the phone. "Why? What's wrong?"

"That son of a bitch—" She paused and drew a sharp breath. "Make sure he gets that part. Tell him I'm not doing this. Period. We're finished. I'll be out of here tomorrow or the next day. Max."

"Rachel, wait. Please." Elijah had relayed her previous message, and Dwight had promised to take care of it first thing. "I take it he didn't send you anything."

"Oh, he sent something. But it was no better than a check written with disappearing ink. And now the bastard won't return my calls. Screw him."

Part of Elijah wanted to deck Dwight. For multiple reasons. He tried to separate them.

Professionally, Elijah needed Rachel's help. Getting someone else in at this point would waste time. Personally, he just wanted to be around her. She professed to hate him, but at some point they had to push past that anger. That's what he wanted. If she left now, she'd only build higher walls.

"What about making a deal with me? I can get info on Nick. And more." For a moment, he thought the line was already dead.

"What do you mean, more?"

Elijah hesitated, but only for a second. "I can tell you about some of the assignments we were on. And what we did afterward. The good times."

Once again silence greeted him. The fact she didn't hang up gave him hope.

He pressed on. "This will be just between us, Rach. I'll still relay your message to Dwight, in hopes he'll make things right."

She snorted. "And what makes you any more trustworthy than Dwight?"

"Look," Elijah continued. "We need to talk face to face. Meet me at my place at ten. If you don't like what you hear, you can walk. You have nothing to lose."

"I'll think about it." And she hung up.

Rachel trudged back to her dorm later that afternoon. Sitting in class, pretending to be interested was torture. This job couldn't end soon enough. For a lot of reasons.

She noticed the note she'd stuck on Emily's door was gone. She had left a phone message earlier, wanting to meet the other girl for dinner. But Emily hadn't called back, which was unusual.

While she'd agreed to talk with Elijah later, Rachel was in wrapping-up mode. He and Dwight were peas from the same CIA pod, so she doubted she'd get much from him.

Her plan for tonight was to visit Mason's office once again to search for Cindy's counseling records. She was prepared to accept that, like the pregnancy test she'd been unable to verify, Cindy's counseling records simply might not be accessible. *So be it.*

Rachel would also search for the video file the senator had mentioned, which would likely be a waste of time, but that was as far as she'd go. Then she'd close the case.

Only one question remained unresolved. What to do about the high incidence of adoption at

Shepherd's Cross? Ultimately someone needed to locate and speak with the birth mothers, to see if they'd been coerced into giving up their children. That someone wouldn't be her, though.

She knocked on Emily's door. Megan, the pretty redhead Rachel had met at the social, answered. "Hi!"

"Hello. I was looking for Emily, but I can come back if she's busy."

Megan's smile widened. "She's already gone. She left a phone message, asking if I'd come by to water her plants."

"I'll catch her tomorrow, then," Rachel turned to leave, but Megan stopped her.

"Didn't you hear? One of the student ambassadors who was supposed to go overseas got sick. Emily volunteered to take her place."

The news was unexpected, though Rachel knew Emily would have jumped at the chance to go again. Emily had talked about their summer trip as if it were a visit to Mecca.

"How long will she be gone?"

"Two weeks."

Rachel would be gone before she returned. Why did that make her feel sad? She shrugged it off. "Thanks."

Since it was Friday night, the cafeteria was practically deserted, which suited Rachel. Still, when Dwight called there were other students within hearing range, which prevented her from using the F-word-peppered speech she'd planned.

"You have to keep helping us," Dwight said. "I sent you something."

"What you sent was no different from your dissolving e-mail." Rachel dumped her food tray, appetite gone, and hurried outside where she could talk in private. "I'm not going to play this game every time."

"I have hard copies of those photos and more. What I sent was merely a preview."

"That's not what we agreed to."

"It's the best I can do."

"Then my job is done." Rachel hung up on him. To stay on the line and wait for a response weakened her position. If he wanted to play her way, he'd call back. But she already knew he wouldn't.

It was more proof the rat bastard had planned to screw her all along. She never should have trusted Dwight.

Back at her dorm, she made a cup of coffee. As much as she hated to admit it, part of her still held out hope that Elijah would offer something tangible on Nick. Those thumbnail prints she'd glimpsed this morning had left her empty. Aching.

Desperate.

All the more reason she needed to decide exactly what information she wanted from Elijah in return for helping him. For starters, she'd ask about photographs. She had so few and none within the last two years of his life.

She also wanted to know what jobs Elijah and Nick had worked together. Part of that was a test to see if it tallied with what Nick had told her. Providing Nick had been honest. Her brother wasn't above lying to protect the Company. Or her feelings.

She understood that what Nick did was classified. She respected that. To a point . . .

The bottom line was, she really wanted to know about Nick's final assignment. How and where he'd

Zebra Contemporary

Whatever your taste in contemporary romance – Romantic Suspense … Character-Driven … Light and Whimsical … Heartwarming … Humorous – we have it at Zebra!

And now Zebra has created a Book Club for readers like yourself who enjoy fine Contemporary Romance written by today's best-selling authors.

Authors like Lori Foster… Janet Dailey… Fern Michaels… Janelle Taylor… Kasey Michaels… Lisa Jackson… Shannon Drake… Kat Martin… to name but a few!

These are the finest contemporary romances available anywhere today!

But don't take our word for it! Accept our gift of 3 FREE Zebra Contemporary Romances – and see for yourself. You only pay $1.99 for shipping and handling.

Once you've read them, we're sure you'll want to continue receiving the newest Zebra Contemporaries as soon as they're published each month! And you can by becoming a member of the Zebra Contemporary Romance Book Club!

As a member of Zebra Contemporary Romance Book Club,

- You'll receive three books every month. Each book will be by one of Zebra's best-selling authors.

- You'll have variety – you'll never receive two of the same kind of story in one month.

- You'll get your books hot off the press, usually before they appear in bookstores.

- You'll ALWAYS save up to 20% off the cover price.

SEND FOR YOUR FREE BOOKS TODAY!

To start your membership, simply complete and return the Free Book Certificate. You'll receive your Introductory Shipment of 3 FREE Zebra Contemporary Romances, you only pay $1.99 for shipping and handling. Then, each month you will receive the 3 newest Zebra Contemporary Romances. Each shipment will be yours to examine FREE for 10 days. If you decide to keep the books, you'll pay the preferred subscriber price (a savings of up to 20% off the cover price), plus shipping and handling. If you want us to stop sending books, just say the word… it's that simple.

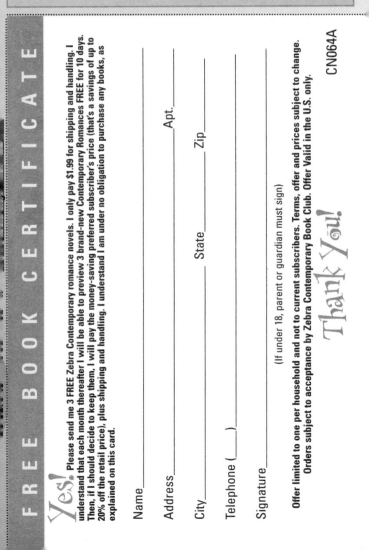

FREE BOOK CERTIFICATE

Yes! Please send me 3 FREE Zebra Contemporary romance novels. I only pay $1.99 for shipping and handling. I understand that each month thereafter I will be able to preview 3 brand-new Contemporary Romances FREE for 10 days. Then, if I should decide to keep them, I will pay the money-saving preferred subscriber's price (that's a savings of up to 20% off the retail price), plus shipping and handling. I understand I am under no obligation to purchase any books, as explained on this card.

Name _____

Address _____ Apt. _____

City _____ State _____ Zip _____

Telephone (____) _____

Signature _____

(If under 18, parent or guardian must sign)

Thank You!

Offer limited to one per household and not to current subscribers. Terms, offer and prices subject to change. Orders subject to acceptance by Zebra Contemporary Book Club. Offer Valid in the U.S. only.

CN064A

THE BENEFITS OF BOOK CLUB MEMBERSHIP

- You'll get your books hot off the press, usually before they appear in bookstores.
- You'll ALWAYS save up to 20% off the cover price.
- You'll get our FREE monthly newsletter filled with author interviews, book previews, special offers and MORE!
- There's no obligation — you can cancel at any time and you have no minimum number of books to buy.
- And—if you decide you don't like the books you receive, you can return them. (You always have ten days to decide.)

lll..l.ll....llll.l.ll.l.l..ll.l..l..lll.l.lll..l

Zebra Contemporary Romance Book Club

Zebra Home Subscription Service, Inc.

P.O. Box 5214

Clifton , NJ 07015-5214

died. She needed it for closure. She'd take the information to her grave, which probably wouldn't sway Elijah.

So she'd already come up with a plan. She'd ask Elijah where Howie Stevens was now, then she'd contact Howie.

She'd duped Howie for information once. Would he fall for it again? And just how far was she willing to go to get what she sought?

With Howie . . . not far. Dwight? Forget it. But Elijah?

She set her coffee aside and paced. What would it take to convince Elijah to give her whatever she wanted? Whatever he wanted? Did that include sex?

In spite of her resolve to forget it, she recalled their kiss from the other night. Elijah had wanted her. Or at least he'd responded to her. How powerful was the lure of wanting what you can't have? Could she use it against him?

Or could she get away with teasing Elijah into thinking she'd sleep with him in exchange for information, then renege? She rejected the idea immediately. Unlike Dwight, she couldn't promise, then not deliver. She'd have to sleep with Elijah.

Yeah, right. Who was she kidding?

Rachel could never have sex with anyone as a means to an end. Period. The only reason she was even considering this was because the thought of sleeping with Elijah wasn't totally repulsive.

Elijah had been a fantastic lover. Demanding. Greedy. Generous. They couldn't seem to make love enough, for even on the heels of mind-blowing satisfaction came a new desire. More intense.

There had never been another man like him.

And that admission made her want to flee the campus.

She checked the time, then hurried toward the closet. She had a meeting with Mason this evening, which would give her a chance to scope out his office and see if anything seemed different after she caught Hanson's bodyguard there.

After changing clothes, she glanced at the mirror. Without thought, she'd chosen a red and black plaid skirt and a silky white blouse. And it looked nice. Rachel gritted her teeth. God, this place was starting to rub off on her.

She arrived ten minutes early at the administration building. Mason's secretary's desk was deserted, so she knocked on his office door. When she got no answer, she twisted the knob. The door opened without noise, but the office was empty. Where was he?

Retreating and closing the door, she studied the file cabinets behind Mason's secretary's desk. Was Cindy Benjamin's counseling file in one of those?

Just as she stepped toward the desk, Mason's office door swung open behind her.

"Rachel! I didn't mean to startle you. I was just coming out to meet you."

"I, uh, was going to leave a note. I knocked, but when I didn't get an answer, I thought perhaps I'd come on the wrong day."

"My apologies! I heard you knock, but I was on the phone." Mason held his door wide. "Come on in."

The moment he turned his back, Rachel frowned. She knew damn good and well he hadn't been on the phone. But perhaps his office had a private bathroom and that was just an excuse.

"Have a seat." Mason walked toward a sofa. Once again he poured a glass of juice for her. "How has your first week been?"

"Better than I anticipated. Everyone is quite friendly."

"We pride ourselves on that. In fact, we consider ourselves one big family here. Have you read Reverend Hanson's newest book, *The Model Family*?"

She shook her head. "I've been meaning to, but—"

"Don't apologize, my dear. With class and study requirements, few students have time for extra reading. I was just going to comment on Hanson's chapter about social families."

While Mason explained the premise, Rachel finished her juice. "I'll have to make a point to get the book," she said when he was done.

"Have you used the relaxation CD I gave you?"

Rachel nodded. At least this wasn't a total lie. "I listened to it last night."

"Excellent. We'll start like we did the other night, then. The headphones are right beside you." He moved to open the cabinet above the fireplace.

As he turned on the television, Rachel noticed the fireplace was set forward almost seven feet from the rest of the wall, yet the cabinet space above was barely a foot deep. She eyed the bookcases lining the fireplace. They had similar dimensions, meaning there was something on the other side. A secret room?

She narrowed her eyes. If there was a small room or closet behind the cabinet, where was the door?

"Here we go." Mason stepped back. "I'll give you a few minutes to relax."

Lying on the sofa, Rachel slipped the headphones on. Mason's voice came over the headphones, telling her to take a deep breath. She did, but this time she had no intention of falling asleep, wanting to be aware of the entire session.

"Relax," his voice urged. "And go deeper."

Rachel took a deep breath.

"Wake up, Rachel."

She shook her head, then blinked to clear her vision. Once again, Mason was beside the couch, smiling wide.

"Did I fall asleep again?"

"It's common. Don't feel bad. The relaxation exercises are very effective. How do you feel?"

Rachel stretched. Like before, she had that feeling of well-being, and for a moment, she wondered if she had been drugged.

Except she felt no ill effects. She checked the time. Tonight they'd only met for an hour. There wasn't any drug she knew of that could knock a person out and let them revive an hour later without feeling a trace.

Sitting up, she set the headphones aside. "I don't remember what we talked about."

Mason moved to his notepad and picked it up. He ran his finger down a list. "We did an exercise where you described your perfect day. Then we broke it down in segments, trying to define the reason behind each action. You seek a higher sense of freedom, Rachel. It's what makes you most happy."

Oddly, she had a vague recollection of that. Still, she rubbed her head, uncomfortable to think she'd discussed that with a virtual stranger.

The phone rang. Mason answered and put the caller on hold. "If you'll excuse me, I have to take this call. Can you find your way out?"

"Sure."

Outside, Rachel continued to puzzle over their meeting. She had been determined not to succumb this time, yet she had. The relaxation technique Mason used was indeed powerful. Which made her apprehensive.

She needed to listen to the tape wide-awake and without headphones to see exactly what it said.

EIGHT

Kito Mzuzi picked up the phone on the fourth ring, just before it went to the answering machine. He knew Mason would call back, and just to make a point, he was tempted to ignore the call.

Instead, he answered with a warning. "Don't ever put me on hold."

Mason exhaled noisily. "It was unavoidable. I understand you received my package. The manner in which you took it, however, raised a few eyebrows. I had to do some fast talking to fix it."

Mason was, of course, referring to the fact that Kito had taken possession of the girl immediately. Usually, he waited a week or so, while certain excuses were made.

"If you had kept your word and sent the package on time, that wouldn't have happened. I had made certain arrangements that are costly to reschedule," Kito said. "You promised two shipments in two weeks. I've received one in three. That means you've defaulted on our agreement."

"Which has absolutely no bearing, since you've been in default for months," Mason retorted.

A hostile silence filled the line as Kito once again reminded himself of what was at stake.

The women Mason provided were exquisite. And the illusion they created was impossible to replicate. Others had tried to copy their film techniques, but no one had the same level of success. Outsiders had no idea what was involved. Hell, Kito himself didn't even know all of it. Yet.

But he would. And when he did . . .

"When can I expect the rest of my order?"

"Within a week. Since it's the last one, it has to go through normal channels."

"Very well."

NINE

Rachel was at Elijah's at ten. The friction between them threatened to kindle an inferno, yet he seemed determined to keep things amiable.

"Coffee?" he offered.

At her nod, he poured two mugs and moved to the L-shaped sectional in the living room.

Rachel sat, then turned toward him. "I've considered your offer. If we can come up with agreeable terms, I'll continue to work with you a little longer."

Elijah set his coffee aside. "What did you have in mind?"

"Tell me what happened the night Nick died."

"I wasn't there when the actual attack happened."

She curled her lip. "So I heard. But surely—"

He cut her off. "Heard? I can just imagine your take. Bet it goes something like this: I was off screwing around while my friends died." He didn't hide his anger this time. "That's bullshit, Rach. I was meeting a goddamn snitch. At Nick's request. It was a setup and I was captured. But I didn't even know what happened to them until six months later. And I still didn't believe it. Figured it was more psych ops."

She met his gaze and realized he spoke the truth. "When did you learn the others had died?"

"After I was released. Nearly two and a half years later."

Her hands had fisted so tightly her nails dug into her palms. She flexed her fingers, giving in to the urge to ask about his imprisonment. "Was it bad where you were held?"

He nodded. "But I survived. So, what else do you want to know about Nick?"

That he didn't want to discuss his time in captivity was obvious. She straightened. "When did you and Nick start working together again?"

She knew the two men had a terrible fight after Rachel and Elijah split. Nick had sworn he'd never work with Elijah again. And while she hadn't known it just then, she later realized that Nick had suffered a loss as well. Of the man he'd once considered his brother.

While she had only met Elijah's family once, Nick had spent a fair amount of time at the Trent ranch in Texas. In fact, the few personal photographs Nick had kept were from there.

"We started working together before Nick's last trip home. We had buried our differences long ago, but that was the first time we'd been on an assignment since . . ." Elijah skipped forward. "I can't tell you where we were, but it was cold as hell. Nick tried to teach me to play chess. Clever bastard made chess pieces using wooden matches and thread. Red tip versus blue tip. He claimed blue was his lucky color."

Rachel nodded. Nick had shown her that trick once. While the matchsticks in no way resembled real chessmen, the pieces were distinctly different. So not only did you have to strategize moves, you had to stop and translate what the pieces represented.

Two equal-length match heads side by side: king. Two shorter match heads side by side: queen. The board was drawn on paper. And when you finished with the game, you simply piled the pieces up, crumpled the paper and lit it.

"I had a hard time recalling bishop from rook," Elijah continued. "No sooner had I memorized it then I caught him telling someone else the opposite of what he'd told me. I called him on it and things got a little out of hand. We were snowed in and we'd been drinking. When we went outside to settle our disagreement, Nick slipped on a patch of ice and busted his ass. We learned later he'd broken two fingers in the process, but at the time he still wanted to fight. First punch had him crying like a little girl. He told me later that he'd blamed the injury on a fight with a Russian jet pilot."

The memory spilled over Rachel like warm honey. Nick had missed Christmas, but came in two weeks later with his fingers splinted. "Goddamn Russians," he'd claimed. "Never know when to keep their mouths shut."

"Nick told me he'd been in a bar and had made a bet about a MiG interior," she said. "He claimed the Russian didn't like the fact he knew that much about their aircraft."

Her brother had also claimed the Russkie had the hardest jaw he'd ever punched.

"You went to Key West that year, right?" Elijah asked.

She nodded. It had been just the two of them. They'd snorkeled, fished, and eaten more than their legal limit in lobster. If only she'd known that would be the last time she saw Nick alive.

Overwhelmed, she closed her eyes, battling tears. What she hadn't counted on were the emotions packed away with each memory. Maybe she wasn't nearly as prepared to hear about Nick as she thought.

Elijah handed her an envelope that was on the coffee table. "Dwight sent copies of the photos. Legit ones. You can have them without obligation. I'll still honor our agreement and tell you what I can."

Rachel fingered the envelope. She'd look at them later. Right now . . .

She cleared her throat and stood. "It's almost eleven. We should get going."

He followed her to the kitchen and put their mugs in the sink. "One more thing. The man we saw last night is named Nigel Kowicki. I haven't come up with anything on him, which makes me suspicious. He's too clean for a bodyguard. No military. No police record. And he's still in town, so I suggest we work together to cover for each other."

"What if we both need to be different places?"

"We'll take turns. You can go first. What are your plans for tonight?"

She shifted, not wanting to disclose everything. First she wanted to analyze the keystroke recorder, which had to be done at the media center.

"I've got a few files to check on the network, then I want to go back to Mason's office in the administration building."

"Let's do it, then."

* * *

Working in a separate office at the media center gave Rachel a chance to equalize. Their conversation about Nick had left her on the verge of tears, a place she wasn't comfortable.

Her thoughts circled like vultures around Elijah's denial that he hadn't been screwing around. Had he been honest, or was he playing word games? Okay, so he called it *meeting a snitch*. Had the snitch been beautiful? With long red nails? *Meeting a snatch*, perhaps?

After the disaster in Venice, Elijah had claimed that was all he'd been doing there, too. He'd vehemently denied sleeping with anyone but Rachel since they met. "It's all part of the act, Rach. No different then the time you posed as a hooker to get info."

In the end, though, Rachel found she couldn't get that picture from her mind. And Elijah couldn't handle her lack of trust.

The computer beeped, indicating the contents of the keystroke recorder had been downloaded. Grateful for something else to focus on, she retraced Elijah's steps on the college and church network.

The first night, he'd gone all over the place, checking the system out. After that, he seemed to split his time between two activities. Deposit records and *video files*.

Why was Elijah looking for a video file? And how coincidental was it that the senator had just asked her to search for the same thing? Granted, Elijah wasn't searching for it by a file name, but still . . .

Since Dwight had the senator's office bugged,

he must have been tipped off about the file before the senator called Rachel.

Damn Dwight! He was still playing both sides of the fence.

Rachel opened a few of the video files Elijah had looked at. They were all taped sermons of William Hanson. In fact, Elijah had started at the top, with the newest files, and was methodically working his way down, checking every single one.

The video directory was huge. How many years of sermons did they have stored there? She briefly debated asking Elijah about what he was looking for, but decided not to. It would tip him off that she knew what he was doing.

As Rachel studied the file names, though, she noticed they were slightly different from the one the senator had given her. The video file names Elijah searched all had six digits. Month, date, year.

The senator had only given her four digits. But the data retrieved from Cindy's computer had been corrupt, so perhaps it wasn't a complete file name.

Typing quickly, Rachel did a wild-card search on 0913.MPG. Nine hits came back over different years. She opened each and watched a few seconds of Hanson preaching before closing the file.

Well, so much for the senator's lead. At least she could honestly say she'd searched. She shut down her computer and went next door. "I'm ready to go to Mason's office."

Elijah made a few notes, then moved so she could shut the unit down.

"When we get there, you can go in," he said. "I'll set the alarms at one set of doors and watch the other. If we get company I'll buzz you."

Once inside Mason's office, Rachel searched the locked file in the credenza, but found only church-related papers. Then she recalled her curiosity about how the wall stuck out for no apparent reason.

She checked the fireplace, a shallow electric faux unit that was no deeper than the bookcases flanking it. Beyond the bookcases was a smooth stretch of wall. She tapped and found it hollow.

The hair on her neck lifted. There had to be a door here. She ran her fingers along the edges and felt it give. Pressing on it, she lifted. A section of wall slid on a track like a pocket door.

Rachel shined her flashlight into the small room. It was lined with metal cabinets. She tugged on one and found it locked.

"Well, well."

After digging out her pick, she opened a two-drawer cabinet first and flipped through the tabs. There was a file on each of the Eve's Circle girls. She peeked inside hers and found nothing but a note about their meeting time.

In the very back was a file with Cindy Benjamin's name on it. Rachel pulled it out. A shiny CD slipped out and hit the ground, making noise. Rachel flinched and grabbed the disc. Cindy's name was written on it.

Working quickly, she unpacked her laptop and inserted the CD. While she waited for it to load, she flipped through the papers in the manila folder and grew excited.

Was this Cindy's missing counseling file?

Ignoring the preprinted waivers and disclaimers Cindy had signed, Rachel found the initial referral sheet. The note said Cindy had been sent for counseling after a pregnancy test *came back negative.*

Rachel read it twice.

Well, that answered the question of Cindy's pregnancy, even though Rachel hadn't seen the actual blood test results. She swallowed her disappointment and realized that she'd actually hoped to find an answer that would give the senator's wife hope.

She turned back to her computer screen to review the directory. The disk held the file she'd been searching for: 0913.MPG.

Since it appeared Cindy hadn't been pregnant, Rachel doubted this video would be of a child. Still, she'd check it out, simply to assure the senator she'd done everything.

She clicked Play, but the screen flashed an error message. "Great!" Had she damaged the file when she dropped it?

Running a quick diagnostic revealed the problem. The disc was recorded for Region Three. Rachel changed her drive to read the region—Southeast Asia—and this time the video played.

Cindy Benjamin's face came into view, but she was agitated and crying. She turned away from the camera as if talking to someone behind her.

Rachel clicked the audio controls, which she typically kept muted. Who was Cindy was talking to?

The other person came into view. *Senator Benjamin.* His lips moved without sound as he stepped closer. When he reached Cindy, he took her by the shoulders and shook her. Hard. When she tried to get away, he slapped her. Open handed, across the face.

Rachel's temper exploded as Cindy staggered

backward from the force of the blow and fell to the floor. That dirty, rotten bastard!

On screen, the senator stood over Cindy and began unfastening his belt.

"Don't you dare strike her with that." Rachel fidgeted with the volume, jumping when the senator's voice boomed through the tiny speakers.

"You selfish little bitch. After all I've done, you'll do exactly as I say." He let go of the belt and unzipped his pants, then lowered them, exposing his erection. "Get on your knees and show me that you're sorry."

Rachel wanted to throw up as the video got worse.

Ignoring his stepdaughter's repeated requests to stop, the senator physically forced her to perform oral sex. With each protest, he berated Cindy more loudly, more viciously. And when she failed to *go faster,* he slapped her again. "Now, start over."

Cindy's anguish and horror were evident. So, too, was her stepfather's perverted enjoyment in subjugating her.

Words could not describe Rachel's anger. She wanted to take action, to smash or shoot something. Preferably the senator, who was moaning on the video now, lost in the throes of a depraved climax.

When the video stopped abruptly, Rachel sucked in air, realizing she had held her breath. For a moment, it seemed time had collapsed into a black void, when actually only five or six minutes had passed. She tried to will her mind to calmness. *Stop and think rationally.* Reacting violently in response to violence was no answer.

At least for now.

Pity for Cindy welled beneath Rachel's rib cage. The girl's checkered past—drugs, alcohol—all made sense now. Their estrangement, too.

Even the lies had been cries for help. Cindy had in all probability been enduring this for years. The sad truth was that while she had protested, her objections were weak and ineffective, indicating a certain level of conditioning.

Emily had mentioned that before the car accident Cindy was going to confront her parents. Was this the *trouble* Emily alluded to? Obviously, yes. And if Rachel hadn't been so damn fixated on the pregnancy aspect, she might have asked Emily better questions.

Instead, Rachel had developed a blind spot that made it easier for the senator to use her. The whole story of Cindy being pregnant had been an elaborate ruse. Benjamin had played on Rachel's soft spot for kids.

He'd also exploited his connections to her cousin to find the chinks in her armor. Rachel no longer blamed Jimmy. The senator had taken advantage of Jimmy's loyalty to weave a plot against her. There was value in knowing a person's strengths, but to control them, you needed to know their weaknesses.

And Nick was Rachel's Achilles' heel.

With that insight came a second realization about why the senator had gone to such lengths to get her to take the case. He couldn't just walk into an investigator's office and hire them to retrieve a video of him abusing his stepchild. No legitimate firm would have taken that case.

Which left the shady firms. The ones who'd do anything for a buck. But with them, Benjamin ran a huge risk of copies being made and sold to the media. To the highest bidder.

If it weren't for the fact that Cindy was in the film, Rachel would have seriously considered sending the video to all the major networks herself. The senator damn sure deserved it and much worse.

But not Cindy . . .

The repulsive images still burned in Rachel's mind. That the senator had physically and sexually abused his stepdaughter was horrible. But why was it on film? Who had taped them? When was it made and where?

And how in the hell did it end up in Mason Wright's possession?

The answer to her last question was glaringly evident. A career-destroying video like this existed for only one reason: blackmail. Which explained why the senator had interfered with the IRS audit of the church's records.

All of this made Rachel feel like the worst kind of fool. In retrospect, she realized that parts of Benjamin's story hadn't clicked from the beginning, but she had let her desire to get information on her brother cloud her judgment.

When the senator had given her the video file name, he had known exactly what she would find. And while he would have also known she would be upset to view this, the arrogant bastard had tucked two damage-control aces up his sleeve.

First was her cousin Jimmy's future with the senator. Benjamin had seriously overestimated her cousin's sway.

Second was the senator's quasi-promise of information on Nick. Initially, she'd been worried he wouldn't produce anything. Now, she'd have bet her life's savings that the senator already had information on her brother but was waiting to use it to negotiate for her silence and the video.

She scrubbed a hand over her face. Revolted. With everyone.

So, what were the other players after? Like Mason Wright? How had he obtained the video in the first place? Had Cindy made it herself, then perhaps showed it to him as part of their counseling?

Was this what Nigel Kowicki, Hanson's bodyguard, had been after? How many people knew about the video's existence? The senator's political opponents, perhaps? Did Nigel work for one of them? Leaking this during reelection could ruin the senator and anyone connected to him.

Which brought her back to Dwight Davis and the fact she knew Elijah had been searching for a video file, too. It had to be connected. Did that mean Dwight's whole story of deposits traced to terrorists was false? Probably.

It didn't explain why Dwight wanted the video, though. This type of case—abuse—was outside the scope of the CIA. Unless Dwight had his own plan for blackmail. She wouldn't have put it past him.

Didn't anyone but Rachel feel sorry for Cindy's suffering? Elijah had a sister the same age. How would he have felt if this video had been of his sister?

Mentally shoving her disgust aside, Rachel turned back to her laptop. She needed to make a copy of this.

While the video duplicated onto her hard drive, she went back to the paper file. This was indeed Cindy's counseling record, but as she flipped through it, she discovered the majority of pages were missing.

The log sheet indicated there had been three meetings after Cindy's initial appointment. *See notes*, the comments read. Except the notes were gone. The very last page noted that Cindy had requested her counseling be transferred to Mason Wright to *resolve issues of parental incest.*

Had Mason even tried to help Cindy? Or had he simply milked her for blackmail material?

And was this an isolated case, or did Mason regularly troll for exploitive information? Perhaps while he had subjects in a trance? Rachel recalled her own sessions with him, how powerful the trances had been.

She eyed the rest of the locked cabinets lining the wall. What else did Mason have hidden in here? She picked the lock of the tall double-door cabinet beside her and swung one of the doors open. She was disappointed to find office supplies: blank discs, paper, pens.

She peeked at the other side, in a hurry to move on. Her hand froze, then pushed the door wide. The other side of the cabinet was a virtual chemistry lab. Beakers. Test tubes. A small scale. She recalled the mortar and pestle on Mason's desk. He had mentioned his father was a pharmacologist. Was this more of his father's equipment?

Several glass jars lined a lower shelf. She swept her flashlight over them. The label on one jumped out at her. RACHEL. Two others caught her eye as well. EMILY and ALISA.

She opened the jar bearing her own name, found a white powder was inside. Cautious, she sniffed above it, but could discern no scent.

And while Rachel didn't know what it was, her gut confirmed an awful suspicion. She had been drugged. Via the orange juice. Both visits, Mason had poured her a glass, but never drank any himself.

She recalled the feelings of euphoria she'd had after a session with Mason. They'd faded rapidly, leaving her feeling normal once she left his office. What had he given her? And what the hell had he done while she was under?

Rachel scanned the rest of the jars. Some of the larger ones had strange abbreviations, like NqDA. Ingredients? The jars with the other two girls' names seemed to contain the identical powder that Rachel's did. But why separate them unless they were different?

Did Emily or Alisa even suspect they were being drugged? Knowing she probably was not the only one given drugs didn't make Rachel feel any better.

Helping herself to a sheet of paper, she tore it into three squares and wrote the names from the labels. Then she opened each jar and shook out a small amount to have analyzed.

After folding the paper carefully to keep the powder trapped inside, Rachel sealed the edges with tape.

From outside, a loud noise exploded, shaking the building. She nearly dropped one of the jars. It had only been thunder, but still . . .

Her phone vibrated, which caused her to panic anew. She'd been so caught up in her discoveries, she'd forgotten Elijah was outside. He could be warning her someone was coming. She jammed the drug packets in her front pocket as she answered her phone.

"Yes."

"We've got a line of severe storms moving in. The wind's blowing like hell already, and it looks like most of the campus has lost power."

Rachel glanced at the laptop's screen and found the video had finished copying. "I'll be down in two minutes."

Shutting her phone, she made certain that everything was as she'd found it in the cabinet. Then she removed the disc from her laptop and replaced it in Cindy's file.

She cast one last glance at the room before slipping out. What else did Mason have hidden in here? "Tomorrow night," she whispered.

The wind buffeted her, blowing bits of sand and dirt into her face when she stepped outside. Elijah moved up, then motioned her around to the side of the building, which offered slight protection from the wind.

"Any luck?" he asked.

Rachel flicked on her flashlight, wanting to see his eyes. "Be honest with me. The video you're searching for. Do you have any idea how repulsive the content is?"

Elijah nodded, then glanced away, no doubt trying to figure out how she knew what he'd been up to. "If you found it, we need to talk. And I need to see it."

"I have a copy." She didn't want to tell him about the hidden room. Not until she'd had a chance to go back and explore it fully herself. And not before she knew what Dwight intended to do with it.

Thunder burst again, directly overhead, as lightning shattered the darkness. Elijah swore, drawing close. "Let's hightail it before all hell breaks loose. We can talk at my place."

Rachel heard rain hit the leaves high above her head as they took off jogging. Seconds later, the drops became buckets full, soaking her to the skin. Lightning splintered the sky, strobing upward to ignite towering thunderclouds.

"Come on." Elijah cut across campus, running full tilt. She stayed at his heels. The rain came down so hard it stung her skin. She kept her eyes downcast as much as possible.

Elijah's apartment had no power. He flipped on his flashlight. "I'll grab some towels."

She popped the red filter off her own flashlight and set it on the counter as she toed off her wet sneakers and stepped away from the lake that had formed near the door. Peeling off her backpack, she checked her laptop, relieved to find the heavy canvas had kept it dry. She set the laptop on the kitchen table and propped the bag against the chair.

"Here." He handed her a towel, then tossed a couple on the floor.

Unfolding the towel, Rachel ran it over her hair and face, then down her arms, trying to wick some of the excess water from her clothes.

"I can lend you a dry shirt." Elijah had moved into the shadows near the sink. He peeled off his wet T-shirt and tossed it aside before rubbing a towel over his chest. "You've got to be freezing."

Rachel nodded, unable to tear her gaze from his bare chest. The man had sinfully broad shoulders. Even in the murky light, she could see the way his dark chest hair spread between his nipples, then narrowed down, down, toward his . . .

The windows rattled as the storm's intensity increased. Suddenly her shivering seemed to snowball. With it came an expanded sensation of lightness and well-being that was similar to what she'd felt after her session with Mason Wright.

The drugs.

"Shit!" Frantic, Rachel dug into her pocket where she'd stuck the samples. The neatly taped packets were squishy wet and stained a dark color.

Elijah moved closer, his expression concerned. "What's wrong?"

She pointed to the wet wads of paper she'd dumped on the counter. "I took some samples from Mason's office tonight. To have them analyzed. I, I, think he drugged me before."

"Before? When?"

"Our meetings. Counseling sessions."

Elijah grabbed the flashlight and held her hand up in the beam. The tips of her fingers were stained red. "Do you have any idea what this is?"

She shook her head. Even as she recognized that she'd been drugged, she couldn't fight the effects. "I'm feeling it, though."

"Describe it."

"It's not unpleasant. Just strange. Like I'm on a cloud. But then I slip off and . . . another cloud catches me." She looked at his hands, which were still holding hers, aware that her skin, her muscles were tingling.

"You had these in your pocket?"

Rachel nodded, which set off new waves of sensation.

"Whatever it was, it's started to dissolve. You probably absorbed some of it through your skin." Elijah's voice was distorted. "We need to get you out of these wet clothes. Fast."

She grabbed at her shirt, but couldn't find the hem, her fingers numb. His hands came over hers, stripping off her jeans and shirt.

He pointed to the red stain the powder had left on her upper thigh. "We need to get this off your skin."

"It looks like a Rorschach blot, doesn't it?"

"If you say so." Elijah swung her up into his arms. Until then she hadn't even realized she'd swooned. It felt good to be held. Heat radiated from him. "I'm c-c-cold."

Even as she said it, Rachel realized it was a side effect. *This will pass. Just stay calm. Enjoy it. What follows is even better.* How did she know that?

Mason had told her. Mason had whispered delightful promises in her ear.

Colors swirled behind her eyelids now. Bright colors. Red, like fire, passion. Then orange. The colors shifted again, kaleidoscopic. Magical. They shimmered like ethereal northern lights.

Elijah carried her into the bathroom and propped the flashlight on the back of the commode. Then he sat her on the counter.

"Hold on, Rachel." He turned away to adjust the water.

And to get a grip on his temper. What the hell was Mason Wright doing drugging her? And what had he done during these so-called counseling sessions?

When the water was warm, Elijah moved back to her. She had leaned against the mirror, her arms crossed over her stomach as if to ward off the trembling. He checked her pulse, found it elevated but steady.

He glanced at her wet, transparent underwear.

For as little as it hid, she might as well have been naked.

"Can you stand up?" he asked.

At her nod, Elijah swung her, underwear and all, beneath the spray of water. He grabbed a cloth and soap, then scrubbed her leg until the stain washed free.

Next he grabbed her hand and lathered her fingers. When he was satisfied he'd removed all visible traces, he shut off the water and lifted her from the tub.

"Strip off your underwear," Elijah instructed after wrapping a large towel around her.

He had expected her to keep the towel in place as she did it. She didn't. Or perhaps she couldn't. The towel fell to the floor unheeded as she struggled with the clasp of her bra, unable to undo it.

Reaching forward, Elijah unfastened it then peeled off her panties. Retrieving the towel, he wrapped it snugly around her. She was shaking again, her skin cool.

"Let's get you warm," he said.

He carried her to his bed. Setting the flashlight on the nightstand freed one hand, allowing him to toss back the covers. She curled onto her side, hugging the towel as fierce tremors racked her frame.

"I'm freezing," she whispered.

Elijah pulled the covers over her, then moved away to peel off his wet pants. He put on a dry pair of boxers and climbed into the bed before tugging her into his arms.

"You'll be warm in a minute." Drawing her legs between his, he ran his hands briskly up and down her arms. Once again, he checked her pulse. It was unchanged.

Pressing her close, he wrapped his arms fully around her. If she got worse, he wouldn't hesitate to take her to the hospital, though he wasn't sure the one in town was the best choice. Unfortunately, the closest one beyond here was an hour away. However, in a life-threatening emergency, Shepherd's Cross would do just fine.

Rain slashed against the window above their heads, thunder rolling in the distance. After another few minutes, her tremors subsided. She sighed, her breathing more relaxed as well.

"Feeling better?" he asked.

"Much. I knew it would pass." Rachel lifted a hand and began stroking his chin. "And in its place is something better. Kiss me, Elijah. Please."

Even as she said it, she shimmied up and pressed her lips to his. Her tongue swept boldly into his mouth. She nibbled his bottom lip before sucking on it. The move caught him off guard even as he recognized it was the drug.

Just keep it to mouth contact, he told himself as she deepened the kiss.

She wiggled, rolling onto his chest and straddling his abdomen. The towel remained securely in place around her breasts. But around her hips it bunched up, the soft curls of her pubis brushing his belly, providing a visual and tactile reminder that she was naked beneath.

Then Rachel scooted lower and thrust her bottom against Elijah's straining erection. She rubbed against his shaft fully, undulating her hips and twisting the fabric of his boxers with each move. Lowering her mouth, she kissed his chest, scraping his nipple with her teeth.

Elijah hissed. There was no mistaking the raw

sexual invitation of her moves. The woman was a gifted seductress who could render him senseless with a touch, a taste.

The problem was she didn't realize what she was doing.

Still, his resolution to limit contact to a kiss was severely strained. It didn't help that he'd wanted her since he'd first laid eyes on her. Hard and fast, without preliminaries. Without foreplay. Without apology.

"We have to stop, Rachel," he said.

"But we haven't even started." Raising slightly, she tugged the towel free and tossed it to the floor, then lowered back against him.

Elijah groaned as her bare flesh scalded his, the hard pebbles of her nipples dragging across his chest.

"I want you to make love to me," she begged. "And I won't take no for an answer."

Sliding off his chest, she propped up at his side, then boldly slipped her fingers beneath his boxers. Her hand curled around his cock, stroking the hard length with a firm grip.

Swearing, Elijah swung his legs off the mattress and sat up.

Rachel followed, pressing herself against his back before leaning forward to nip the top of his shoulder as her hands circled around to fondle him.

"I need this," she pleaded. "And you can do anything. Anything."

"You don't know what you're saying, Rachel. Or doing."

Grabbing her wrists, Elijah tugged her around and onto his lap. Her eyes were fully dilated, her pupils the size of dimes. Pushing to his feet with her in his arms, he tugged the bedspread back and evened it out.

"You'll thank me for this in the morning," he whispered.

Catching her lips in a kiss, he laid her down on the bed and pinned her beneath him.

"Yes." She practically purred. "You know exactly what I want."

Moving quickly, Elijah flipped her over and rolled her up in the bedspread, as tightly as he could.

At first Rachel struggled, then she gave up. "What did I do wrong?" She was crying now, and her helplessness tore at him.

"You've done nothing wrong."

"Then make love to me," she begged, confirming that he had no choice but to restrain her.

He brushed the hair away from her brow and made soothing noises. He also made promises he had no intention of keeping.

"Close your eyes and sleep. We'll make love when you wake up."

"Promise?"

At his nod, she calmed. Within minutes she drifted off.

Elijah checked her pulse at her carotid artery, found it was even and slower. Satisfied the worst was over, he straightened, watched her.

While Rachel had obviously been subjected to an overdose tonight, he didn't like the thought that she might have reacted this way with Mason Wright. Even now, while she wasn't begging for sex, she was virtually unconscious. The thought that someone could take advantage of her while she was out cold like this didn't sit well.

He had a million questions, all of which would have to wait until later. She said she'd found the video. Christ, which one? Not that it mattered. They were all equally brutal. He had some explaining to do. As did she. Obviously, they were both guilty of omission.

Still, the fact that Rachel had known what he'd been searching for didn't bother him nearly as much as knowing she'd had to view that garbage without warning. After all these years, part of him still wanted to shield her.

Yes, Elijah would continue to need her help, maybe now more than ever. But he needed to rethink working with her if it endangered her. *If she endangered herself.*

He rubbed the back of his neck and felt the tension. The tiredness. He checked the clock. It was two. As long as he had her back in her dorm by five, they'd be okay.

Setting the alarm on his watch for four-thirty, he checked her pulse, then stretched out on the bed beside her and closed his eyes. He needed sleep just as badly as she did.

TEN

Rachel awoke to a tiny, annoying beeping, her head throbbing. She groaned and tried to open her eyes. They were heavy, swollen, the inside of her mouth dry.

She felt a hand on her back. Her bare back.

Instinctively, she shoved away. Why was she sleeping with someone?

And where were her clothes?

"Rachel. It's Elijah." His embrace tightened briefly. "You're all right."

Recognizing his voice made it easier to breathe even as it raised more questions. She was sprawled across his chest, his bare chest, her legs tangled in the sheets. "Did we . . . ?"

"Make love? No. I took your clothes off because they were wet."

For some reason that answer wasn't reassuring. She shoved the hair off her face and squinted at the bedside clock that flashed on and off. She shut her eyes as the pain in her temples escalated.

Elijah sat up and shoved the clock away. "Power's back on. I'll make coffee. Need anything?"

"Water," she croaked. "And aspirin."

The mattress shifted as he moved off the bed. A drawer opened and closed, followed by muffled sounds as he pulled on clothes.

As soon as he was gone, Rachel tried to sit up, but had to settle for simply propping higher on the pillow. Snatching the sheet closer, she glanced around the room. Light shined in from the hall, keeping most of the room in shadow. But what she saw had her doubting Elijah's prior denial. The bed was wrecked, the spread twisted. Like way back when . . .

Elijah padded back into the room and handed her a glass. When she almost dropped it, his hand circled hers, steadying it as she brought it to her mouth. Only now did she realize he also held her head up. She took a sip, then another.

"Here's your aspirin. Open." He slipped two tablets against her tongue and offered more water. "Coffee's brewing."

"Thanks."

He let her head slip back down and sat beside her on the bed. "How much do you remember?"

"Give me a minute." Concentrating, she closed her eyes. "We'd gotten caught in the storm. Before that . . ." Her eyes opened wide with recall. "I was in Mason's office. I took samples of three drugs. They got wet in the rain, right?"

He nodded. "The powders dissolved and combined. Then they were absorbed through your skin. Any idea what it was?"

"No. That's why I wanted to have it tested. Is there enough left to analyze?"

"I spread the papers out to dry. It appears there's residue of each, though I'm not sure how pure the samples are."

"Then I'll get more tonight. I have to know what it is."

"I agree. But tonight we'll go together." Standing, Elijah crossed to his dresser. "Here are some clothes. I'll go check on the coffee."

Rachel sat up, slowly. Her head still pounded, but at least it felt like her own head. She tugged on the sweats he'd left. They were miles too big, but at least they covered her. She used the bathroom and then splashed water on her face. It helped clear the cobwebs.

Until she walked back in the bedroom. Recollections bombarded her, most wispy and incomplete. But there were distinct memories of her and Elijah naked, of bare skin pressed to bare skin.

She tried to focus. "Remember, damn it!" She could recall everything until she got out of the shower. After that there was an odd montage of erotic pictures. Some were images from her nightmares, people she didn't recognize. And still others were snippets from the past when she and Elijah had dated.

The ones that were most disturbing right now, though, were the ones she knew were from this morning. She recalled kissing him. Teasing him. Even stroking his penis. God, the things she had wanted to do to him.

Elijah had assured her they hadn't had sex, but what about other things?

She made her way to the kitchen, nearly running into him in the hall. He had two mugs of coffee in his hands. Retreating, he set the cups on the table and pulled a chair out for her before taking the one opposite.

Rachel sipped the coffee. "I'm, uh, having flashbacks to some pretty hot moments. Were they imagined?"

"It got a little dicey." His voice gave away the fact that he'd been turned on by whatever had happened.

"Define dicey."

He lowered his mug. "You were literally begging for sex, Rachel. I know you're not happy to hear that."

"You're right." She grimaced.

"You didn't know what you were doing. While I'd never take advantage of you, someone else might have. And that bothers me. You said you thought Mason Wright had drugged you before? When?"

Instead of answering, she held up her mug. "Can I have more coffee?" It was a stall. Last night, Rachel had been determined not to show her hand. Now, though . . .

He stalked to the counter. When he returned she took the mug from his hand. "Counseling sessions with Mason are required for members of Eve's Circle. I've met with him twice."

"Is that when you believe he drugged you?"

"Yes. It had to have been in the juice. Both times I fell asleep. At first I thought it was simply that the hypnosis techniques he used were ultraeffective." She explained about the audio and video Mason used.

"I don't like the sound of this."

"It gets worse. Last time I was there, I noticed what turned out to be a hidden storage room. That's where I found the drugs. And the disc with the video."

Elijah shifted guiltily. "Which is something else we need to talk about."

"We? You." She looked at him. "Did you know the whole thing with Cindy was a ruse? That Senator Benjamin was only after that video of him abusing her?" Rachel shook her head. "I expected this from Dwight, but you—"

"Whoa." He shifted forward, brows knitted. "The video you found is of the senator? And his stepdaughter?"

"Don't play dumb." Rachel glanced to where her laptop still sat on the table, exactly where she'd left it. "Last night you said you knew how vile that video was. That it was what you were looking for."

"I'm not playing dumb, but I think we're on two different wavelengths here." Hesitating for only a moment, he went on. "What I'm about to tell you is highly classified."

She rolled her eyes. "And that's your excuse for not telling me this beforehand, right?"

"You know the drill, Rach."

Unfortunately, she did. Almost everything Nick was ever involved in was classified. "Go on."

"The type of video I'm looking for is extremely violent pornography. Highly specialized and sadistic with a capital *S*. We've suspected for a while that profits from it support certain terrorist activities, but we only recently learned that the guy who makes it and the guy who distributes it are one and the same. His name is Kito Mzuzi. We also suspect he uses the mission's overseas video facilities to replicate the stuff."

It was Rachel's turn to be confused. "The church is in on this?"

"That's where it gets muddy. At first it was believed the church was simply leasing the facilities, after hours. When we couldn't trace any rental income, though, we figured they might be bartering use of the facility for security purposes. Protection money. Then we got word that unedited samples of the films were sent here, with the accounting records. That means someone here at Shepherd's Cross knows."

She absorbed what he'd told her. Getting angry at Dwight's subterfuge was like getting mad at the wind for blowing. "Was anything Dwight told me true?"

Now Elijah stood and refilled his own mug. Stalling. "The transfer Dwight told you about was legit, but we can't find anything to prove it was more than an error. I can't build a case on that."

"Finding pornographic video here—that was made overseas—would tie them together, right?"

"Precisely. Up until now, I had suspected Hanson himself was involved. He's back and forth between the missions monthly. After tonight, though, I wonder if it's Mason."

"But the tape I found of the senator, while it's vile, doesn't sound like the same thing you've been searching for."

"True. However, what you've found sounds like the perfect impetus for derailing a tax audit." Elijah checked his watch. "We don't have much time. And I'd like to see this video of the senator."

For a moment, Rachel was tempted not to show him. To give him a dose of his own medicine and let him know how it felt to be left out in the cold. Except being left out in the cold was SOP for the CIA.

"Hand me my laptop." Firing it up, she set the video to Play. While she knew what to expect, the scene still revolted her. When it ended she shut the laptop off. "Sickening, isn't it?"

"Yes. But I'll warn you; the stuff I'm looking for makes that look tame. What are you going to do with it?"

"I haven't decided."

"Will you give me a chance to check a few things? I know you're upset. You have every right to be. But revealing this too soon could blow my case."

The fact that he asked for her cooperation mollified her. "I'll hold off until we've had a chance to discuss it further."

"That's all I ask." Elijah climbed to his feet. "We need to get you back to your room."

"I can find my own way."

"I know, but considering what you've been through, I'll feel better if I make sure."

Outside, the ground was littered with leaves and branches ripped free in the storm. When they drew close to Rachel's dorm, Elijah stopped.

"I'm going to take those drug samples in for testing this morning. But I'll have my cell phone, so call if you need anything." He turned to leave.

Rachel reached out and grasped his sleeve. "Wait." She found it difficult to say what needed to be said. "Thank you for taking care of me."

To her surprise, he picked up her fingers and brushed a light kiss across her knuckles. "You're welcome. Now get some sleep."

Elijah spent the day haunted by memories. Memories of Rachel naked, in his bed, in his arms. Some recollections were from that morning. Some were from their past. All were tinged with regret.

For all their ups and downs—and if he was honest, there had been a lot of those—the one place they'd always gotten along had been in bed.

It had taken him a long time to realize that what made their physical relationship so profound though, was their emotional one.

He had loved Rachel like no other. Consequently, no other relationship came close, emotionally or physically, to what they'd shared. And for years, he had damn sure tried to prove it wrong. Physically, at least.

That all changed during the time he'd been imprisoned, when he'd had nothing better to do than relive and reexamine every aspect of his life. Particularly the puzzle of his feelings for Rachel versus other females.

It had been difficult to admit it was love that made the sex great. And with that admission came another realization: he couldn't love anyone else because he still loved Rachel.

Elijah had choked on that one. He'd also tried to rationalize it away. After all, he'd used the countless memories of her as a means to maintain his sanity while being tortured. Consequently, he'd made her larger than life.

It was only after he had been released from captivity that he recognized the truth. *He had never stopped loving Rachel.* Sure, he'd been furious that night in Venice. She could have blown a job he'd been working for months.

He'd also been livid over her accusations of infidelity. Granted, it had looked bad, but it was an act. Elijah knew exactly where the lines were drawn between right and wrong. He might have danced close to the edge, but he never stepped over it.

And instead of being understanding and realizing how it had looked from Rachel's point of view, he'd listened to his ego and accused her of not trusting him.

In the end, they'd both blamed the incident for the relationship's demise, but the truth was they had been teetering on the brink for over a year.

Everything took a toll: the weeks between phone calls; the way his plans always changed at the last minute. The countless times he'd run late or even stood her up.

He and Rachel both had unusually demanding jobs that required them to work long distances from each other. Maintaining a relationship with someone undercover was tough enough. But when those same undercover jobs required a person to disappear for months at a time, it could be hell.

Because she had a brother who did the same thing, and because she did a similar type of work, Rachel had a unique awareness of what Elijah did. Unfortunately, he'd taken advantage of her understanding. Worse, he hadn't reciprocated, hadn't shown her the same level of thoughtfulness.

In other words, he'd been an asshole. And that admission changed nothing now. Time had worked against them, closing any avenue of hope.

Elijah brought his thoughts ruefully back to the present. He had just met a courier and turned over what was left of the drug samples. He wanted them analyzed, pronto. The courier had also given him some new equipment and supplies, including glass vials and latex gloves to take additional drug samples.

Just as he drove back into Shepherd's Cross, his

cell phone rang. It was Dwight. "I got your message. You found something?"

"Not what we're looking for, but potentially significant." Elijah filled him in on the video of Senator Benjamin. When he told Dwight about the drugs, however, he omitted the specific details of their effect.

Dwight was flabbergasted. "Holy shit! Rachel's okay?"

"Seems to be. She's eager to know what she was exposed to, naturally."

"I'll rush the lab results. Tell me more about this video of Benjamin. Have you seen it?"

"Yep. And it's as sick as it sounds."

"You said Rachel found it. Where? And any idea how it got there? Or if there's more than one?"

"A lot of the details are sketchy. After the fiasco with the drugs, there wasn't a lot of time to talk. I'll know more after tonight."

"Will there be any issues with containment? If this leaks . . ."

"I'm working on it."

"I want a copy of that video," Dwight said. "Call me first thing tomorrow."

After disconnecting, Elijah checked the time. It was after four. He called Rachel. While he had yet to get any sleep, he hoped she had.

"How are you feeling?" he asked when she answered.

"Fine. Whatever it was seems to be out of my system."

"The samples are on their way to the lab."

"How long before you'll get results?"

"It's being expedited, but I doubt I'll hear anything before tomorrow. You still feel up to meeting tonight?"

"Absolutely."

"Then I'll meet you at the administration building."

Shortly before eleven, Rachel slipped out the back door of her dorm. The night was cool; pensive. Perfect for her mood.

It had taken her the better part of the afternoon to come to grips with her anger at Mason Wright. How dare he drug her!

Part of her longed to confront him face to face. Which she couldn't do. Yet. But when she could . . .

And what about Emily and Alisa? Did they have any idea what Mason was up to? Rachel suspected they were being drugged, too, since their names had been listed on some of the glass jars.

But what about the other Circle members? Was Mason drugging them as well? Tonight she'd check all the labels carefully to see what all was there.

Her second dilemma was what to do about the video she'd uncovered of Senator Benjamin.

The thought of publicly exposing him seemed a fitting retaliation. Except that it exposed the victim. And Cindy had suffered enough in life. If anyone deserved to rest in peace, she did.

Rachel had watched the video several times that afternoon in an attempt to place the setting. In one scene, she'd spotted a small plaque on the back of the door. While she couldn't zoom in close enough to see details, it looked like one of those checkout policies posted at hotels. Or, judging by the furnishings, a nice inn.

The question of how Mason Wright had come to possess the video remained unanswered. The bottom line was, he had it. She suspected he'd already used it against the senator, hence her being hired.

Dropping to one knee, Rachel tightened a shoelace. Even as she did, she recognized she was delaying. Giving herself one last chance to gather her wits before facing Elijah.

All afternoon, she'd had flashbacks from the night before. Or at least she thought they were flashbacks. She could recall little after arriving back at Elijah's apartment. But what she did recall was scorching. And the memory seemed to trigger an even sharper desire.

For Elijah.

With that admission came the unsettling knowledge that while she had managed years ago to accept that their relationship was over, the explosive attraction between them was as fierce as ever. She should have recognized that when it flared to life the first time she'd seen him back in Richmond.

But acknowledging desire didn't make the other problems between them go away. Their hurtful past. The tangled circumstances of Nick's death.

And what about this case she and Elijah were involved in now? Did she trust him? Hell, she didn't even know how much of Mason's secret room she wanted to share with Elijah. Would he take a page from Dwight's handbook and try to freeze her out?

Earlier today, she'd sent copies of the video to both Sheila and Chase. Just in case.

Part of her was still annoyed that neither Elijah nor Dwight had told her up front about the pornography. She understood that it was an ongoing investigation. The thought that profits from pornography—made at the church's facility—supported terrorism enraged her. It also made her realize that her case was truly secondary to Elijah's case.

Which meant that exposing the senator and Mason Wright might have to wait indefinitely.

She had reached the administration building now. Elijah was near the corner of the building, smoking a cigar.

She walked up and held out her hand. Bemusement crossed his face as he passed her the cigar.

"I forgot you're a reformed smoker," he said.

Nodding, she drew in, then blew out a streamer of smoke. The fragrant cigar was unbelievably smooth. "Cuban?"

"Your brother got me started on them."

"Nick loved a cigar and cognac." Rachel handed the Cuban back. "I don't suppose you've got a flask?"

"No, but I'll requisition one." Elijah extinguished the cigar. "I picked up extra door alarms, by the way, so we can both go in."

"I'm not sure I'm ready to share."

He straightened. "Seeing as I know where the stuff is now, I could have gone in alone. Instead, I'm trying to work with you. But will you work with me?"

"What assurance do I have that you won't eventually shut me out?"

"My word. On Nick's grave."

She stared at him. "There's nothing more sacred."

Inside the building, Rachel watched as he rigged a wireless device at the doors. When he finished, he handed her an earpiece. "You'll be monitoring the front doors. One beep means someone's coming through the east door; two beeps, west."

She nodded, then led the way to Mason's office and showed him the room hidden behind the bookcases. The small quarters were cramped with two people.

Elijah pointed to the cabinets. "What's in those?"

"I'm not sure. I didn't have the chance to open all of them last night. Let's start here." Rachel opened the drug cabinet first. Everything appeared to be just as she'd left it last night. "Those three jars are what I sampled."

She bent down and scanned the labels, reassuring herself that none of the others were Circle member names.

Elijah pulled a small camera out of his pocket and photographed each shelf. Then he pulled on latex gloves and took samples of the drugs Rachel took last night.

He pointed to the larger jars in the back, that had labels like HqNO, RB2h. "Any idea what those are?"

She shrugged. "Ingredients, maybe? The labels mean nothing."

"I'll sample them, too."

While Elijah worked on that, Rachel opened a second file cabinet. Inside were three rectangular plastic boxes. She flipped the lid of one and saw it contained more CDs.

"And what have we here?" she said. "A whole library on the senator, perhaps?"

Elijah peeled off his gloves, then peered over her shoulder. "Let's take a look."

Rachel flipped past the first disc, which wasn't labeled. The second one, however, had a single name scrawled across it.

Emily.

She grabbed the disk and quickly set up her laptop. This time, when the video flickered to life, Rachel recognized the setting. It was Mason's office.

A naked woman crawled back and forth—racing, practically—across the floor on her hands and knees. She was sobbing pathetically, begging not to be sent away.

Rachel's throat tightened as she realized the woman was Emily.

The camera zoomed closer. She focused on Emily's eyes. They were dilated, almost totally black. Knowing the other girl had been drugged didn't make it any easier to watch.

Worse, it appeared that the drug was starting to take effect, slowing Emily's movements. She went from hysterical to calm, from denial to acceptance, all the while remaining on her hands and knees.

And where her previous words had been that she didn't want to leave, now she stated calmly that she'd do anything. That she only wanted to please and serve. That getting into the Kingdom was all that mattered.

Rachel wanted to turn away, but couldn't. This wasn't the Emily she knew. It was a stranger who now crawled calmly toward the sofa. But instead of sitting, Emily raised up and bent her waist across the padded arm, exposing her bare buttocks to the camera.

Then she tranquilly glanced over one shoulder and began confessing her sins. They were vague. "I've been bad. I haven't obeyed." On and on the litany went until finally Emily was out of breath. "I am ready for my chastisement now."

A shadow drew closer, but her punisher kept out

of sight as a black leather strap—a belt—swung into view. It struck Emily's buttocks with a loud crack.

Emily barely flinched. In fact, she seemed to enjoy it, her face softening in elation before she calmly asked for more. "But harder, please."

How many times the ghastly act repeated, Rachel didn't know. Abruptly, the video stopped, flickering grey.

But the last frame remained burned in her mind. Emily's buttocks were swollen and beaten bright red, yet still she asked for more.

Rachel was trembling with anger. "I swear I'm going to kill that bastard."

"I'll help." Elijah put a hand on her shoulder.

She shrugged it off, her fingers flying to the keyboard.

"Are you trying to copy it or destroy it?" he asked.

"I want to see when this file was created."

"That doesn't matter—"

"It does! Emily left to go overseas. Didn't you hear her begging not to be sent away? And the day before she left, she was limping. She told me she'd fallen in the shower. God, I should have known!"

"How? How could you have possibly have known?"

She met his gaze, hated that he was right. And still she was seething inside. "I might not have known before, but now that I do . . ."

"You have every right to be angry."

Elijah's understanding helped little. Emily was so sweet. So trusting. Especially of Mason. She had plainly adored the man, and look what he gave her in return.

"She was just so damn . . . eager to please."

"It was the drug, Rachel. Combined with who-knows-what kind of brainwashing."

Her mind flew back to her own sessions with Mason. The way she'd felt drawn to him afterward. She shook her head in denial. "Even at that, I can't imagine letting anyone do those things to me."

"Emily's been here longer. And she may be getting a different, or stronger, drug. Having this stuff tested will shed light on it." Elijah reached down inside the cabinet and started flipping through the other discs in the case. "These all appear to be of Emily."

"You're kidding! There must be fifty CDs in there."

Rachel moved in beside Elijah again as he opened the lid of the second box. These discs were different brands and colors and had preprinted labels.

"These look like the ones I've been searching for." He read a couple of labels, then opened the third and final box.

The disc in front had a familiar name scrawled across it. *Rachel.* She drew a sharp breath. "Give it to me."

Elijah handed it to her, then quickly flipped through the rest. "That's the only one with your name. The rest are labeled *Alisa.*"

Rachel had already moved back to the laptop and opened the drive. When he moved in behind her, she looked over her shoulder and met his gaze.

"I'm not sure I want you to see this."

"I know." He made no attempt to move away. "But we both need to see it."

Drawing a noisy breath, she started the video.

An image of her face, eyes closed, filled the

screen. Then the camera skimmed down her body. Her blouse was unbuttoned, her front-clasp bra spread wide, leaving her breasts exposed fully to the camera.

"Oh, God, no." Rachel recognized the black and red plaid skirt she'd worn for her session yesterday.

Mason's voice came across the speakers. "Your breasts are lovely, Rachel. From now on, each time you undress, I want you to imagine that I'm watching. I want you to imagine how wonderful my touch would feel upon them."

His hand came into view then, hovering inches from her nipple, but not making contact. "You're on fire for my touch. You sense my fingers, here, and you fervently wish I would give in and pinch you." He withdrew his hand. "But I won't. Each time you listen to this recording, your longing for my touch will increase until it becomes unbearable, and it feels like you will die without it. And then you'll beg me."

Revulsion rolled over Rachel as the camera zoomed in close, then panned back out and swept the length of her body. The fact that only her blouse was disturbed didn't lessen her fury.

Mason gave a final command. "I'd like you to wear a dress next time, Rachel. Something that buttons all the way down the front. And no underwear. It will be your wicked little secret. Now relax and listen. You will awaken to my touch, feeling invigorated and remembering only pleasure."

The video ended. She stared at the screen in shock, recalling her own denial of moments before. Seeing it with her own eyes made it no easier to accept.

"Killing that bastard isn't enough," Rachel said finally. "I want to castrate him. After I break every bone in his body."

"Think you can beat me to it?"

"Don't even think about getting in my way." She shook her head, avoiding looking at him. "Besides, this isn't your problem. It's mine."

"The problem is Mason Wright. What he did was wrong. To you and to Emily. Probably Alisa, too."

She nodded toward the drawers. "You're sure that's the only one of me?"

"Yes. Why?"

"This ran less than two minutes. Yesterday, I was there for an hour. The time before that . . ." Chilled, she rubbed her arms. "I can't stand the thought of what he might have done the rest of the time I was unconscious. Look what he did to Emily."

Elijah hovered closer. "I doubt it's an overnight process. And Emily's been here two years. Judging by the number of discs here, I suspect this has been going on for a long time. It's apparent you were drugged, Rachel, and in a deep trance. I'm betting the audio and video both have embedded subliminal commands as well."

She made a strangled noise. "I didn't even think of that. He even gave me a copy of the audio for home use."

"Did you use it?"

"Once. It gave me nightmares."

"If I can get a copy, I'll have it analyzed." Elijah turned and grabbed one of the discs from the middle box. "After watching that tape of Emily and seeing the effects of those drugs, these may make more sense."

Rachel looked at the CD he held. It was one of the ones with a neatly typed label. "I don't understand."

"Remember the pornography I mentioned earlier? Those women appear drugged and their behavior is aberrant. Now I'm wondering if these women aren't being programmed with this same technique. It would explain their willingness."

"Willingness for what? To have sex on film? Some people do that for a living."

"They're eager to be brutally punished, Rach." Elijah handed her the disc. "Play this. And I'll warn you, it will be shocking."

Turning back, she removed the disc with her name on it and set it aside. "It's hard to imagine anything worse than what I've already seen."

When the video started, Rachel noticed immediately that it was different. The quality was higher. More professional. The setting was totally different, too. A dungeon? Metal brackets in the wall held flickering torches, but the room was well lit from other sources, suggesting a movie stage.

In the background, drumbeats sounded low and easy as the camera slowly panned to a nude woman who was leaning over a crude wooden table. She was blond, but Rachel couldn't see her face.

The woman was bent at the waist and stood on the tips of her toes, which thrust her buttocks up. There were metal shackles at the corners of the table, but the woman wasn't locked in them. Instead, she had her arms spread wide as she gripped the cuffs and begged to be allowed to prove she was worthy.

Two men stepped into the scene, naked and fully erect. Both wore hoods concealing their identities. They held long bamboo poles that Rachel thought looked similar to the kendo-type sticks used in martial arts. A knot formed in her stomach.

The woman was undulating her hips, begging for redemption in a singsong chant that matched the tempo of the drums. As the men took their places on either side of the woman, she spread her legs and arched her hips, as if welcoming the horrible caning that Rachel knew would follow.

But how could I know that?

The woman never screamed as her buttocks and thighs were lashed over and over. "Yes, yes," the woman murmured. "Harder."

As the drumbeats grew louder, faster, the blows kept pace. The muscles in the men's arms bunched with the increasing force of their blows. The woman was crying out loudly now, pleading for sexual release.

The camera panned upward, showing the woman's face. She had a dreamy, faraway expression, as if she were honestly enjoying this.

Once again, Rachel had the feeling she'd seen this before. Then she realized the woman was indeed familiar.

"That's one of the Eve's Circle girls!"

ELEVEN

Elijah stopped the video. "You know her?"

"No. But I've seen group photographs of prior members. They're in the meeting room. She's in one of them. I should have picked up on the blond hair sooner." Rachel looked at the cabinets around them. "What the hell's going on here, Elijah? I feel like I've stepped into an alternate universe."

"Me, too. I had dismissed as irrelevant the question of where they found the girls to do these movies. It's obvious they're not underage." He ran his hands through his hair. "I figured they were high and doing it to support their drug habits."

"Wait a minute. Are you saying Mason is training the girls here? Then sending them overseas to do this?"

"It would seem so. The films all have a particular look. Blue-eyed blondes with nice figures are a popular sexual icon in the international porn industry. It also means Mason is more involved in this."

Rachel groaned. "Is this what Emily's going to be used for?"

"I don't know. We've got some contacts at the mission. I can see if Emily arrived."

"Some of those scenes were . . ." She massaged her temples. "Familiar. And not just because of the woman. I think the nightmares I had contained those images. And worse."

Elijah moved closer. "Did you say that you watched a video along with the tape? I'm betting some of the images and sounds from these are inserted in what you saw and listened to."

"But why?" She scowled, disgusted. "Seeing this doesn't make me like it."

"Over time it desensitizes you to violence. Intermingle it with subliminal audio that gives your subconscious the message that this is normal, or even desirable, and then combine it with the drugs. You wouldn't know what hit you."

Rachel looked at him. "Did I . . . Did I behave like that last night? Begging to be disciplined?"

When he responded, his voice was tight. "You weren't begging to be punished, but yes, you begged for something else. And while I know this may not make you any happier, I think your reaction last night was heightened by desire from our past, combined with the drug, versus mental stimulus from Mason."

Embarrassed, Rachel looked away. "None of it makes me happy, but I can browbeat myself later. For now we need to figure out what we do with all this."

"I can't take any originals. And we don't have time to copy everything." He checked the time, then dragged out his laptop from his backpack. "I'm glad I brought this. I'll duplicate what I can onto my hard drive. In the meantime, can you get

me the names and photographs of all the Eve's
Circle girls? All the girls in the videos I've seen
have been blond. I want to see if I can identify any
of the others."

She nodded. "Set your machine for the lowest
compression. It'll copy quicker and use less space.
Hand me some of the ones you want copied. It'll
be faster if we both do them. I can transfer them
onto your computer when we're back at your
place."

Elijah pointed to the disc that she'd set off to
one side. *The disc with her name on it.* "You know you
can't take that, Rachel. Since it's recent, Mason's
more likely to miss it."

"Do you really think I'm going to leave this here
for that pervert to watch?" She held up a hand to
ward off his protests. "And what about when the
CIA seizes all this? Do you know how many people
I know there? It's bad enough you saw it. But at
least you . . . I mean we . . ."

"I understand. And believe me, I don't want
anyone else to see it either." Turning away, Elijah
opened the cabinet that held supplies. "How's
your forgery skills these days?"

"Passable."

"Here's a matching blank disc. Copy your name
on it, then put a small scratch on the back. If
Mason tries to play it, hopefully he'll just think it
was a damaged disc. Then you can take the original. I never saw it. But . . ." He paused. "Think
twice before you destroy it. It is evidence of a crime
against you. It's totally your call, but later you may
decide to take action."

Before he could move away, she laid a hand on

his arm. That he gave her a choice and protected her privacy meant a lot. She'd follow his advice and keep the disc, for now. "Thank you."

They worked for two hours. While Elijah oversaw the copying processes, Rachel logged on to Mason's secretary's computer and printed the rosters of Eve's Circle. Then she copied personal data and a photograph for each member.

While several girls had been members for multiple years, like Emily, Cindy, and Alisa, there were still twenty distinct names. How many of these girls had been abused? All? Some?

Neither of them spoke until they arrived back at Elijah's apartment.

"Do you think Senator Benjamin is in on all this?" Rachel asked.

Elijah rubbed his jaw, then shook his head. "If Benjamin knows what Mason is doing with these girls, the video of his stepdaughter loses its leverage. My gut says the senator is running scared—desperate to get that video before the next presidential election."

His explanation made sense. What Senator Benjamin had done to his stepdaughter was appalling, but she resisted labeling Mason's actions as *worse* because it seemed to suggest that Benjamin wasn't quite as vile.

This was why Rachel preferred to view things as black and white. Screw the shades of gray. Something was either right or wrong. Period. Degrees of separation lost meaning if the basic issue was simply good versus bad.

She pointed to the kitchen table. "I suggest we set up our laptops here. And I'll download directly to yours."

After a few false starts, she was able to establish a link and start a data transfer. "This will take a few minutes."

"Good."

Rachel straightened, very aware of Elijah standing right behind her. Bits and pieces of memories from last night surfaced, heightening her awareness.

She expected him to back up when she turned. He didn't, leaving them dangerously close.

"So what happens next?" she asked. "How soon can you bust Mason?"

"Not fast enough, I'm afraid. If we expose him too soon, we risk Kito Mzuzi destroying evidence and taking off."

"And in the meantime, Mason gets to keep on abusing these girls? And I'm supposed to act like nothing's wrong next time I see him?"

Elijah's brow darkened. "I want you to leave, Rachel. What you've done is incredibly helpful and I swear to God, I'll keep you fully informed of everything. I'll also get you a full analysis of those drugs and the tapes. Plus everything I can get my hands on pertaining to Nick."

"I'm not leaving," Rachel said. "Not as long as you're here. I'm involved in this and I want to know everything you know."

For a moment she thought Elijah would argue. Or try to pull rank.

"Then you should know this." He moved impossibly closer, forcing her to take a step backward. The table blocked further retreat. "If we keep working together, something's liable to happen. Like this."

His arm circled her, pressing her fully against

his chest. His other hand cupped the back of her neck, holding her steady as his mouth took hers.

Rachel groaned as Elijah's tongue swept boldly into her mouth. *This* was a kiss. Pure heat. Pure passion.

She opened hungrily, inviting him in. Taking what he offered. He angled his chin, his hands cupping her face.

The desire she'd been fighting flared to life. God, she was tired of struggling, of debating her every thought of this man. Right now, she simply wanted to feel. To remember. She sighed, breathing him in. Intoxicated.

No one had ever touched her body, or her soul, like this man. And that knowledge frightened her even as it excited her.

Her hands slid down to caress his chest, his waist. He moaned, encouraging her as his mouth shifted lower to graze the side of her neck, trailing kisses down her throat.

She shuddered against the burning, blinding longing that threatened to engulf her as he captured her lips once again and pulled her close. He filled her senses, making her crazy for more as he pressed his full erection against her abdomen.

She wanted to touch him *there*. To take him inside her, now. She was wet and hot and desperate for him.

The thought terrified and aroused her simultaneously. She pushed away, suddenly desperate for space. For sanity, reason.

Few things in life frightened Rachel Anderson. But the ferocity of this need, of such an all-consuming desire, scared her witless. Especially when, for so many years, she had told herself she abhorred this man, had purposely fanned the fires of hate.

Now she knew why.

By shouting to herself that she despised Elijah, she avoided hearing that small, persistent voice that said maybe she still cared for him.

Maybe I never stopped caring.

Behind her, her computer beeped, indicating the file transfer was completed. Finished.

"I can't deal with this right now." Rachel wanted to flee, needing to be alone with her thoughts and feelings to sort them out. Turning away, she shut down her laptop before cramming it into her bag. The zipper caught, refusing to budge.

Elijah's hand came over hers, stilling the frantic motion. He tugged the zipper backward, reversing it onto the track. Then he stepped away, giving her space. "The last thing I want is to cause you more distress. But sooner or later, we have to deal with it, Rachel."

"I vote later."

His jaw tightened. "Later, then. I still need to go to your dorm with you, to get the relaxation CD Mason gave you."

She started to tell him she'd bring it tomorrow, but instead she nodded. Getting the audio transcribed and analyzed was important.

They didn't speak again until they were almost to her place. "I'll wait here," Elijah said.

When she came back out, she handed him the CD. "I'll need to get that back, in case Mason asks for it. And I want a complete transcript of what's on it."

"I'll make certain of that. Good night."

Back inside her room, Rachel left the lights off,

moving comfortably through the darkness. She accepted that sleep would elude her tonight.

And not just because of Elijah. Part of her was worried she'd have those nightmares again. Knowing the images had been real made them more frightening.

The videos they'd discovered tonight, with their graphic violence entwined with sex, had been deeply disturbing. Knowing those women had been drugged and manipulated only increased her sense of outrage. And her sense of helplessness.

Rachel typically dealt with violence by separating her reaction to it from the act itself. But how could she do that this time? Images of Emily, sweet innocent Emily, blurred the lines of separation.

Guilt over the fact that she had tried to develop a friendship with Emily simply to gather information for her own case ate at her. Compared to what Mason Wright and the others were doing, it was a minor sin. But it continued to bother her.

Seeing herself on video tonight had been sobering, too. At first Rachel had felt violated, ravaged even. Until she saw what the others had been subjected to. Then she'd felt somewhat fortunate.

And the thought that she'd been drugged and exposed to God-knew-what subliminal commands was alarming. She had to find out exactly what suggestions had been implanted in her mind. Then she could figure out how to remove them.

In the meantime, she had to wonder if these intense feelings for Elijah were merely a result of the drugs or the mind manipulation. When he had kissed her tonight, her brain had simply shut down, leaving her awash in an ocean of sexual awareness.

Until she was certain *she* was in control, she needed to avoid being alone with him.

To keep up the act, Rachel attended classes the next day, but found it difficult to concentrate. And to stay awake.

When she returned to her dorm at four, she called Elijah and told him she was skipping his computer class.

"Is something wrong?" he asked.

Where to start? "I'm sleep deprived and your class is the only one I can skip without being marked absent."

He chuckled, which irritated her. "Get some rest. I'll see you later, then."

She fell into a deep, dreamless sleep. It was dark when she awoke six hours later, grumpy but refreshed. She knew grumpy was a sign that it had been a normal rest.

Impatient, she dressed and arrived at Elijah's apartment at ten-forty-five. He was on his cell phone, but pointed to the coffeepot, indicating she should help herself.

Rachel sat on the couch and watched him pace as he listened. Judging by the circles beneath his eyes, she guessed he'd had little sleep.

When Elijah finally hung up, he sat opposite her.

"Long day?" she asked.

"Yeah, but productive. The stuff we found last night broke the logjam. I've been in overload most of the day. That was the lab, by the way."

"What did they say?"

"The results are preliminary, but basically you, Emily, and Alisa were given different drugs. The base ingredients are the same, but in varying ratios. Yours was the weakest. Plus Emily's and Alisa's had substances yours didn't. They're still trying to isolate the different elements. It's very different from anything the lab has seen before and they're eager to do more extensive tests."

"Were the base ingredients in the other jars we sampled?"

"Some, but not all. It's probable Mason has another lab somewhere."

"Perhaps at his home?"

"More than likely. Which makes it hard to search at night because he's there." Elijah picked up his mug of coffee. "At any rate, the lab feels the main purpose of the drug is to enhance mind control."

"Gee. And now the CIA has it. Small wonder they're eager to do more tests," Rachel said. "What about long term affects?"

He arched an eyebrow. "They're still assessing that. Some of the compounds had sedative qualities, while others had stimulant properties. Emily's and Alisa's contained a mild hallucinogenic that's nonaddictive. While you'd probably have one hell of a trip, the lab assured me that unless consumed in huge quantities, it won't kill a person, per se."

"Unless of course they hallucinate they can fly and jump off a building," she snapped. "Or they let someone asphyxiate them while having sex. What's Mason trying to do?"

"Who knows? But think about it. If you combine the drugs with the right subliminal messages, you could program someone to do virtually anything."

"It makes me ill to think about it. Any word on what they found on the audio disc?"

"Not yet. They're trying to unravel it. There are multiple layers of sound, specific noise patterns, music and voice. I suspect the CD you had contained basic—but by no means less powerful—techniques designed to break down defenses while laying the groundwork for other stronger mind-control methods." Elijah tilted his head to one side, studying her. "Would you rather not hear all of this?"

"Keep going. I have to know. And not just for me, but to understand what Mason has done to the others."

"You have to remember this is a multistep process. Over time, he most likely increases or changes the drugs while simultaneously increasing his level of mastery through hypnosis and subliminals. If he works with someone long enough, he probably reaches a point where he's embedded enough commands and suggestions that he can control them verbally. I'm betting that's what gets his rocks off."

"And once they're completely broken, he loses interest," Rachel finished. "Mason told me his father was a pharmacologist. Any chance he got help with this?"

Elijah shrugged. "His old man died over twenty years ago. Did he mention that most of his father's work was done in South America, outside the auspices of the FDA? Mason spent nearly ten years traveling in the rain forests with his father. At eighteen, he returned to the states for college. Guess it won't surprise you to learn Mason interned with a professor who was experimenting in subliminal techniques, NLP, Ericksonian hypnosis, etc."

"Knowing how Frankenstein was created doesn't

make him any less a monster." Rachel closed her eyes. "Did you get any word on Emily?"

"She left Los Angeles two days ago, but we haven't confirmed her arrival at the mission. Which isn't unusual. Getting to the mission involves planes, automobiles, and donkey carts." Standing, Elijah pointed to her mug. "Want more coffee?"

Nodding, she followed him to the kitchen. "So, what next?"

"I need to copy as many of the rest of those videos as I can. You don't have to go, if you'd rather not."

"Try to keep me away."

"Look, Rach—" He raised a hand, then dropped it. "This job has been nothing but hell for you. And I know working with me hasn't been much better. But without you . . . Well, none of this would be coming together."

The sincerity and admiration she saw in his eyes made her feel good. And more. She squelched it. "Just promise you won't shut me out, Elijah. I don't give a damn what Dwight says, or what your commitment is to the Company. I want to see this through to the end. With you."

For a moment she thought he'd argue. Instead he nodded, then set his mug aside. "We should go, then."

Once again Rachel wore an earpiece monitoring the front doors of the administration building. They had barely slipped inside the secret room in Mason's office, though, when two beeps sounded in her ear.

"Alarm," she hissed. "The west door."

Elijah signaled to leave. Grabbing her pack, she slipped out and made a beeline out of the office.

Footsteps echoed down the hall, headed their way. Whoever it was made no attempt to disguise their presence, so she doubted it was Nigel Kowicki. She tugged Elijah into the small, dark lobby situated directly across from Mason's secretary's desk.

He flattened himself behind a couch while she dove behind a chair. The area was open. If anyone turned on a light, they could easily be spotted.

Rachel held her breath as she recognized Mason Wright's tall frame striding into sight. He went directly into his office and snapped on the light. She shrank back and prayed they hadn't left anything out of place.

After a few moments, she leaned her head forward. Mason had left the door partly open. While she couldn't see him, she could hear him talking. He was on his phone.

She looked at Elijah and held her hand to her ear, mimicking a phone. He inched forward, peering around the edge of the couch. Nodding his head sharply toward the hall, he raised up.

Rachel leaned forward, regaining her balance. Mason was talking louder, a good indication he believed he was alone. When Elijah crept toward the dark hall, she followed.

She didn't breathe again until they were outside. They stepped around the side of the building.

Leaning against the building's rough brick wall, Rachel tried to suck oxygen into her lungs as quietly as possible. That had been too close.

She sensed Elijah hovering in front of her and opened her eyes. He didn't say a word, yet they were silently communicating through the adrenaline pumping in their veins.

It was a familiar sensation. The thrill of escape. Danger had passed, leaving the pent-up energy of apprehension to morph into something else.

Excitement.

Her heart thudded loudly in her ears. So did his.

She and Elijah had always shared this rare quality. A bond born in mutual passion.

"Shall we make a run for it?" His voice was so low, she had to lean forward to catch his words.

They didn't stop until they reached his apartment. Inside, Rachel dropped her backpack and bent at the waist, her hands on her knees.

She heard the refrigerator door open, then felt something cold touch her arm. She accepted the bottle of water, gulping it down. "That was too damn close."

"You can say that again." Elijah drained his bottle, then moved to the cabinet beside the sink. "I think that calls for a drink. Cognac?" He set a pint bottle on the counter beside her.

She read the label and nodded in approval. "Got any more of those Cubans?"

"Of course." He reached around her and snapped off the light, throwing the kitchen into darkness. "Let's smoke this outside. Grab the cognac."

Rachel expected for them to take off toward the woods, so when Elijah grabbed her around the waist and hauled her backward against him, it startled her.

"Sorry." He kept his voice low, but didn't move his hand from her abdomen. "The apartment next door is empty. As long as we're quiet, we're fine right here."

She lifted her hand to press over his, acknowledging that his touch felt good, but he stepped away. Feeling awkward, she turned and waved toward the chair.

"Go ahead. I feel like standing."

Elijah caught her hand and tugged her. "Actually, since you've got the cognac and I've got the cigar, I thought we'd share the chair." He sat, pulling her down and across his lap.

She twisted the cap from the bottle as he lit the cigar. The fragrant smoke dissipated in the light breeze. She took a sip and closed her eyes, savoring the cognac's warmth. Passing the bottle to him, she accepted the cigar and drew on it. Tasting him.

Rachel handed it back and waited as he took another sip of cognac before pressing the bottle back in her hand.

"You were great back there," he said. "We make a great team. We always did."

It was true. And oddly, it didn't hurt to admit that. On the contrary, it felt . . .

She took another sip of cognac, but waved off the cigar. "No more for me. I should probably be going soon."

"Please stay." Elijah set the cigar on the ground, then tugged the bottle from her hand and set it away, too. "I don't want you to go yet."

And she didn't want to leave.

He wrapped his arms around her and pulled her close. For long moments they just sat quietly, listening to the soft chirrup of tree frogs and crickets. His hand swept up and down her arm, the light friction soothing. Inviting.

That wordless communication was back. When she tilted her head up, his lips met hers. As she knew they would. She opened her mouth, welcoming the sweep of his tongue. He tasted of tobacco and cognac and mint.

Heat and passion, too. Rachel's hands pressed against his chest, kneading the solid muscles beneath his shirt as her fingers touched the top button, sliding it free, then the next and the next, until finally she was able to slide her hands inside and caress his bare chest.

He groaned, deepening the kiss. She felt him tug the hem of her turtleneck free of her jeans, his hand skimming beneath it to brush the bare skin of her abdomen. There was a slight tug as he unsnapped her bra, then his hand eased the lacy cups aside before capturing her breast.

She reveled in the way he molded her flesh, caressing and teasing before catching the nipple between his thumb and forefinger and pressing lightly. It wasn't enough and he knew it.

The warmth and tension that had been building just below her navel sank lower. She felt his burgeoning erection and pulled back slightly to gain access to the region below his belt. He growled when her hand traced boldly over him, squeezing his shaft through the now-tight denim.

She wanted him. Period. And the fact it was an honest need, her own honest need, nearly overwhelmed her. She tugged at the snap of his jeans, suddenly eager to touch him.

Elijah broke the kiss, his breathing ragged. "Rachel, we need to—"

"Don't tell me to stop," she pleaded. "Not tonight."

He caught her face in his hands, shifting her

eyes to meet his. "I don't want you to stop. But I need to know you're sure."

His words carried multiple meanings. Their complex past. Their uncertain future. The concern for what Mason Wright had done to her.

Rachel shut her eyes, closing out everything except this wild longing that burned inside her. It was familiar. And it was real. It was also the same feeling she'd had the first time she ever saw him.

"I'm sure, Elijah. I want this. I want you."

His lips caught hers again, and this time there was no holding back. This was the kiss she never wanted to end. Or rather, that she wanted to see morph into something more.

He stood, carrying her inside, swearing each time he had to stop kissing her. To open the door, to shut it.

Once they were inside, Rachel's fervor consumed her patience. She tugged his shirt off his shoulders, then shrugged to help him peel off her shirt. Their motions grew frantic again, until they were both naked and panting.

The inferno she'd been struggling to contain for days now flared to life. She welcomed the heat and fanned the flame as Elijah lifted her up.

His mouth latched onto her breast, suckling. She wrapped her legs around his waist, offering herself up fully to his mouth, even as she pressed her bottom down, frantic to feel him inside of her.

He swore, struggling for control. "Do you mind hard and fast?"

"Anything!" She kissed him, sucking on his tongue as she rolled her hips once more.

Elijah pushed her away, but before she could pro-

test, he settled back against her. This time the head
of his penis was poised directly at her opening.

He felt huge, and Rachel thought she'd die if he
didn't complete the act. She turned her head from
side to side, the pressure unbearable. "Please."

She felt one of Elijah's hands squeeze her but-
tock as his other slid lower, guiding his penis to
her moist center. That first touch of heat on heat
was shocking.

He shuddered, then growled. "God, you're wet.
And hot. Ready?"

She rocked her hips, trying to rush him. "I've
been ready."

"Hold on." He pressed in, burying himself completely with a swiftness that shocked and delighted
her.

She had forgotten how large he was, how his
thickness made her feel as if she couldn't possibly
hold him all. And yet she did.

She crossed her ankles behind him, taking him
even deeper as he plunged into her again and
again. She felt a scream build as her release spi-
raled upward and out of control.

But instead of screaming, she bit his shoulder,
felt him stiffen. His hands shifted to her hips,
holding her as he pistoned in and out, faster and
harder as they climaxed together.

She collapsed against his chest, grateful he still
held her.

"You okay?" he whispered.

"Mmm. You can put me down."

"Like hell. We never made it out of the kitchen,
Rach. We're going back to the bedroom."

He was still hard and still inside her. The desire

that had been totally sated minutes ago sprang back to life as he moved.

In the bedroom, he set her down, then stepped away to turn on a lamp. She knew by the way his gaze drifted over her that he found her as desirable as he ever did. "You're so beautiful. And so help me, I want you again."

"Ditto." Rachel's eyes glided over him, taking in his sheer male beauty, the way his broad shoulders tapered down to a narrow waist and slim hips.

He was fully erect again, his penis jutting out from a dark patch of pubic hair. It was long and thick, curving slightly. The head was deep crimson, the skin so taut it looked painful.

Her heart beat faster, in awe, anticipation, as desire bloomed low, making her wonder if she had ever *not* wanted this man.

Stepping closer, she looped her arms around his neck, pressing herself fully against his erection as she tugged his head down and pressed her lips to his.

With a groan, Elijah picked her up and carried her to the bed, laying her down as if she were made of spun glass. He leaned over, covering her, yet holding back as he caught her lips in a more leisurely kiss.

"I want to devour you." He trailed kisses down her neck, savoring her soft throat.

Moving lower, he ran his tongue along the curve of her breast, kissing and teasing each hardened nipple, until she groaned. Then he latched on and sucked. She'd always had sensitive breasts. Lucky him.

He drew back slightly, catching the tip between his teeth and tugging. She arched beneath him, encouraging without words, as he switched to her other breast and sucked, teased.

Moving lower, he grazed his teeth along her ribs, spreading kisses across her abdomen and lower, until at last his tongue lapped along the moist folds of her center and closed over her clitoris. Rachel raised off the bed at the onslaught. Her hands splayed through his hair, guiding, encouraging.

She quickly climaxed . . . and still Elijah pressed on, unmerciful, until she came a second time. Then he relented, kissing his way back up to her breasts.

Leaning on his forearms, he looked at her. "I should have asked this earlier. Do I need to use protection?"

"I'm on the pill."

Relieved, he brushed the lightest of kisses on her lips as he settled between her legs and let his throbbing erection kiss the heat of her slick opening. She raised her knees, trying to rush him, but he pressed in slowly, moving deliberately, easing into her.

"How are you feeling?" he whispered.

"On . . . the edge. Like I'm being teased. Tormented." She drew a sharp breath as he flexed in. "That helps, but I still need more."

He grinned. "Relax and enjoy the ride." Rotating his hips, he rubbed against her clitoris slowly, drawing her into a seductive rhythm. "That's it. Now wrap your legs around my hips."

Rachel raised one leg and felt him slide deeper, igniting more fireworks. What this man did to her was mind-boggling. She arched, drawing his mouth into a kiss, capturing his tongue and sucking on it as she moved her other leg up. The new angle caused him to sink even further into her sheath.

Then he pulled back, nearly withdrawing completely. His erection was burning hot and felt too thick, like it wouldn't fit. Yet it did, again and again.

Elijah kept at it, pulling back, sinking in, until Rachel was mindless with sensation. She drew a sharp breath.

"I think . . . I'm coming," she hissed.

"Don't think. Do it." He took her breast in his mouth once again, laving the nipple with his tongue before scraping his teeth against the nipple.

Her reaction was immediate. She panted now, her hips bucking as she chased the sensation. He pumped in and out. Watching her beneath him had him on the brink again.

As her orgasm exploded, her fingernails raked down his back. "Elijah!"

He struggled to prolong the moment, to hold off what was going to be the most powerful climax of his life. But it was like trying to stop the sun from rising. He groaned and tugged back. Then lost it.

With a shout he pumped his hips, felt her tight body clutch his cock. He ground his hips from side to side, bringing them both to a shattering close before pressing deep and letting his release shoot into her.

TWELVE

The ringing of Elijah's telephone shattered the moment. He was tempted to ignore it, but knew he couldn't. For someone to call at this hour of the morning, it had to be important.

"I have to answer that."

At her nod, he snatched the cordless phone from the bedside table. The caller ID was blocked. Propping the phone between his ear and shoulder, he climbed from bed and grabbed a pair of jeans from a drawer, pulling them on.

"Hello." He fumbled with the zipper as he turned back toward her. "*Shit.*" His cock hardened immediately.

She was sitting up in the center of the bed, her legs curled to one side as she watched him dress. That she made no attempt to shield her nudity pleased him even as it made him want her anew.

And seeing her in his bed again—

"Is this a bad time?" It was Dwight.

Elijah turned away and headed toward the living room. He couldn't talk while looking at her naked.

"It's fine. It took me a minute to find my phone." He detoured to the kitchen to start coffee, but found their clothes scattered around on the floor. He snatched them up and carried them back to the bedroom, only to find that Rachel was in the bathroom.

He debated taking the clothes back with him, wanting to see her naked again. Instead, he left them on the bed and headed back to the kitchen. "What's up?"

"A lot." The rasp of a lighter came across the phone. Dwight inhaled before continuing. "I barely know where to start. After years of picking at loose threads, it looks like we finally got one that's going to unravel the whole fucking tapestry. Thanks to Rachel. How's she doing, by the way? Any aftereffects from the drugs?"

"None that we've seen." When things first heated up on the patio, Elijah had worried about that. And while she had reassured him with words, it was the language of their lovemaking that had ultimately convinced him. It was as it had been before. Only better.

At that moment, she walked into the room and moved straight to the coffeepot. She was fully dressed, which relieved and disappointed him at the same time. Even though the coffee wasn't finished brewing, she grabbed two mugs and filled them.

He accepted the coffee with a wink. "Rachel's here now."

At the mention of her name, her eyes flared. "Dwight?" she mouthed.

He nodded before continuing. "We had planned to copy more video tonight, but ran into problems."

"Anything serious?" Dwight asked.

"Mason decided to work late. Check tonight's phone logs. I'm eager to know who he was talking to."

"This late, it had to be an overseas call. You might hold off on going back until I get the transcripts and make certain he's not onto us," Dwight continued. "And if Rachel's there, you might as well put me on speakerphone. You'll both want to hear what I've got to say."

Motioning for her to follow, Elijah grabbed the speakerphone and padded into the living room. The cord caught.

"I got it." Rachel unplugged the cord and stretched it out enough to allow it to reach the coffee table. After she plugged the phone back in, Elijah hit the speaker button.

"You still there?" Elijah asked.

"Yep. Rachel? It's Dwight." His voice was tinny. "I was just saying that we owe all this progress to you."

Elijah knew the remark caught her off guard. And while she kept a restrained look, he sensed it pleased her to hear Dwight acknowledge her contribution.

He patted the couch cushion beside him, moving the phone sideways so they'd have equal access.

She sat beside him, addressing Dwight. "I hope you'll remember how much I helped when it comes time to settle the tab. I'll expect the reward to be commensurate with results."

Elijah noticed Dwight didn't acknowledge her statement, but instead pushed on to another subject.

"Here's what we ran down today. Over the last two years, there are four other Eve's Circle girls—besides Emily Jarrett—who have gone to the church's Thailand mission and basically never returned. Three of them have been identified in the movies."

"How can they simply disappear like that?" Rachel asked. "Without anyone missing them?"

"Mason covers his tracks well. The mission staff overseas are accustomed to students coming and going, only staying a few days before moving on to another site. No one gets to know them well, and most never return. Plus the mission staff has a high turnover rate, too. Everyone at the college thinks the girls are simply somewhere else until their withdrawal paperwork comes through. Then they fall off everyone's radar."

Dwight lit another cigarette, the sound echoing through the speaker. "Equally important, though, is the fact that Mason selects his targets with care. Every one of these missing girls has a similar background. No family, no close friends. And they all spent at least two years at Shepherd's Cross, working closely with Mason Wright. It doesn't look like he works with more than two or three girls at a time."

"And he's drugged and brainwashed them just to send overseas for these movies?" Rachel's voice was strained. Elijah knew she was trying to figure out where she herself fit into Mason's perverted scheme.

"We suspect he targets at least one to keep for himself—sorry, Rachel—just to get his rocks off on campus. It was damn lucky he never got you alone."

Reaching for her hand, Elijah squeezed it briefly,

then let go. The fact that Dwight didn't know the entire story of Rachel's encounter with Mason was probably not much comfort.

"Do you know where Emily and the others are now?" Elijah asked.

"It's hard to say. Kito Mzuzi's estate is close to the mission. Under the guise of philanthropy, Kito allows the church to use his private airstrip to ferry personnel and supplies in and out. He also makes his private pilot available on certain occasions. They may still be at Kito's compound. Or he may have moved them elsewhere. The girls have all been special guests at dinner parties Kito throws just for them."

"And no one at the mission notices Kito being extra nice to these girls?"

"He makes a point of entertaining all the student ambassadors, male and female. The church sponsors a steady stream of students from all over, not just the girls from the college. The students all return to the mission singing Kito's praises. These girls were invited to his compound several times while they were overseas, which lowered their guard even further."

Rachel pushed to her feet and began pacing. "So where are these films made? At Kito's compound?"

"No. And we've heard he never uses the same location. The props and sets are probably crated up and transported with the girls." Dwight exhaled noisily. "Kito seems to have developed a pattern with making the movies. The earlier ones featured the same two girls, sometimes simultaneously. But as the flicks grew in violence and popularity, it seemed like he alternated the girls' usage, probably to allow them to heal between shootings. From what we can gather, the filming sessions have grown increasingly longer, sixteen to eighteen hours at one pop. Meaning he gets enough material from one day to produce eight or ten videos."

Rachel stopped pacing and stared at the phone. Elijah could guess what she was thinking: how could these women endure the severity of punishments some of the films demonstrated?

Elijah wished there were a way to sugarcoat this, but there wasn't. "They're probably drugged continually while filming. The pain simply doesn't register until later."

"You said that was the first two girls," she asked Dwight. "What about the others?"

"Their stuff hasn't hit the market yet. Kito's creating buzz, with rumors that the new releases will have even more violence. Consequently, the price has doubled and demand is higher than ever. Who knows what he'll do to top this."

"You have to get Emily out of there. Now." Rachel paced back toward the couch.

"I'm working on that," Dwight said. "But we're walking on eggshells here. If Kito suspects anything, he'll go underground. The girls are—"

"Don't you dare say they're expendable," she snapped. "I know you want Kito Mzuzi, but he's not worth their lives."

The sound of shuffling papers came through the speakers before Dwight spoke again, his voice weary. "I've already told you more than I should have, Rachel. Hell, even Elijah doesn't know everything, but at least he realizes there's more at stake—"

"Let me guess: national security?" Rachel sniped.

"Always." Dwight grew quiet. "Look, it's late. Elijah, we'll talk soon."

A dial tone came across the line. Elijah hit the button, disconnecting, then watched Rachel sit down on the opposite couch. He sensed her need for distance and forced himself to honor it.

He didn't want her to withdraw again—not when they'd come this far. Yet in light of what they'd just learned, a discussion of their relationship seemed out of place. It made him wonder if the time would ever be right.

Unable to resist touching her, Elijah scooted close and reached for her hand. That she didn't pull back or flinch made him feel deliriously happy. He squeezed her fingers briefly, then released them, not wanting to push his luck.

"Was Dwight telling the truth when he said even you didn't know everything?" she asked. "Or was he blowing smoke?"

"Smoke comes with the territory, Rach. I know that and still I'm the first to admit it's not always easy to accept. Your brother said the trick was keeping the faith that all the pieces of the puzzle were being gathered."

"That's where Nick and I always differed. I have trouble with the concept of blind faith."

Her simple statement struck Elijah hard. Rachel had lost more than most. "If it makes you feel any better, all this information about these girls is as new to me as it is to you."

She met his eyes, studying them for a moment before nodding. "So what now? Should we try to hit Mason's office again?"

"Dwight suggested we lay low until we're sure

Mason isn't suspicious. He's probably right. Let's call it a night and regroup tomorrow."

Rachel nodded and stood, but before she could step away, Elijah pushed up and tugged her into his arms. He felt her momentary resistance, then she relaxed and leaned into him.

Relief flooded his veins. "I'd like you to stay with me tonight," he whispered. "At least for a while. We haven't had a chance to discuss us."

"I'm not sure I'm ready to discuss that." She leaned back and looked up at him. "I can't deny that I enjoyed making love with you earlier. But I'm not ready to delve into what it does or doesn't mean. Can we leave it at that for now?"

"For now." There was little he could deny this woman. The fact she acknowledged enjoying their lovemaking was enough. "At least let me walk you back."

They made their way across campus in silence. A comfortable silence. "You're not going back out after I go in, are you?" she asked when they stopped.

"No. I promise."

"Good night, then."

She stepped away, but not before he saw the slight hesitation. As if she'd been uncertain how to part ways. A kiss? A hug? Nothing?

He caught her hand and brought it to his lips before gently releasing it. Her tremulous smile reassured him.

"Sweet dreams, Rachel," he whispered before disappearing into the darkness.

The next morning, Mason Wright's secretary left a phone message while Rachel was in class, scheduling an appointment for later that afternoon.

The call induced a sense of panic, which was quickly replaced by fury. Particularly when out of the blue she felt a small longing to see him.

She immediately recognized and rejected the thought, but still it gave credence to just how powerful Mason's techniques were. The yearning had been so subtle that if she hadn't known about Mason's duplicity, she would have acted on it.

Rachel realized that his scheduling an appointment, as promised, meant he wasn't onto her and Elijah. However, there was no way she would meet alone with Mason again. Not knowing what she knew about herself, Emily, and the others.

She'd have to shoot him.

Dialing Mason's office, she pretended to have a sore throat while talking with his secretary. "I think I'm running a fever, too."

"I'm sure Reverend Wright would want to postpone. There's a bug going around, you know. Have you been to the clinic yet?"

"I'm headed there now."

"Good," the woman said. "Why don't we tentatively reschedule for Thursday afternoon at four? You can call me that morning to confirm."

That takes care of today, Rachel thought when she hung up. She'd deal with Thursday later. While she and Elijah hadn't discussed what the next step would be, she doubted she'd be on campus much longer.

Before returning to her dorm, Rachel stopped at the student clinic, to lend credence to her excuse. Just last week she'd considered faking an illness to have a chance to talk with Sarah Wetherington.

Now . . . Well, in light of everything she'd learned, the adoption scam was the least of her worries. Which still didn't make it right.

The nurse who took her vital signs commented on her lack of fever.

Rachel grimaced and rubbed her abdomen. "Perhaps my fever broke. Does that mean my stomach problems will go away now?"

The nurse shook her head. "Sorry. Are you having vomiting or diarrhea? Or both?"

What the hell. "Both."

"We're seeing a lot of that. Step in there and slip on a gown. The doctor will be with you in a moment."

While Rachel didn't want a physical exam, she complied. A few minutes later, Sarah Wetherington breezed in, all smiles and warmth. Did the doctor greet frightened young pregnant girls this same way? Or did she come in with an air of disapproval?

"Hello, Rachel. Sorry to be meeting under these circumstance. Stomach virus?"

She nodded. "The nurse indicated something's going around."

"'Tis the season. This happens every year after the students return from overseas. Someone brings back a foreign germ and just about the time it runs its course, flu season hits." Moving to the exam table, Sarah felt the glands beneath Rachel's jaw. Then she pulled a stethoscope from her pocket. "Deep breath."

Rachel's stomach gurgled, a loud reminder that she hadn't eaten breakfast. Or lunch.

Sarah interpreted it as something different and made a sympathetic noise.

"I'll give you something to help that. Just make sure you drink plenty of fluids to avoid dehydration. My nurse will add you to the quarantine list, which simply means your meals will be delivered to your dorm. We're trying to minimize the spread of this, so I'd like you stay in your room today and tomorrow. If you're better by Thursday, you may go back to class."

The news she had a two-day pass from class cheered Rachel. "Thank you."

Sarah made notes in her file. "Aside from being sick, how are you adjusting to a new campus?"

"Fine." At least she could say that with a frown now and blame it on her illness. "The biggest challenge is juggling my time. I've got a remedial class in the evening, plus I've joined a social group. How on earth do you manage it? Someone told me you work at the hospital and volunteer at a local clinic. Is that true?"

"It's all in proper scheduling," Sarah said smugly. "Actually, I volunteer at several clinics. Some of the surrounding areas are economically depressed. It's rather sad to think that if it weren't for my free visits, some young women would never receive proper care."

Sarah paused and Rachel realized she expected a compliment. For preying on disadvantaged young girls? Bitch. "It's very sad." *For them.*

"Go ahead and get dressed. My nurse will be in with some medicine. If you're not noticeably better by Thursday or if it gets any worse, call us."

Rachel was almost back to her dorm when her cell phone rang.

"It's Elijah. Where are you?"

"I just left the clinic." She explained about

Mason's secretary calling to schedule an appointment.

"Good thinking. Look, can you slip away for a while?"

"Now? Sure." She pressed the phone closer, trying to discern his tone. "What's up?"

"I'd rather tell you in person. There's a state park about ten miles south of here, on Highway 80. Meet me there in fifteen."

Whatever it was had to be important for them to be meeting during the day. Rachel went straight to her car and was at the park in twelve minutes.

Elijah was already there, sitting in a midsized pickup truck. She hurried toward him, but instead of climbing out, he pushed the passenger side door open.

"Jump in. We'll talk while I drive."

She fastened her seat belt as he accelerated, tires squealing slightly. "It's Emily, isn't it? Something bad has happened."

He pulled on to the main highway and continued south, away from the college. "We got a transcript of Mason's phone conversation last night. He called the mission director in Thailand and told him that Emily was needed in Sri Lanka, right away. He said he was sending another student ambassador to take Emily's place."

"Can Dwight interfere?"

"It's too late. Emily's already disappeared. She was last seen boarding one of Kito Mzuzi's planes."

An invisible fist hit Rachel in the stomach. "Could she still be in Thailand?"

"We don't know. One of Kito's planes did go to Sri Lanka, but no female passengers were spotted."

"Do you think Mason is really sending another student over? Or is he just trying to draw attention away from Emily's departure?"

Elijah's voice was gruff when he spoke. "He booked Alisa Avery on a flight for day after tomorrow."

Rachel shook her head. "Dwight has to stop this. Now! Before it gets worse."

"Believe me, it gets worse." Elijah glanced at her, only taking his eyes from the road for a second. "Dwight—" He stopped and swore. "Dwight wants to substitute you for Alisa and send you overseas."

It took a moment for his words to register. "I'd go to Thailand as Alisa?" That basically meant the Company would abduct Alisa and keep her under wraps. "Does anyone over there know her?"

"According to Dwight, no. This summer, the students weren't in one place for long, and Mason keeps the Circle girls isolated." Downshifting, Elijah slowed and pulled onto a scenic overlook. Gravel crunched under the tires as he slammed the car in Park and shut off the engine. "I don't like it, Rachel. And I told Dwight it's a bad idea."

"That decision isn't yours to make."

"No. It's not. But that doesn't mean I have to support it."

Rachel stared out her window, collecting her thoughts. The overlook was perched like a crooked little tooth that jutted away from the mountain. A valley spread peacefully below them, but the serenity didn't touch her.

"You know as well as I do that it's a great opportunity," she began. "To find Emily and the others. It's also a chance to get someone inside Kito's compound. You said that has been impossible to do."

"It's also dangerous as hell. Especially for a woman. You saw those movies, Rachel. That tells you exactly how Kito and his men treat women."

"Dwight said he typically invites them to his compound a couple of times before they leave. Going in once or twice would give me a chance to scope things out."

When Elijah didn't respond, she reached for his hand, tugging it off his thigh. At first he resisted, then suddenly he relaxed, his fingers entwining with hers as he squeezed her hand.

"Damn it! I care, Rachel. I know this isn't the time or place. Hell, I know you have every reason to hate me. But I don't want you to do this."

She looked down at their hands, at her fingers dwarfed by his. She wasn't so sure she still hated him. For reasons that were probably crazy. But everything about this man, this case, had been crazy from day one.

"You're right that this isn't the time or place," she began softly. "Our sleeping together last night doesn't help matters."

"It's not about sex, Rachel. It's about caring."

"Same thing. Getting personally involved wrecks your objectivity."

"I lost my objectivity on this years ago." He turned toward her. "There's more. Remember I told you Kito dabbled in a lot of things? One of them is brokering info. He buys intelligence data and resells it to interested parties. He sold the information of where we were five years ago. The bastard profited from Nick's and the other agents' deaths. It was because of Kito that I was captured. This has been personal from the get-go. Your getting involved won't help."

Rachel closed her eyes, struggling against an angry swell of grief. She'd never met Kito Mzuzi, yet he'd hurt three people she cared for. Nick. Emily. And Elijah.

"Can we talk about this as if it's happening to someone else?" she asked.

"Why?"

"To gain perspective."

"Fine. Here's my new perspective: I don't want them to go either."

She ignored his sarcasm, knowing it was simply his way of dealing with uncomfortable emotions. She did the same thing sometimes.

"This is a perfect chance to get someone inside Kito's home. What if that person could plant listening devices? Take photographs? If it's someone they don't suspect, it will be that much easier."

Elijah's lips flattened. "Only a fool would deny that would be helpful. But what if this same person were given drugs? Held against their will? A female would be particularly vulnerable. Particularly if the female was believed to be experienced in their type of sexual deviation. Not to mention being used to taking a certain combination of drugs."

"The danger is extreme," Rachel agreed. "Which means the person needs to be experienced; able to take care of themselves. How much support will the Company provide? Will they send in backup? Open their bag of tricks?"

"They'll dump the whole damn bag at the person's feet," Elijah said. "Everything you've said is right, Rachel. Dwight said the same damn thing. But it doesn't change my mind."

"And it doesn't change mine. I have to do it."

She paused. "Remember when we first met in Richmond? You said the woman you knew would always do the right thing."

"I take it back."

"You can't."

He pinched the bridge of his nose. "Shit. We need to get back before someone notices you're gone. You're supposed to be confined to quarters."

"I'll grab some ginger ale on my way back. There's no soda on campus."

He started the car, but before putting it in gear, he wrapped a hand at her neck and tugged her close. The kiss was frantic and fast, fraught with unspoken anxiety. And desire.

"We'll discuss it more tonight," he whispered.

Rachel was grateful for her quarantine, needing time alone. To think.

Dwight's suggestion that she go to Thailand as Alisa was frightening. Elijah didn't need to spell out the dangers. She'd seen it on the video.

What if it all went bad and Rachel was subjected to that? To be drugged, then tortured. To beg for cruel acts of sex . . .

Because of what Mason had done—filmed her with her blouse open—her usual line of defense, "that will never happen to me," didn't apply.

Chase Scoggs had taught her to be brutally honest. To always look at the worst-case scenario before taking something on. To most people, worst case involved death.

Losing Nick had taken that fear from Rachel. While she wasn't suicidal or careless, she honestly didn't fear dying. But she had other fears.

Her worst case usually involved a physical disability from which she couldn't recover. To become paralyzed or blind was frightening to her. So was rape.

But today, when she assessed the worst evil that could befall her, she was shocked to realize that death was a concern again.

Because it means not seeing Elijah again.

She refused to consider why it mattered. Simply admitting it was hard enough. Her feelings were a jangled mess when it came to him.

Unfortunately, the entire case was personal. There was Senator Benjamin's horrible deception. There was Mason Wright and what he'd done to Rachel. And to Emily. Finally, there was Kito Mzuzi, a man she'd never met but whom she hated. A man responsible for Elijah's imprisonment. And her brother's death.

The bottom line was suddenly crystal clear. While nothing would bring Nick back, there were still other women in danger here. And if Kito and Mason weren't stopped, how many more would suffer? Rachel had to take this on.

Once her mind was made up, she began thinking about what she had to do before going overseas. Alisa was scheduled to leave in two days, which didn't leave much time.

That meant Rachel needed to leave the campus as soon as possible. Probably in the morning. Concocting a story that her aunt was terminally ill would allow her to leave in a hurry. She'd get Dwight to come up with some backup in case the school checked on her.

Leaving her personal life behind was pathetically easy. She did that all the time. Her townhouse in Atlanta could stay locked up for weeks. She had no plants, no pet. Her personal mail went to the office and all her bills were paid electronically.

Her business was a different story. Fortunately, all the investigators who worked for her were self-reliant. When they had problems, they automatically went to Sheila because Rachel was usually gone. Hell, Rachel went to Sheila when she had problems.

And while Sheila would be curious about this job, she'd accept Rachel's I-can't-tell-you-now excuse and cover for her.

There was only one person Rachel dreaded calling. Chase Scoggs. He'd raise five shades of holy hell when she told him what she was doing.

And she didn't give a damn what Dwight or anyone else said about the matter: she would tell Chase the whole truth. Someone had to know.

If the worst-case scenario happened . . . Chase would know what to do. He was executor of her estate.

She slipped into Elijah's apartment later that night. He was right there, waiting, and immediately tugged her into his arms and simply held her. No kiss. No words.

The tension between them was different than before. Sharper. More poignant. She had told him earlier, by phone, that she was going through with it. With or without his support.

They had argued, which she expected. But since she had just gone through those same arguments with Chase, she had been prepared. Chase could be . . . impossible to reason with sometimes.

And while Elijah hadn't liked it, she knew that once he worked through his own bottom-line analysis, he'd admit she was right. Before they hung up, he'd reluctantly agreed to let Dwight know of her decision.

Now she rested her head against his chest, drawing strength from the beat of his heart. For a moment, she regretted another decision she'd made today. But she knew she had to see it through as well.

She straightened. "What have you heard from Dwight?"

"He wants you out of here first thing. An emergency call about your aunt will be made to the office in the morning, so there will be no question about you rushing to her side. Drive to Charleston and leave the car in the airport garage. Dwight's made all the arrangements. You'll fly to Los Angeles. He'll meet you there and brief you."

"What about you?"

Elijah met her gaze. "Later tomorrow, I'll make sure one of the teachers spots the bottle of cognac in my briefcase. They have a zero-tolerance policy, so I should be sacked pronto. I'll meet you and Dwight in L.A. We'll part ways there, but I'll be in contact once you hit Thailand."

"You're going too?"

"Absolutely."

Knowing he would be nearby made it seem more tolerable. "I'm glad."

Taking her hand, Elijah tugged her into the living room, but they didn't sit down. "There's a lot to be done."

"I took care of all my personal and business arrangements this afternoon. Except one: I have to tell Senator Benjamin something since I'll be leaving the campus. I suppose flying to Richmond and shooting him is out."

He gave her a half smile. "Tell him you've reviewed every available record and concluded that Cindy wasn't pregnant. Let him know you've discreetly questioned friends and teachers, which also supports your conclusion. As far as the video—" The smile disappeared. "Assure him you've searched high and low, but found nothing. Therefore you don't believe it exists. Then simply tell him you're on another assignment."

"I've already worked an alibi with Sheila. She thinks I'm working a case for one of Chase's friends."

Elijah handed her an envelope. "Inside is a full chemical analysis of the drug Mason gave you. You didn't ingest enough of it to have any long-term affect. There's also a transcript of the audio."

Opening the envelope, Rachel scanned the transcript. The audio commands were mostly instructions for her to obey and desire Mason. She shivered in revulsion. "It feels like he stuck a finger in my brain."

"Dwight said he knows a couple of therapists who can give you reverse commands." Elijah looked at her. "I did a little checking on my own, though, and three different sources have confirmed that you probably weren't exposed to it long enough to have a lasting effect. Particularly now that you know it happened and exactly what was said."

That he'd gone through the trouble of doing that for her touched her. "Chase Scoggs suggested the same things, but I feel better knowing you checked."

"Your airline tickets and fake identification are

in the envelope, too. Dwight wants you traveling to Los Angeles under an alias."

"Makes sense." By morning she'd be gone. "So what's up tonight?"

"Here? Nothing. I spotted Kowicki sneaking around the church's office last night. I still don't know what he's after, but today he had to leave with William Hanson. Right now no one suspects anything, so I suggest we leave well enough alone."

Rachel nodded. "I'll head back, then."

"Actually, I hoped you'd stay here for a while, so we could—"

She pressed a finger to his mouth. "I think it's best if we shelve our physical relationship until this is over. It's hard enough."

His fingers closed over hers, pressing them close as he planted a kiss. "You have no idea how hard it is. Until it's over, then. Which means we agree it's temporary. Once this job is wrapped, Rachel, we're going someplace private. And we're going to put all the cards on the table once and for all. Agreed?"

"Agreed."

He moved closer. "I've got one Cuban left. And we barely made a dent in the cognac. Interested?"

For long seconds she stared at him, sorely tempted. Then she shook her head. "I'm not that strong, Elijah. Sharing a cigar means touching you. And I can't touch you without wanting to kiss you. And kissing you . . ."

For a moment she thought he'd pull her into his arms anyway. Wished for it . . . Instead, he nodded. "Can I walk you back?"

"No. Because that won't make it any easier."

And because she had one more thing to do.

THIRTEEN

One of the college administrators was at Rachel's door early the next morning, looking very concerned. "I'm afraid I have some bad news. It's your aunt. They've been trying to reach you."

The bad news was a broken hip, complicated by a stroke. No one questioned Rachel's decision to withdraw from school so she could be closer to her aunt. "We'll look forward to having you return in the spring," the woman said.

Since Rachel had packed the night before, it was easy to load her car. Unable to toss what was left of the little fern Emily had given her, she carried it down to Megan's room.

She explained about her aunt, then thrust the sad little fern forward. "I have a huge favor. Would you take care of this until I come back?"

"Huge is right." Megan looked at the plant dubiously. "What did you do to it?"

"Nothing. I swear. Can you save it?"

Megan smiled. "I'll try."

Relieved, Rachel headed back to her room. As she carried the last box to her car, Alisa Avery hurried up to her.

"I was just at the office and heard about your aunt, Rachel! I'm so sorry."

"Thank you. I spoke with her doctor and he feels confident she'll recover. Of course, she'll need a lot of therapy." Rachel bit her lip. "She's always been there for me."

"Can I help with anything?"

"I think this is it. I just threw things in boxes to hurry."

"I'll let the other Circle members know. We'll keep her, and you, in our prayers. I'm sure Reverend Wright will, too."

It was difficult not to grab Alisa and shake the serene look off her face. If she only knew . . .

"Tell everyone I'll see them when I get back," Rachel said instead. "And when Emily returns, will you tell her I'll call her when everything settles down with my aunt?"

Alisa nodded, then grinned. "Actually, I'll be seeing Emily myself in a few days. I didn't want to mention it with your bad news, but I've been awarded a student ambassadorship! I'm leaving tomorrow for Thailand. I'm so lucky."

Rachel's cheeks grew hard. *You have no idea how lucky.* "Congratulations. Have a safe journey and a wonderful time."

She drove straight to Charleston, making one stop before going to the airport, at a pack-and-ship place. To the boxes of Sheila's daughter's clothes, she added a generous check to cover dry cleaning. Dwight had assured her the Company would get everything she needed for travel before she left L.A. He also reminded her not to take any personal items.

Rachel sent her laptop to Chase Scoggs, who promised to lock it in his gun safe, a safe Fort Knox would envy, until she returned.

At the airport, she called Senator Benjamin while she waited for her flight. He wasn't happy to learn she'd already left campus.

"I've exhausted every lead," Rachel said. "While I realize you'd hoped otherwise, I found nothing that indicates Cindy was pregnant. Perhaps the diary entry was based on a false alarm."

"But . . . the video," he sputtered.

She was grateful he couldn't see her face just then. "I searched everywhere and found nothing. I don't believe the file was downloaded from campus."

The senator cleared his throat. "I could check a few more of Cindy's belongings, see if there are more clues or—"

She cut him off. "I'm sorry, but as I indicated when I accepted this job, I have several pressing commitments that I simply can't postpone any longer. I'll be unavailable for the next week or two—but if you'd like, I'll contact you when I'm back in town."

At that moment, a voice came across the airport's public address system, making conversation impossible.

"I'm afraid I have to go," Rachel said. "That was my final boarding call." It wasn't, but she used it anyway.

"As soon as you're back, then, please contact me. I just hope there is still time . . ." He let his voice waver. It sounded fake now.

Rachel hung up. There had to be a special place in hell for men like Thurston Benjamin. And Mason Wright. She still hadn't decided on a fitting retribution for either man. Nothing seemed cruel enough.

By the time she landed in California it was still mid-afternoon, thanks largely to the time change. She scanned the name placards held up by limo drivers, spotting her alias. The uniformed man holding the card was familiar.

"How they hanging, Franklin?" she whispered.

"Wouldn't you like to know?" The agent returned her wink and reluctantly extended a hand. "Give me your bag so this looks legit."

He led her to a Lincoln Town Car, but they didn't travel far. Before entering the hotel, Franklin ditched the uniform and donned a tie and jacket. He also didn't offer to carry her bag.

They went straight to Dwight's business suite on the sixth floor.

"Déjà vu?" Dwight quipped.

She shrugged, looking around. Besides Dwight and Franklin, there were two other men in the room. One was an agent. The other? He looked like a cross between a mad scientist and a junkie.

"Introduce me?" Rachel prompted.

Dwight ignored the junkie, waving the other agent forward first. "Carlton's a paramedic. A full RN. I've checked your shot records. Most of your vaccines were current since you just went to Honduras two months ago, so you're in better shape than most. There are a couple you'll need before traveling."

"I wish you'd ask *before* you violate my privacy."

"No time."

Carlton opened his med kit and tugged on a pair of latex gloves. "I need you to roll up both sleeves."

"What am I getting?" she asked.

"Tetanus and hepatitis."

After administering the shots, Carlton held up a swab and asked her to open her mouth.

"DNA?" She looked at Dwight.

"These days it's SOP for everyone," he said.

Worst-case scenario, Rachel thought. She turned back and found Carlton holding up a large syringe.

"Have you ever had a microchip implant?" he asked.

"No. And I'm not sure I want to start now."

Carlton gave her an I-don't-blame-you shrug but didn't back down. "It goes on the underside of your arm."

"What does it do?"

"Besides possibly save your life? Beats the hell out of me." Carlton swabbed her arm with alcohol. "My job is to make sure it's embedded properly."

The injection hurt like hell, but out of principle, Rachel didn't flinch.

As soon as Carlton left, Dwight introduced the second man. "This is Mikey. He's the equivalent of James Bond's Q."

"Only better." Mikey wagged his eyebrows. "And younger."

"Before we start, I need your John Hancock." Dwight shoved a sheaf of papers toward her. "I'm making you a contract employee, Rachel. It eliminates a lot of the clearance issues."

Eager to be done, she glanced through the

forms and quickly signed them. When she finished, Dwight turned to Mikey.

"Show her what you've got."

Rachel's first impression of Mikey as a mad scientist wasn't too far off. He opened a suitcase containing a variety of common cosmetics, jewelry, and other feminine paraphernalia.

"The earrings have wireless microphones," Mikey began.

"Where's the transmitter and batteries?"

"They're configured into the cell phone you'll be given." Mikey picked up one of the necklaces. "This choker, those necklaces, and the brooches are all fitted with nano-microdigital cameras. You can mix and match these so you're not wearing the same pieces every day." He picked up a silver choker with a simple yet tasteful black cabochon slide.

"You activate it like so." Mikey touched the slide. "Women fidget with their jewelry all the time, so you can easily turn it on and off. It will take three images a minute and will store roughly two hours of pictures. If you need more than two hours, wear multiple pieces and activate them one at a time. I'll show you how to change the media discs later."

Rachel shook her head in amazement. "Slick. Auto-focus?"

"Yep. It's point-and-shoot technology. Basically, whatever direction your knockers are pointed in, that's where the lens is focused."

Behind her, Franklin snickered.

Mikey looked up. "What? He told me not to call them boobs."

"And you didn't," Rachel assured him. "What about the brooches?"

"They operate the same way as the necklaces. The watch is the only piece that's different. It has two lenses. At twelve o'clock we have a fixed zoom. Use it for anything over twenty feet. At six o'clock, there's a close-up lens. Hold it like so." Mikey held it about ten inches above a sheet of paper on the table. "And it's like having a photocopier on your wrist. The electronics are all shielded, so they're virtually undetectable."

Rachel picked up one of the necklaces and found it only slightly heavier than she expected. She fastened it around her neck to get a feel for the switches, then turned to face Franklin. "Say cheese."

"I want all of these back," Dwight said. "They're useless without the proper media—and I've got that particular market cornered."

The media for the cameras looked like tiny wafers and required a minuscule pair of tweezers to handle—all of which Mikey had hidden in lipstick tubes.

"I hope you like the shade." He swiveled a lipstick up to demonstrate its functionality.

"*Ahem.* I'll have the used discs picked up daily," Dwight cut in. "But we'll discuss that later. Let's move on."

Mikey handed her a silver filigree compact. "Looks like I matched your skin tone." He showed her the powder. Then he lowered the mirror. Tiny silver dots the size of match heads lined it. "Ears. Take one out like so. There's little grippers and adhesive. Tug this thread, it exposes the glue. Otherwise, the grippers should hold. The ones on the bottom have no teeth—for stuff like glass or metal. Refills are here."

"Is that it?" she asked Mikey as he closed the case. "No weapons?"

Mikey hooked a thumb toward Dwight and shrugged. "I wanted to send along poison darts. He said you'd use them out of spite. Just kidding. Actually, he said you were pretty capable of taking care of yourself."

"I'd feel better with poison darts."

Mikey snapped his fingers. "I almost forgot about the microchip in your arm. You'll be tracked twenty-four/seven. If you need immediate extraction, crack this bubble with your fingernail." He helped her locate it. "You really have to press hard to bust it. If it burns like hell, that means help is on the way."

When Mikey left, Franklin followed, leaving just Dwight and Rachel in the suite.

"I take it the bugs are for Kito's house."

Dwight nodded. "But don't take any unnecessary chances planting them."

"Anything in particular you want pictures of?"

"Interiors—doors, windows—the usual stuff. Any papers or correspondence on Kito's desk would be helpful, but again, don't take risks."

"Why are you being so thoughtful all of a sudden?"

He snorted. "Just tired, I guess. I'm sure it will pass." Crossing to the bar, he poured a drink. "Want anything?"

"No. Thanks." She rubbed the muscle of her arm where she'd been given a shot. "What else have we got to cover?"

"Lots. I've got the rundown on the mission, Kito's compound, et cetera, but I suggest we cover that in the morning when Elijah gets in. And I've calls to make. Let's plan on meeting early."

The news that she would see Elijah tomorrow made her feel better. "Where am I staying?"

Dwight handed her a key card. "Two doors down. Room 611. There's clothes, luggage, new IDs, everything. We'll add Mikey's toys in the morning."

"How are you going to substitute me for Alisa?"

"She changes planes in Atlanta. We'll take her out there and have a look-alike fly to Los Angeles. Then we'll substitute you tomorrow afternoon."

"How long will you hold her?"

"As long as it takes. She'll be treated well, Rachel. Trust me. And it's a hell of a lot better than what Mason Wright had planned for her."

"She'll need counseling."

"I imagine a lot of people will."

Rachel stood and headed for the door. Dwight followed her.

"What you're doing is above and beyond," he began. "Your brother would be proud."

"Nick would kick both our asses and you know it," she scoffed. "Elijah's too."

"Speaking of him . . . Has it been difficult?"

"Yes. But then, you knew it would be, didn't you? However, in light of everything that's happened, we've agreed to table our differences."

Dwight looked at her, his expression unreadable. "There's a box of photographs in your room. You can't take any of them with you overseas. But when you're ready, you can have the front desk ship them to Chase. I already spoke with him, so he knows to expect them."

"You called Chase?"

"If it makes you feel any better, the crazy bastard threatened to kill me. Even though he knows damn good and well the call was recorded."

"He's a good friend."

"Maybe after this you'll put in a good word for me. The son of a bitch is too young to be retired. I could use a man like him. If he'd dry out."

Rachel opened her mouth to deny the accusation. She couldn't. The fact that she understood *why* Chase drank didn't make it right.

Still, the instinct to defend her friend was strong. "He's free to drown his pain in whatever way he chooses. I know what it's like to suffer the type of loss Chase did."

Dwight held her gaze. "Understanding and enabling are two different things. Killing himself with alcohol won't bring his son back to life."

Rachel ordered dinner from room service, but could barely eat.

The box of photographs Dwight had left in her room was a veritable treasure chest and included photographs that spanned Nick's entire six-year career with the CIA.

None of the photographs had backgrounds that were readily identifiable, which she didn't mind. Most were black and white, taken from surveillance cameras, but some were color. And all had date stamps. After going through the box once, she arranged the photographs in chronological order.

Over the years, her brother's look changed from photo to photo. Long hair, short hair, even wigs. The hair color varied with the style. In some shots Nick was clean shaven, in others he sported beards, mustaches, goatees, even a soul patch. The disguises were so good in some she had to look twice.

I miss you, Nick.

Before going to bed, she called Chase. "You already heard I'm sending you another box. But this one has my heart in it."

"I'll keep it safe. Until you get your scrawny little ass back here, that is. Be careful, kid," he hiccupped. "If you need anything, call."

She hung up and stared at the phone. As much as she hated admitting Dwight was right, she needed to deal with Chase's drinking—and her own attitude about it—when she got back.

She fell into a deep sleep, but was awakened when the phone rang. Disoriented, she grabbed it and dropped it.

"This better be damn good, Dwight."

"It's Elijah."

Immediately she was alert, her heart pounding painfully. She closed her eyes against the ache in her chest. Why the hell hadn't she stayed that last night with him in West Virginia?

"I'm sorry," she whispered. "Where are you?"

"I just got in."

She sat straight up, glanced at the time. One o'clock. "You're at the airport?"

"I'm right next door."

Her eyes flew to the locked door that separated her room from the adjoining one. She'd assumed Franklin or another agent was staying there.

Without a word, she hung up and flew to the door, then twisted the lock. His side was already open, soft light spilling forth.

Then Elijah filled the doorway. He reached for her, tugging her across the portal into his room and into his arms as he captured her mouth in a forceful kiss.

One hand came up, cradling her head, his fingers sliding through her hair, drawing her closer as his tongue swept deeper. His fingers slid down the silk of her short nightgown to cradle her buttocks.

His kiss was like fire and she melted against him, defenseless.

"It's not fair," she whispered.

He pulled back. "What?"

"You're fully dressed. I'm not."

Grinning, he pressed a kiss to her temple. "There's two ways to fix that." He tugged the shirt over his head and tossed it aside. "Better?"

"Hmm. Not quite." She unsnapped his jeans before boldly unzipping them. Spreading them wide, she carefully pushed them down until his penis sprang free.

The engorged shaft poked straight out, swaying slightly. Long, hard, and ready. The sight of him fully erect stole her breath, inviting her to touch. And in her hand, he grew even harder. Her fingers slid over the swollen head, then shifted lower to grip him fully.

Her eyes drifted up, taking in the muscles of his abdomen, the dark hair on his chest. She stroked again, reveling in his size and strength. She knew exactly what she wanted to do to him tonight.

"This is much better," she agreed.

He bent down, his mouth brushing her ear. "But now we have a new problem. You're wearing more than I am."

"There's only one way to settle this." With a sigh,

she stepped back and slid the nightie over her head, letting it drop to the floor as he kicked away from his pants.

Elijah drew a sharp breath, letting his eyes rove freely over her body, aware that she did the same.

"You are perfect." He closed the distance between them.

He wasn't prepared for the jolt that swept through him as her rock-hard nipples teased his chest. She stood on tiptoe, rubbing her body against his as she eagerly accepted his kiss.

His hands tightened at her waist. He wanted her on the bed, beneath him, and carrying her was the fastest way to accomplish that.

But when he shifted to pick her up, she put her hands on his arms, pushing slightly away. "Wait. Watch."

She pressed kisses across his chest, then caught his nipple with her mouth, laving it with her tongue before biting gently. He hissed.

Her hand was on his erection again, her touch too light. He closed his fingers over hers, pumping his flesh.

"Harder?" she asked. She licked his nipple again, then blew air across it.

The sensation shot straight to his groin. "Harder. You know what I like."

Nodding, Rachel moved lower, pressing kisses down his ribs. She kissed the tender skin below his navel as she lowered to her knees.

Elijah groaned. His hands closed over her breasts, caressing, teasing her nipples as he watched. Waited.

She had his erection caged in her hands as she stroked him. Fluid seeped from the tip of his penis.

She moved closer to run her tongue across it, then she withdrew, pumping him even harder with her hands.

Elijah bucked.

"Spread your legs," she whispered.

He complied, and felt her mouth run along the inside of his thigh and down. She nibbled softly at the side of his knee, then switched to the other leg and slowly worked her way up.

He waited, wanting desperately to feel her mouth on his flesh again, but she held back, stroking him only with her hands. Unable to hold back, he pumped forward, groaning as if in pain.

"Shh," she soothed. "I know what you need."

With that, she lowered her mouth to the pulsing head of his penis, licking it yet again. A shudder rocked him as her mouth dipped lower, her tongue tracing the veins to the base.

He felt her hand cup his testicles, squeezing gently as her mouth closed fully over his cock. He jerked, struggling for control.

Rachel drew back, flicking her tongue on the underside of his penis. She crooned softly, then took the swollen head into her mouth again. Her teeth grazed carefully along the ridge, weakening him. God, what this woman did to him!

He looked down, watching her mouth work very deliberately down his cock. She glanced up, boldly returning his stare as she tightened her mouth over the head and sucked.

Elijah swore, unable to tear his gaze away. Emboldened, Rachel took him deeper, then drew back, repeating the motion over and over until his shaft disappeared into her hungry mouth.

"Rachel! I can't take much more of this," he hissed.

She pulled back, peering up, her hand continuing the motion. "Tell me when to stop, then."

Lowering her mouth, she resumed the strokes with her lips, but this time the pace was faster. Then she started sucking again. Harder.

His hand speared through her hair, holding her in place. Urging her on. Fire burst inside his mind as sensation wound tighter. The feeling built, his limbs growing more taut.

Elijah convulsed. "Stop!"

She did, and immediately, he swept her into his arms and carried her to the bed. "You drive me crazy, Rachel."

"Crazy good?"

"Always." He pressed a kiss to her mouth, gently nibbling at her bottom lip before delving deeply into her mouth and capturing her tongue.

Moving lower, he trailed his mouth to her breast and took her nipple between his teeth, tugging lightly. She inhaled sharply, encouraging him. As he sucked and teased, his hand moved down to the damp tangle of curls between her thighs.

Gently he parted her, his thumb flicking over her swollen clit. She was wet and hot.

"Elijah, please!" She writhed beneath his hand. "I want you inside me."

He wished he had more willpower, but her words undid him. Moving over her, he lowered his body to hers. She raised her knees, taking him home. He pressed forward, not stopping until he was all the way in. Her orgasm hit fast and furious, and with a shout he pumped furiously, taking them both over the edge.

* * *

They fell asleep in each other's arms, waking at dawn to make love once again. Rachel was sore. But sated.

"I need to go back to my room," she said. "I've got to meet Dwight in an hour. You'll be there too?"

He nodded. "Yeah. But there's one thing we need to talk about before seeing Dwight, Rachel. Cindy Benjamin's video was blank."

She didn't bother denying that she'd substituted another blank disc. Chase Scoggs had the original.

"I couldn't leave that one there either. I guess because Cindy's not here to defend herself. And it's not like the other tapes that Mason has or is making, where he's manipulating these girls."

"It was still risky."

"Perhaps. But I doubt Mason goes back to watch that one. We both know it's rather tame for his tastes. It exists merely for blackmail."

"Which, unfortunately for Cindy, ties in to this case." Elijah cupped her chin, tilting her head. "She's not the only victim here. I feel bad for all the women who have been affected by this, but destroying the evidence of what was done doesn't make it go away. If anything, it does the opposite and lets the perpetrator get away."

She closed her eyes, wishing it weren't so. Then she nodded. "You're right. When we're back from Thailand, I'll hand the disc over to Dwight."

When Rachel arrived at Dwight's suite, Elijah was already there.

"I took the liberty of ordering your breakfast,"

Dwight said. "Room service will be up any minute. Help yourself to coffee."

She poured a cup, then sat in a chair opposite the two men.

"We were just going over Elijah's itinerary," Dwight explained.

Elijah nodded. "I'm going in by private means, so I won't arrive until the day after you."

"And he'll be working behind the scenes, Rachel, so you probably won't see him."

Rachel frowned. "I thought you said you had contacts at the mission."

"I do. Howie Stevens. He'll relay messages and film, and track the microchip in your arm."

This surprised her. Howie had been the one who'd told her the rumors about Elijah. In retrospect, she realized Howie had simply been repeating what he'd heard. Garbage in, garbage out.

She exchanged a brief glance with Elijah. "Howie's in Thailand? I wondered where you shipped him off to."

"Yes, and he'll be your primary contact," Dwight said. "He'll relay any messages you have for me and vice versa."

A knock sounded at the door. Franklin wheeled in a table laden with covered trays. He winked at Rachel, then left. The scowl Elijah directed at the other man's back left her feeling . . . good.

"Dig in. They're all the same. Ham-and-cheese omelets." Dwight snapped his napkin open. "I brought Elijah up to speed on the equipment you're taking. I want to emphasize that all we want you to do, Rachel, is take whatever pictures you can, plant bugs if you can, and get out. My men will work the rest."

"But what about looking for Emily and the others?"

"We'll handle that," Dwight said. "I know you're concerned, but if you saw her, she'd recognize you. Which could blow your cover. You have to trust that there are other plans in place. Do your part, and it will all work fine."

Trust? She took a bite of toast, then chewed thoughtfully. "How will I get out of the country without Kito Mzuzi's assistance? And without raising questions?"

"The day before you're supposed to leave, Howie will get you away from the mission, to a safe transport out of the country. We're already laying groundwork for simultaneous raids here and there. If it's not coordinated perfectly . . ."

"I don't envy you that part," Rachel admitted. Working with foreign governments on joint projects was a nightmare.

After breakfast, they spent several hours reviewing surveillance data. Dwight had maps and photographs of the mission complex and its key personnel. Since Alisa had just been there this past summer, Rachel needed to feign some familiarity.

"These are all people Alisa would have met when she was there. The good news is, she wasn't there long and most of her time was spent sightseeing with Mason. Tom Robbins is the mission director, and Howie's confirmed that Robbins is expecting you," Dwight said. "By the way, Kito was gone this summer, so Alisa never met him."

Rachel studied the photographs of Kito Mzuzi.

He was a striking man and looked younger than thirty-nine. His mother had been Thai, while his father had been Dutch, which gave him an exotic look that some might find attractive. She didn't.

He wore his ebony, shoulder-length hair slicked back in a ponytail and favored aviator-style sunglasses that hid the scar at his temple. When she saw a shot of him without sunglasses, she noted the cruel light in his eyes.

"He was educated in London and is fluent in five languages, including English," Dwight told her.

"Why does he have a cane in some shots?" She pointed to the silver-handled walking cane. "But not others?"

"It's a prop, but there's a wicked little sword inside," Dwight continued. "He carries it more for effect than self-defense. Kito's arrogant and vain. He also considers himself a ladies' man. He'll try to be a gentleman, but he'll pour on the charm."

"At least in the beginning," Elijah warned. "We all know that's an act."

"We're hoping you'll have multiple chances to survey the compound. Kito's the type who would respond favorably to a request for a tour. He also has a collection of artwork that he'll tell you are originals. They're forgeries, but playing along will lower his guard."

Dwight checked his watch. "That's it for now. We need to get ready to go." He turned to Elijah. "I'll ride in the limo with Rachel, do a last minute recap. Franklin will pick you up in fifteen. Good luck to both of you."

She looked at Elijah, uncertain of what to say.

Particularly with Dwight present. She had hoped they'd have a moment alone at the airport.

She stuck out her hand. "I'll see you in Thailand. Good-bye."

FOURTEEN

Rachel breathed an enormous sigh when the rickety cargo plane finally touched down on Kito Mzuzi's private airstrip. It was late afternoon, local time, and in spite of the sleep Rachel had on the plane, her body clock screamed it was the middle of the night. The time difference left her feeling out of sync.

Though the jet's cargo hold was filled with supplies, she had been the only passenger on the final leg of the journey.

"You get off now," the Thai copilot said, pointing to the door.

Two flatbed trucks and a Jeep pulled up as she exited the plane. She recognized the man who climbed out of the Jeep and strode toward her. Tom Robbins was the mission director.

"Alisa, right? Welcome back." Tom took her bag. "We met briefly this summer, I believe, though to be honest, I'm terrible with names and faces. I get my own grandkids mixed up."

Rachel smiled. "It's nice to see you again, Mr. Robbins. How's your wife?"

"Great. She's waiting back at the mission for us." Tom lifted her suitcase into the back of the open Jeep. "I need to speak with the pilot about off-loading our supplies. I won't be long."

"Take your time. It feels good to stretch."

Another car approached, dust spinning up as it sped toward them. Tom nodded. "That looks like Kito Mzuzi's men. We frequently get deliveries at the same time."

As Tom moved away, the other car, a massive black Mercedes that looked and sounded more like a small tank, pulled up behind the Jeep.

The driver nodded curtly in Rachel's direction before loping off toward the plane. She started to turn away just as the passenger door of the Mercedes opened and a second man stepped out.

Kito Mzuzi. Grasping his cane in one hand, he strode directly toward her.

Pasting on a smile was difficult. This man was responsible for her brother's death. She straightened, smoothing her hair and adjusting her necklace. *On.*

"You must be one of the visiting students." He extended his hand. "I'm Kito Mzuzi. Welcome to our humble land."

"Thank you." She shook his hand, resisting the urge to yank hers back when he held it for a few seconds. "I'm Alisa Avery. I was here this summer, but I don't believe we met."

"Then I'm very glad you returned. Did you have a pleasant trip?" He waved toward the plane. "Or as pleasant as one can get on that monstrosity."

She nodded. "After the third plane change, they all looked and felt alike."

To Rachel's relief, Tom joined them. The two men greeted each other warmly. Of course, Tom and the others here at the mission viewed Kito as a generous benefactor. If they only knew what Kito *really* did.

"I'm sure Alisa is exhausted," Tom said. "I'll take her back to the mission. My men will get the supplies."

Kito pushed his sunglasses back against his nose. "I'm having a small dinner party tomorrow night to welcome you and the other students, Alisa. I hope to see you then."

"I'll look forward to it."

Twirling his cane, Kito strolled back to his vehicle.

Tom helped Rachel into the Jeep, then took off. Her first glimpse of Kito's compound had been through the dirty window of the airplane. In the late-afternoon sun, it had looked like a prison, the building and grounds austere, the countryside desolate.

As they approached the mission, Tom offered to give Rachel a refresher tour, pointing out a few landmarks. The three largest buildings—the church, the hospital, and the media center—looked garishly out of place, the modern structures sitting mere yards from thatch-roofed shacks.

"Did you visit the open-air markets while you were here?"

She nodded. "It was pretty crowded that day, though."

"That part hasn't changed." He pointed to another building. "You remember the dining hall.

Breakfast is still served at seven. I think dinner is an hour earlier than when you were here this summer."

"Six?" Rachel guessed.

Tom pulled up to one of the thatched-roof shacks. "Last time, your group stayed at the little boarding house next to the church. But we had a small group of students from India arrive yesterday. Since they're all males, my wife and I felt it would be more appropriate to put you up here. The McKays are on vacation right now. Martha and I live right next door, if you need anything."

Tom carried her suitcase inside and showed her around the two-room cabin. While primitive, it was cleaner and cooler than Rachel had expected.

"The well water is safe for cleaning, but it has to be treated for drinking." He showed her where the McKays kept their water purification tablets. "I'll let you get settled. I'll tell Martha you'll meet us at the dining hall for dinner."

"That sounds perfect."

Alone at last, Rachel unpacked her bag. As they had all day, her thoughts wandered back to Elijah. Where was he? And when would she hear from him?

She hadn't seen or heard from him once she'd left the hotel with Dwight. Already she'd regretted that their good-bye hadn't been more private. More personal.

She struggled, trying to avoid questions about their relationship. Did she and Elijah have a future? Or were they simply dealing with an isolated circumstance that was complicated by their past? Meaning once this job was over . . . so were they.

After drawing water from the well behind the

house, she bathed using an old-fashioned pitcher and basin. She changed into khaki pants and a shirt, then headed to the dining hall shortly before six.

Tom's tour, coupled with the photographs and maps she'd seen, helped minimize her sense of disorientation. When she reached the hall, Martha Robbins greeted her enthusiastically.

"You were the one who giggled a lot."

Rachel forced an extra-large smile. "I feel too tired to giggle tonight."

"Jet lag. Give it a day or two, and you'll be right back to your usual perky self."

After they ate, Martha introduced her to everyone. There were twenty-two full-time missionaries at the church's complex. Over half of them worked at the media center.

While a few of them claimed to have met her that summer, no one questioned her act as Alisa. And outside of Martha's giggle remark, no one had any remarkable memories.

Rachel shifted her eyes toward the one familiar face at the table. Howie Stevens. Or *Harold Popper*, as he was known here.

Martha explained that Howie was their newest staff member. "Tom says Harold's a whiz at computers."

"Sound digitizing," Howie corrected. "It's nice to meet you, Alisa."

When Martha stepped away to talk with someone else, Howie shifted closer. "We need to talk. Leave your back door unlatched tonight. I'll come by after eleven."

After dinner, the missionaries had a group prayer meeting, but Martha took pity on her. "You look exhausted. Why don't you run on and get some sleep."

Since she had over four hours until Howie came, sleep was exactly what Rachel did. She had worried she wouldn't hear him come in, yet at the soft squeak of the back screen door, she bolted upright on the sofa, wide-awake.

"Rachel?" Howie whispered.

"I'm in the living room."

The room, while dark, wasn't pitch black. Howie moved into the chair beside the sofa. "Trying to catch up on sleep?"

"Trying."

"The time change is a bitch here. It took me a week to adjust."

"Yeah, well, I have to compress that." Rachel hoped to be out of there in a week. "What's up? Have you heard from Dwight or Elijah?"

"Elijah gets in tomorrow, but he'll be at a base camp south of here. Dwight knows you arrived but wants to know if you had any problems with your cover."

"None. Tell him I met Kito at the airstrip. He's having a little soirée tomorrow night."

"I heard. He came by earlier and invited the other students as well, which doesn't raise any eyebrows here." Howie reached in his shirt pocket and withdrew a small square of plastic, barely one inch wide and no thicker than a stick of gum. "Dwight also said to give you this. It will copy the contents of Kito's PDA."

She frowned. "And how in the hell am I supposed to get his PDA?"

"You don't. But if you get access to his office, you just pop this baby on the hot-sync device beside his computer. It will download the contents automatically."

She grabbed the square. Damn Dwight! How typical of him to assure her she only had to do certain things, only to pull a fast one at the last minute. "Why didn't he give this to me earlier?"

Howie shrugged. "Maybe he didn't want Elijah to know?"

Considering Elijah hadn't been there when Rachel and Dwight had met with Mikey, she doubted that was the case. She started to give Howie a scathing message to relay back, but changed her mind. She'd wait and chew Dwight out in person.

"Dwight said I should give you the media discs from the cameras. How do we handle that?"

"I'll come by here tomorrow night, same time, and pick them up. I'm sure Dwight will be eager to get a briefing on the party, too." Howie stood. "I'll let you get back to sleep."

"Wait, Howie." Rachel cleared her throat. "I understand I put you in an awkward position. Before . . . When I asked about my brother. If I caused you trouble, I apologize."

He smiled. "Thanks. But it was my own damn fault. I was pretty green to have fallen for it, but I learned a lot. And Dwight's already assured me this assignment will put me back on the fast track with the Company, so all's well that ends well."

Rachel ate breakfast in the dining hall. The rations—oatmeal, pancakes, and stewed fruit—were as bland as dinner the night before. But she perked up to see an industrial-sized urn of coffee.

She looked for Howie Stevens, but didn't see

him. As soon as she finished, Martha Robbins latched onto her arm.

"Tom suggested you accompany me today, to get a feel for what a typical mission day is like."

"Sounds good." Rachel was eager to see and learn more about the area and its inhabitants. Particularly Kito Mzuzi.

"Most days, I start with paperwork," Martha said as she led the way to the mission offices that were housed in the media center. "Inevitably I get called away, so whatever I get done in the morning is usually it for the day. As you can see, I'm a bit behind."

A bit? Rachel looked at the crowded office. Two desks were crammed inside, the surfaces stacked high. It looked as if a paper blizzard had struck and no one had shoveled out. Obviously the clutter-free, caffeine-free anomaly was limited to West Virginia.

"A mission director's wife is expected to be a jack-of-all-trades. Bookkeeper, janitor, purchasing agent, secretary. Sometimes I even cook." Martha waved a hand at the paper. "Did I mention file clerk? Probably not. I've learned to tackle the deadline stuff first; supply orders and end-of-the-month accounting. Everything else waits."

"What can I do to help?"

"Can you type?"

"Reasonably."

"I'll let you enter purchase orders." Martha pointed to the larger desk. "You can use Tom's desk."

Rachel surveyed the desktop. The computer was a stand-alone PC. No network, no password, and, of course, no modem. One thing caught her eye: a PDA resting in a cradle beside the computer.

She pointed to it. "Did your husband forget his PDA?"

Martha laughed. "Oh, he forgot it, all right. Right after Kito gave it to him. I'm not making fun; it was a lovely gesture. Kito gave us both one for Christmas last year, but they're not really practical here. I gave mine away, but Tom worries he'll offend Kito, so he kept his."

"Mr. Mzuzi seems quite generous." Rachel choked on the words.

"He's been a godsend. With his connections, and money, he cuts through red tape like this." Martha snapped her fingers. "Few people realize how instrumental he was in getting the media center built."

And even fewer people realize how the bastard profits from it, Rachel thought. "Your husband mentioned a welcoming party this evening."

"Kito makes a point of entertaining the student ambassadors, which we heartily endorse. Our mission has the highest ratio of students who return after graduation, thanks in large part to the favorable impression he makes. Some of the other locations are begging for student assistants." Martha handed her a sheaf of papers. "Now, if I don't hush, we'll never get any work done."

They spent the morning in the office. At lunchtime, Rachel met the four other student ambassadors, who were all from New Delhi. They agreed on a meeting time for going to Kito's.

She spent the afternoon inventorying hospital supplies with Martha. When she finally returned to her quarters, it was time to get ready for Kito's party.

She prepared carefully, wearing a short-sleeve navy sheath that she dressed up with a light wrap. She had purposely selected a dress with a pocket to keep a few of the electronic bugs easily accessible.

Glancing in the mirror, she eyed her jewelry critically. She was wearing a choker, a brooch, and the watch. Still, she would have felt better with a gun. Or at least one of Mikey's poison darts. Tucking a few items in a small purse, she took off to meet the others.

They drove Tom's Jeep to Kito's compound, Rachel squeezed in the backseat between two others. While there was no guard at the gate, she spotted a surveillance camera and tried to get a picture. Crowded between the others made it difficult to swing her *knockers* where she wanted.

Kito's home was deceptive in size, the inside much more luxurious than the exterior.

They had barely stepped inside when Kito joined them. "Welcome. Please, make yourselves at home." He shook hands with Rachel first, then greeted the other four.

Turning back to Rachel, he offered to take her wrap. "Allow me." He moved behind her and lifted it from her shoulders. She forced herself not to shudder.

"We can visit in here." Kito offered his arm to Rachel. "Before we eat."

Having no choice, she placed her hand lightly at the crook of his elbow. "You have a lovely home." She nodded toward one of the vases overflowing with roses. "Where do you find fresh flowers over here?"

"I grow them. They are a hobby of sorts. I adore beauty." He let his eyes slide over her quickly.

They were inside a formal sitting room, where four other men stood, drinks in hand. She recognized one as Kito's driver. She shook hands as they were introduced.

Being the only female made her self-conscious, particularly the way Kito's men checked her out.

Hot tea was served. Since it was poured from one pot, Rachel sipped it and found it quite good.

Avoiding the sofa, she took a seat in a cushioned chair and discreetly attached one of the listening devices to the underside of the arm. Kito sat directly across from her, blatantly staring more than once. He asked each of the students about their education and their mission work.

"And you, Alisa. Where do you attend school?"

As if you don't know. "Shepherd's Cross, West Virginia. It's a small campus, but beautiful."

When a uniformed housekeeper appeared at the door, Kito stood. "Dinner, my friends."

Once again, he offered his arm to Rachel, escorting her a short way down the hall to a formal dining room.

He pulled a chair out for her, then sat next to her at the head of the table. Conversation lulled during the multicourse meal, but picked up when dessert was served.

While the others got into a spirited but friendly debate about soccer teams, Kito leaned closer. "The crème brûlée is not to your liking? You barely touched it."

"It was wonderful. But I'm full."

"Perhaps you'd like to stretch your legs while they argue over the World Cup?"

She smiled. "That would be nice. I'd like to see more of your house—if that's not rude to ask."

Kito smiled like a wolf that had just been hired to nanny a lamb. "I would love to show it to you."

In the hall, Kito's housekeeper hovered, uncertain. "Will you excuse me for a moment?"

"Of course. Is there a powder room I can use?"

"Second door down, to the left."

Inside, she tried to eavesdrop, but heard nothing. When she stepped back into the hall, Kito hurried to her side. Once again, she had to take his arm.

"Is this a family home?" she asked.

"No. I acquired it a few years ago. The previous owners had let it run down." He led her into another sitting room, this one much larger and even more formal. "This entire wing is brand new."

"You do a lot of entertaining?"

"When I'm in. My work requires that I travel, so while this one is my favorite, I end up dividing my time between three homes."

"How interesting." Rachel pointed to the painting above the fireplace. Like everything in the house, it was gaudy and ostentatious. "Your travel must allow you to collect all the wonderful works you have displayed."

"Another hobby. Are you familiar with any of the old masters?"

She shook her head. "Not in the depth I'd like to be. But I love art. The way it makes you feel is indescribable."

Kito shifted closer. "We have much in common. That's the same way I feel. Come, I have more to show you."

He squeezed her fingers briefly before placing them back on his arm. Rachel gasped softly—in revulsion. He grinned, obviously thinking she was taken in by his savoir faire.

"This is my private office." He opened a set of

double doors and led her into a dark room. She held her breath until he stepped away to snap on a light.

She feigned amazement at the framed works crowding the walls. "It's like an art gallery in here. May I?"

At his nod, she moved around the room, getting photographs from every angle.

"I believe that's my favorite." She pointed to the one behind his desk. It was an oil painting of roses. The pinks, yellows, and reds looked out of place in the office.

She moved closer, leaning across the credenza and pretending to read the signature as she planted another electronic device. The computer was on, the screen off. Beside it was the hot-sync cradle for his PDA, identical to the one in Tom Robbins' office. "Artists write like doctors . . . It's impossible to read."

Kito moved up beside her and read the name. "It's my favorite painting too. And since you seem to share my passion for flowers, let me show you something else." He led her over to the French doors. "Close your eyes."

Rachel raised her hand over her eyes and heard Kito punch in four digits on the keypad lock. Through slit eyes, she caught the bottom, bottom, top, middle motion of his hand, hoped the cameras caught the digits.

"Keep them closed." Kito swung the door open, then put a hand to her waist.

Rachel jerked.

"Shh." Kito pressed close to her ear. "I didn't mean to startle you. I just wanted to guide you. Step down, then forward. Now open your eyes."

Had she not already known the back of the house was surrounded by gardens, the air would have been a giveaway. The sweet, spicy scent was nearly overpowering.

Though it was dark, small lights shone along stone pathways. From what she could see of its size, the garden had to contain every known species of rose.

"This is beyond belief," she said. "I can't imagine what it must look like in broad daylight."

"Again—you steal my thoughts." Kito reached toward a pure white bud, snapping the stem harshly. Then he held the flower up and traced the delicate petals down the side of her face before presenting it to her with a dramatic flourish. "I will never look at this garden in moonlight without thinking of how it pales in comparison to your beauty."

Rachel bowed her head, staring at the rose, praying the moment would pass. To her horror, Kito's hand cupped her chin. He had moved closer, and for a panicked moment she was afraid he would kiss her. Bile burned the back of her throat.

"You are shy. And no doubt, such strong words from a total stranger frighten you," he whispered. "Forgive me, Alisa, but I have never felt such an immediate attraction to anyone. Particularly to someone who seems to share the things I love."

To her relief, he backed away. "You must see the gardens by day. You will come for lunch tomorrow?"

She paused. "I have to be back at the mission by two. I have another commitment in the afternoon."

He pulled his PDA from his pocket and made a quick note.

"In that case, I'll send one of my men to collect you at eleven." He turned back toward the door and led her inside. "I'm greedy and want to spend as much time as I can with you."

They found the others back in the sitting room. As soon as they entered, Kito thanked them for coming, signaling an end to the evening.

Relieved, Rachel followed the others to the door. Kito's housekeeper stood at the door with her wrap draped over one arm, a large bouquet in the other.

As the others filed outside, Kito hung back. Taking the wrap, he swirled it around Rachel's shoulders, his fingers lingering. Then he pressed the roses into her grasp and squeezed her fingers before releasing them.

"To remember our evening," he whispered. "You will haunt my dreams, Alisa. Good night."

Good riddance. "Good-bye."

The other students talked excitedly on the ride back to the mission and Rachel realized the guys hadn't even noticed she was gone. Kito's driver had given them tickets for an upcoming soccer match when they returned to India.

It was barely ten o'clock when she returned to her cabin. She started to dump the roses in the garbage, but worried someone might notice. And she needed to keep up the act.

She left them on the back porch, out of sight. Before changing clothes, she bathed again, wanting to wash away Kito's presence, which seemed to cling like an oily soot.

His flirtatious act had repulsed her. Was that how he acted with Emily and the others? And had they bought it? Been flattered that a powerful, wealthy man was showing them attention?

After changing clothes, she sat in the dark, waiting on Howie. She wondered if the bugging devices she'd planted were working. While their conversation tonight was worthless, hopefully Kito's other conversations would yield some valuable information.

In spite of her so-called tour, she'd seen very little of Kito's house, perhaps only a third of the bottom floor. Maybe tomorrow she could finagle another tour, particularly of the outlying buildings. If Kito was holding Emily and the others, she doubted they were at the main house.

And in spite of Dwight's insistence that she take no chances, she was determined to search for Emily.

The squeak of the back door opening alerted her to Howie's arrival. She stood, stepping into the kitchen.

She knew immediately it wasn't Howie . . .

"Elijah!" Rachel flung herself into his arms, and was lifted up for a kiss. Then she stepped back. "What are you doing here?"

"I had to see you. I told Howie I'd check in with you and bring back the film." He ran a hand through his hair and moved closer. "Your earrings worked perfectly. We could hear everything. Kito coming on to you like that . . . I wanted to kill him."

She shivered, glad she hadn't known earlier that he would be listening too. "It was no treat on my end. The man is beyond grotesque—"

"You need to let me finish, Rach," he interrupted. "It made me realize how you must have felt in Venice. I was listening tonight knowing damn good and well it was a setup—and still it felt like my heart had been torn out of my chest. I know it's about six years too late, but I'm sorry I did that to you. I realize now that in a committed relationship, there are simply things you don't do, period. Even if it's an act."

A single tear ran down Rachel's cheek. She turned away and wiped her cheek, grateful for the dark. If anyone would have asked her if an apology mattered anymore, she would have denied it. So why the tears now?

Because it did matter. It had always mattered. Because she loved him.

Picking her up, Elijah cradled her against his chest and rocked her in his arms. How long they stood there, she didn't know.

But when she raised her head, he met her lips and as always, what was between them exploded.

"I want you," he growled.

She looped her arms around his neck. "Help yourself."

In seconds they were in the bedroom and naked. Elijah eased her back onto the bed, then drew back. Grasping her ankles, he moved her legs.

He dipped low, pressing a kiss to her knee. Then he spread her legs, moving closer as he ran his mouth up the inside of her thigh. His hand cupped her.

"You're wet," he whispered. He slid one finger into the blond curls, gently probing, then stroked in and out, a delicious prelude of what was to follow.

She moved against his hand, moisture easing his way.

"That's it, sweetheart," Elijah encouraged her.

Rachel felt an increased pressure as he stuck two fingers inside before brushing his thumb over her clitoris. Her body stretched to accept him.

His thumb continued stroking back and forth. A different kind of pressure built now, making Rachel aware that she was already on the verge of climaxing.

"Don't fight it." His hands continued the torment.

Rachel struggled, but lost, as a powerful orgasm melted over her. "I wanted to wait for you."

Elijah pressed a kiss to the inside of her thigh, causing her to jump. "And I was going to see how many orgasms I could bring you first."

He kissed the opposite thigh now, sucking on her skin before nipping lightly. She nearly came off the bed. When she did, he slipped his fingers farther inside.

But before she could savor the fullness, his mouth came down on her. He caught her clitoris in his mouth and sucked.

She released the sheet she'd knotted in her fists, spearing her hands through his damp hair. He was relentless; licking, stroking, sucking. She felt yet another orgasm building.

Elijah didn't let up, tormenting her with his mouth, his fingers working deeper inside.

And just before she went over the edge, he pressed his mouth harder against her and swirled his tongue.

Rachel swallowed a scream.

He moved up over her then, his mouth pausing to tease her breasts before he finally entered her. She marveled at the delicious sensation of being filled. Completed.

"Breathe," Elijah murmured.

Only then did she realize she still held her breath. She relaxed and moved her hips. He drew back and flexed in. The move sent nerve riots across her heated skin.

She wrapped one leg around his waist, taking him even deeper. "Come with me," she begged.

In response, he braced his hands at her sides and started pumping in and out, faster, harder, until reality exploded in a shimmer of sensation.

FIFTEEN

Mason Wright picked up his phone, but the caller was not who he expected.

"It's Thurston Benjamin."

"Senator. Always a pleasure to speak with you. I trust all is well?"

"Spare me your bullshit, *Reverend*. We both know this isn't a social call."

Reaching across his desk, Mason grabbed a lemon drop. "That hasn't prevented us from keeping our interactions amiable."

"That was then. Now? Let's just say you no longer have my nuts in a vise."

The words made Mason choke on the candy. "I don't exactly follow."

"We're making a new deal. My rules. I want the original video. In exchange, I'll destroy the information I've been given on the adoption scam Shepherd's Cross has been running. I've got the names of thirty-three young women who've been conned into giving up their babies. Even if the church survives the lawsuits, they'll never regain credibility. Like politicians, churches and church leaders are held to a higher standard. There are no second chances."

The news had Mason's shoulders sagging with relief. He'd warned both Richard Wetherington and William Hanson that sooner or later, someone would put two and two together on the adoptions.

Mason had nothing to fear in that area. Except that the public scrutiny could expose other areas. Areas where he had more to lose than others.

Shutting his eyes, he drew a deep breath. Mason had already planned to announce his retirement at the end of the month. Once he was out of the country, he'd have no more need for the video. No more need for the favors the video had granted.

"May I ask how you came across this data?"

"Does it matter?" the senator snarled.

"I simply want to make certain no one else stumbles across it in the same manner."

"It wasn't easy to uncover. I had to hire several private investigators and each uncovered a different segment. No one knows the full story but me. Now, do we have a deal or not?"

"We do. How would you like to proceed?"

"It's difficult for me to travel at this time. My wife is in the hospital."

"I could come to Richmond early next week, if that suits you?"

"The sooner the better."

"I'll have my secretary call your office in the morning."

Both men hung up simultaneously. Mason wondered if the senator had the same sense of relief he did.

And on the heels of that relief came a sudden

urge to end it quickly. All of it. Pulling out his appointment calendar, Mason started jotting notes. He'd announce his retirement tomorrow, go see the senator the day after, then leave the country— ostensibly to bid the missions farewell.

Standing, he hurried toward his file room. He'd begin taking this stuff home with him tonight. Unlocking the file cabinet, he removed Cindy Benjamin's file.

The senator was foolish to believe Mason wasn't going to copy this disc before turning it over. One never knew . . .

And he'd already given the senator most of the original documents from Cindy's counseling file. Most damaging had been the ones that described Cindy's reaction to discovering she was pregnant by her stepfather. She'd been despondent, suicidal.

Mason had arranged the abortion and earned Cindy's unwavering trust. Of course, the drugs had helped. And Cindy had never known Mason made the video after purposely encouraging her to confront her stepfather.

If only Emily hadn't pressed the girl to try again, to see both of her parents. Mason had tried to catch Cindy, to stop her . . .

Her death was an accident.

Shaking his head, Mason returned to his desk to copy the CD. But nothing came up on the screen. He checked the directory, which showed the disc was blank.

He pulled it out to examine it closely. That was the second time this week this had happened.

Shit! He flew back to the file room and opened the other cabinet, then he carried all three boxes to his desk. He opened the first one and checked several discs at random, but the fact they all played fine didn't ease him.

The senator's words, "I hired private investigators," were troubling. Had someone been snooping around on campus?

Earlier this week, Mason had had a feeling something was out of place in the drug safe, but he'd shrugged it off. Now . . .

Once again, Mason headed to the small room, but this time he looked at everything skeptically. Was anything else out of order? Or missing?

He scrutinized the drug cabinet. He'd just been in it this morning, so everything looked unchanged. Still, he'd empty this room completely tonight.

He reached under the shelf for the disc he kept hidden there, grateful that he hadn't stored it with the others.

But his hand came up empty.

Swearing, Mason squatted down. The plastic sleeve he'd taped underneath the shelf was empty.

Someone had stolen his drug formulas.

Damn it! Yes, he had copies, but he hadn't filed the patents yet.

If some schlock investigator the senator hired had stumbled across his room, perhaps they didn't even know what they'd found. Which meant Mason had to find out whom the senator had hired . . . no matter what the cost.

First thing in the morning he'd go to visit the senator. But in the meantime, he needed to let Kito know that someone might have seen their videos so Kito could take steps to protect their other interests.

SIXTEEN

Howie slipped her a folded piece of paper at breakfast the next morning. Anticipation elevated her pulse. Was it a note from Elijah?

He hadn't stayed long after they made love last night. She had briefed him on the dinner at Kito's, then given him the media from the cameras. "I think I caught the combination to the door lock, but I'm hoping some of these will confirm it."

Elijah had shaken his head. "You're not thinking about going back there at night, are you?"

"No, but if an opportunity presents itself while I'm there, I'll take it."

"You're taking a big enough risk getting these photos and planting the electronics. Hell, I told Dwight I didn't even want you doing that much."

With that, Rachel knew why Dwight had waited and let Howie tell her about Kito's PDA. Elijah wouldn't like knowing he'd asked her to do that, either.

Outside, she opened the paper Howie had given her. Four digits were scribbled. *7 7 3 4*. The combination. He had been able to read it from the pictures.

"Alisa!"

Rachel turned as Martha Robbins hurried up to her. "Can I enlist your help in the office again this morning?" Martha asked. "I accomplished more yesterday than I have all month. Thanks to you."

"I'm glad to help. I'm supposed to have lunch at Mr. Mzuzi's today, but I could cancel—"

"Don't do that. Just take off whenever you need to." The woman smiled. "And I have a favor to ask."

Rachel looked at her expectantly.

"I told Tom that with your help I could probably get all caught up, and he offered to ask Mason Wright if you could stay on here a few extra days. Would you mind?"

What could she say? "Of course not."

Since her jewelry looked out of place with the khaki pants she wore at the mission, Rachel changed into a simple dress before going to lunch. To keep it more casual, she wore a pair of flats and limited her jewelry to one necklace and the watch.

At eleven o'clock, Kito's driver pulled up to her cabin, bearing a fresh bouquet of roses.

"Mr. Mzuzi has been delayed but asks that you wait for him at the house."

"Let me put these in water." Stepping back inside, Rachel dumped the flowers in the sink. The news that Kito was running late didn't bother her in the least. The less time she spent with the man, the better.

At the compound, the driver showed Rachel into the same sitting room.

"I'll have tea sent in."

A few minutes later, Kito's housekeeper appeared with a tray.

"May I wait for Mr. Mzuzi in the garden?" Rachel wasn't certain if the woman spoke English.

The woman bobbed her head. "Garden? Yes."

Carrying the tray, the housekeeper led Rachel down the hall, past Kito's office, to a smaller dining room off the kitchen. The table was set for two, indicating they'd probably have lunch there.

More French doors opened onto a small patio overlooking the gardens. A wrought-iron table and chairs were tucked in the corner.

The housekeeper set the tray down. "Mr. Mzuzi will be here in twenty minutes."

"That's fine," Rachel assured the woman. "Don't worry about me."

As soon as she was alone, Rachel walked into the rose garden. It was much larger and more elaborate than she'd realized last night. Elaborate stone fountains and statues were everywhere.

She slipped around the rose-covered trellis that shielded the doors to Kito's office. Bending to admire the flowers, she peeked in the windows, confirming it was empty. Sucking in a deep breath, she punched in the numbers on the keypad.

Inside, she went straight to Kito's computer and slipped the square Howie had given her into the empty PDA slot. A green light lit on the cradle, then began flashing.

She counted seconds. "Come on, damn it," she whispered. Howie said ten seconds.

From outside she heard voices. *Kito!* He was back early.

Snatching the square, she hit the reset button of his computer. She moved away from the French doors, toward the interior door leading to the hall. She pressed her ear to it before letting herself out. In another part of the house, a door slammed as Kito yelled at the housekeeper.

Moving quickly, Rachel slipped into the bathroom and slid the square into her bra. That had been too close. To make noise, she flushed the commode and turned on the faucet to wash her hands. Then she opened the door.

"Kito! I mean, Mr. Mzuzi!" She backed up, pretending to be startled.

"I didn't mean to frighten you." A strand of hair had worked loose from his ponytail. He tucked it behind one ear and smiled. "And you must always call me Kito."

Behind him, Rachel saw the housekeeper's relieved look. She took the arm Kito offered and let him lead her back out to the gardens.

"I hope our plans didn't interfere with anything important," Rachel began.

"Our luncheon was far more important, and I apologize for my delay." He held the door for her. "Have you already seen the garden?"

"No. I slipped back in to powder my nose. I hadn't even poured tea yet."

"The maid will bring a fresh pot. In the meantime, allow me to give you the grand tour."

This time, instead of offering his arm, Kito took her hand and entwined their fingers. Rachel wanted to pull away, but knew she couldn't without making him wary. And after almost getting caught earlier . . .

When they reached the far side of the garden, she pointed to the outbuildings. "Your estate is larger than I realized."

"Those are guest quarters. Mostly for my staff. I am quite private and don't like a lot of strangers in my home. Come. Let's eat."

As they dined on salmon and fresh salad, Kito told her stories about some of the archeological sites that had recently been discovered on his property.

Shortly before two, he walked her to the foyer. "I'm going to visit one of those sites in a few days. Would you join me?"

"Mrs. Robbins has me on a project that needs to be completed before I return to school," Rachel said. "Unfortunately, I won't have any free time."

"You must give me a chance to change your mind, Alisa. You've left me awestruck. Have dinner with me tonight?"

She glanced at him. "Alone?"

"As alone as we can get with my staff," he teased. "But, yes, alone. And I sense your concerns, so let me assure you I am a perfect gentleman." He was holding her hand again, stroking his thumb across her knuckles. "I only want a chance to charm you, as you have charmed me."

She wanted to say no. But she didn't. Perhaps tonight she could get him to show her more of the compound. "Very well."

Kito brought her hand to his mouth and pressed a kiss to it. "Until tonight."

* * *

Rachel found Martha at the dining hall, mediating an argument between the mission's cook and the native helpers. Both sides were threatening to walk out.

"This is going to take a while." Martha reached in her pocket and handed Rachel a key. "If you want to go on to the office, I'll be there shortly."

As soon as she reached the office, Rachel tugged the square from her bra and turned on Tom's computer. Because she'd been interrupted, she wasn't certain if she'd gotten anything from Kito's computer. Or if she had, she might have lost the data yanking the chip loose.

"Let's see if this works."

She slipped the square into Tom's hot-sync cradle and uploaded it. The screen flashed several times, then beeped. Grabbing the mouse, Rachel looked at the main directory and selected Calendar.

Kito was obviously a busy man. Each day was packed with notations, but most of his abbreviations made little sense.

The Contacts section, however, was loaded. She scanned the list. Under *B* were listed several banks, a string of numbers following each. Account numbers? She'd bet Dwight would wet his pants when he saw this.

She continued through the list, wondering how many of these people were involved with the pornography. Or were they involved in some of Kito's other endeavors? Bottom line, they were probably all in cahoots in one form or fashion.

Except for one.

Why is Dwight Davis's name in here?

She sat back, stunned, then quickly went through

the rest of the names. None of the others were familiar.

Damn Dwight! This was why he hadn't said anything about downloading the PDA in front of Elijah. The bastard was playing the same game the senator had.

Only worse.

She thought back to what Elijah had told her about Kito selling out their location, where Nick and the others were killed. Kito had to have received that information from someone to begin with. Had Dwight sold his own men out?

She thought of the photographs of her brother he'd given her in Los Angeles. She'd actually softened toward Dwight after that. *When in reality, he killed Nick just as surely as if he'd personally detonated the bomb.*

That meant he was also responsible for Elijah being held. But since Dwight had eventually sprung Elijah from prison, no one suspected a thing. That fucking bastard!

Footsteps sounded in the halls. Rachel stuffed the square back in her bra and hit the power switch. She'd have to come back later to erase the data from Tom's computer.

Diving for a stack of requisitions that needed to be filed, she spread them out on the file cabinet, pretending to sort them.

Martha breezed in. "Aren't you a busy little thing!"

If you only knew, Rachel thought angrily.

Martha got called away later that afternoon. Rachel took advantage of the moment to search for Howie. She found him in a tiny office, surrounded by computer monitors and sound boards.

"I need to talk to Elijah."

Howie looked concerned. "I can get him a message."

She shook her head. Until she talked to Elijah, Rachel didn't want Howie to know she'd downloaded Kito's PDA. Howie was loyal to Dwight, and if he tipped him off . . .

She forced a calm she didn't feel. "It's personal."

Howie's look changed to one of annoyance. "We're on a job here, remember? Focus on planting bugs and downloading the PDA. Then you'll have all the time you want for *personal* stuff."

She ignored the slam. "Can you get ahold of him before I go to Kito's?"

"It's unlikely, but I'll try. Worst case, I'll see if he can meet you again tonight."

She left Howie's office feeling deeply dissatisfied. The last thing she wanted to do was have dinner with Kito, but to back out of it now might raise suspicions.

Rachel filed papers until late, then headed back to her cabin. To her dismay, she found a note tucked in her jewelry box. Elijah had been there and she'd missed him. So much for Howie acting as if he couldn't reach him!

Sorry I missed you. If I don't make it back before six, I'll be here tonight.

She dressed in a hurry, then paced around the small cabin, hoping Elijah would indeed make it back before she left. He didn't. Five minutes be-

fore Kito's driver was due to show up, she scribbled a short note and left it in the same place. Just
in case Elijah came by after she left.

Don't trust Dwight. He's in Kito's PDA.

Kito Mzuzi met the blond man at the airstrip.
The blond handed him an envelope. The one he
received in return was much fatter.

"Another excellent job, Mr. Kowicki," Kito said.

"Yeah, well, next time you want me to play bodyguard for a preacher, it will cost extra."

Kito smiled, knowing there wouldn't be a next
time. "Take a little time off to relax and enjoy.
We'll be filming in three days."

The blond grinned at the news. "I'll see you
then."

No, you won't. Kito watched the plane take off.
By nightfall, the other man would be dead. He
knew way too much.

Besides, he'd been sloppy and had almost gotten them caught.

Mason Wright had called in a panic last night,
concerned because someone had been snooping
around in his office. While Mason didn't come
right out and say someone had stolen his drug for-
mulations, Kito knew that was what really bothered
the man.

Mason would shit if he knew Kito now had those
formulas. Which meant there was no longer any
need for Mason, either.

Climbing back inside his car, Kito poured a
drink, eager to study the drug formulas. To see
what they'd been doing wrong.

He'd spent a lot of money trying to replicate Mason's drugs, only to find out that a few of the ingredients were mysterious. They'd also been damn important. Without them, the girls had not performed the same. Two had died.

But now . . . The formulas presented a whole universe of new opportunities. He was growing tired of doing the movies, and already had a producer lined up to buy him out.

Kito had known all along there would be more money in drugs anyway. And after his own attempts at copying the formulas, he knew no one could rip him off. He'd own the market.

The thought made him smile. Things were definitely looking up. He had a new business venture that excited him. Same with the cunt. He had yet to figure out what it was about Alisa that was different, but the thought of conquering her had him excited in ways nothing had in a long while.

Tonight he'd have her. Then he'd see how long she held his interest. Who knew? Perhaps she'd be different and last more than a week.

Rachel sensed Kito's excitement the moment he greeted her. He hovered, complimenting her profusely as he led her into the sitting room.

While he poured tea, she took a chair in the corner, not wanting him to sit too close. When he walked toward her with a cup and saucer, she noticed another thing. His erection. She quickly averted her eyes.

Coming here tonight was a big mistake. She

eyed the tea he handed her, suddenly suspicious. Was it drugged?

"How was your afternoon?" he asked.

She feigned a sip. "Busy. And yours?"

"I got very little accomplished. Thanks to a certain someone distracting my thoughts."

"I suppose you'll be relieved when that certain someone departs." It was difficult to smile. "So you can work uninterrupted."

"Actually, I'm hoping to change your mind tonight about going to the archeology sites with me." Kito leaned forward. "To that end, I intend to charm you with fine food and excellent company. You'll be begging me to let you stay."

Not on your life.

The only begging Rachel would be doing was later. With Elijah. She wanted out of the mission. Kito was getting too close for comfort. Keeping up a front tonight was going to be tough enough.

His housekeeper appeared, silently signaling that their meal was ready. Kito offered his arm. "I thought we'd eat early tonight so we could have more time afterward."

In the dining room, his housekeeper served them and promptly disappeared after filling their water glasses.

Kito raised his wine glass. "Might I propose a toast?"

While he had offered her wine earlier, Rachel had refused. Still, she picked up her water goblet.

Smiling, he switched glasses, picking up his water too. "To the most beautiful woman I've ever seen. May she grace my house with her presence for a long time to come."

Rachel sipped the water. Since the housekeeper had poured them both from the same pitcher, she was sure it was safe. What she'd have to watch was later, if Kito offered drinks after dinner.

Tonight, they dined on roast duck glazed with cranberries. She ate small bites, unable to swallow much. Kito talked almost nonstop, which was a relief because all she had to do was nod her head.

Rachel was halfway through her meal when she felt it. That sensation of well-being. *I've been drugged.*

The fork dropped from her hand, clattering noisily onto her plate.

"Are you okay?" Kito peered at her, his eyes flashing eagerly.

She shook her head. *Don't blow it.* "I feel . . . a bit queasy. Would you excuse me?"

He stood. "Of course. Do you need help?"

"No. I'm okay."

She felt like she staggered down the hall. Inside the bathroom, she ran water on her wrist. How had he drugged her? His housekeeper had served them from the same dish. Same with her water.

Or had there been something inside her glass that dissolved when mixed with water?

She groaned, felt the trembling. *Elijah.* Her earrings. "I need help," she whispered. "I've been drugged. Elijah, help me!"

A soft tapping sounded outside the door. "Alisa? Are you all right, my dear? Should I call for help?"

The trembling grew worse. Reaching under her arm, she felt around for the microchip and pressed on it. Nothing happened.

The tapping repeated, more urgent. "Alisa! Open up."

Panicking, Rachel ran her thumbnail over the

chip, locating the bubble. Then she pressed as hard as she could.

There was a sharp pain, followed by an awful burning. Mikey hadn't lied.

Behind her the door opened, though she knew she had locked it. Kito stepped in. "Let me help you. Don't fight it."

She tried to back away, but in the small confines there wasn't room.

The trembling had grown violent now. When she tried to form words, she couldn't.

"This will pass," Kito crooned. "You'll be okay in a few minutes. And I'll see to all your needs. Take her upstairs."

Only now did Rachel realize Kito's driver hovered in the hallway.

Run. Fight, she thought. But she couldn't.

The man picked her up and walked down the hall.

Elijah was searching for Howie Stevens. Couldn't find him. He called Dwight back. "The bastard's not answering his phone."

Dwight swore. "Find Rachel and pull out."

"She's with Kito."

Elijah had gone by her cabin moments before and found her note. *Don't trust Dwight. He's in Kito's PDA.* How in the hell did she know that?

She had told Howie she wanted to see Elijah for personal reasons. "Fuck her on your time off," Howie had snapped at Elijah after relaying her message. "We've got a job to do here."

He had wanted to punch Howie. Elijah knew damn good and well Rachel hadn't sent the message to solicit lovemaking. Whatever she had discovered, she obviously hadn't wanted Howie to know about it either.

"I'm sending in backup," Dwight said. "Watch the tracking device to make sure Rachel doesn't leave Kito's compound."

Hurrying back to Howie's cabin, Elijah turned on the laptop. When he found Howie, he'd kill him. Not only was the little jerk supposed to be listening to her conversations with Kito, he was supposed to watch the tracking beacon.

It seemed like it took forever for the laptop to fire up and make a satellite connection.

When it finally beeped, showing it had located her, Elijah's heart stopped. Instead of flashing green, it was flashing red.

Rachel's in trouble!

How long ago had this happened? And had Howie gone to help her?

Rachel slowly became aware of her surroundings. A fire crackled in the background, the heat warming her skin. She was lying on something soft. No . . . Actually, she was curled up on a giant pillow. On the floor. Near a hearth.

And she was naked.

Her senses elevated. The logs in the fireplace were pine, their scent hanging in the air as the sap popped and sizzled, the sound abnormally loud. She lifted her head, her movements awkward. Everything required thought. And thinking was hard. She fought the drug's affects.

"You're awake. Excellent."

Turning, Rachel saw a man sitting on the edge

of the bed. It took her a moment to recognize him. Every time she'd seen Kito, he'd had his hair pulled tightly back in a ponytail.

His hair was loose now and flowed around his shoulders, giving him an effeminate look. Light seemed to radiate around him, like a sparkling aura.

She blinked, willing her vision to clear. He was naked, too. His erection poked straight up from his lap as he fondled himself with one hand. In the other hand he held a riding crop.

He snapped the crop against his leg. "I think you owe me an apology for keeping me waiting." His hand pumped his flesh. "I will give you one chance to show me you're sorry."

The videos . . . Kito expected her to act like the women in those movies. And he no doubt intended to treat her every bit as cruelly. The man was beyond sick and perverted.

She felt no fear, no hesitancy at her nudity. This man was responsible for her brother's death. And for the imprisonment of the man she loved.

He'd pay for both.

Sitting up, she surveyed the room. They were in what she assumed was Kito's bedroom. The fact they were alone encouraged her.

Kito cracked the crop against his leg again. Harder. His hand stroked furiously and she realized he'd enjoyed feeling the sting of the crop.

Rachel eased forward onto her hands and knees. She crawled toward him deliberately, barely inching her way across the floor.

His eyes were glued to her breasts. She rolled her shoulders slightly to enhance their dangling. Anything to keep his attention.

"I've been bad," she began. "But so have you."

Smiling, Kito struck his leg again. He was panting now, practically slapping at his erection.

"You'll pay for that impertinence."

She paused, aware that she was within striking distance. "I'm sorry. I have such wicked thoughts."

"And what thoughts were those, my sweet?" The crop popped his calf, twice. "Be honest or you'll pay an even higher price."

Rachel nodded. "I wondered what it would feel like if the crop struck your cock. Your balls."

Kito's eyes rolled back as his hand closed over his shaft. Rachel didn't waste a moment. She sprang up from the floor, throwing her full weight against him.

Jamming her elbow against his jaw, she heard a satisfying crack. He reacted swiftly, grabbing her as they tumbled off the edge of the bed and onto the floor.

Kito landed on top. He slapped her, the force nearly breaking her neck. She struggled to flip him over and off of her, but suddenly her arms wouldn't cooperate. The drugs . . .

"You little bitch!" He had her pinned to the ground as he tried to force his knees between her legs. She knew rape was only the beginning of what he had in mind.

Behind them, the door crashed open. Footsteps pounded toward them. Rachel's blood ran cold as she realized Kito's men were coming to his aid. She knew what they would do to her.

"Freeze, Kito! And get off her before I blow your goddamn brains out."

Elijah. Rachel struggled to sit up. Someone wrapped a sheet around her, but she kept her eyes on Elijah. He was bearing down on Kito, a gun pointed at his head.

"He didn't touch me," she said.

"That's not what it looked like to me."

"Elijah, please! He didn't—"

The silence grew, heavy and expectant, as Elijah stopped. When he finally turned away from Kito, she released the breath she'd been holding.

She was vaguely aware of other men. Four or five, perhaps. They were all dressed in black, their faces smeared with dark paint, same as Elijah. But the men were all Thai. Who did they work for?

Elijah picked her up and walked out of the room with her, leaving the others to handle Kito. Later, she'd be embarrassed, mortified. For now she was just glad to see him.

"You're sure you're okay?" he asked when they were alone.

"Positive. He drugged me, but I've been aware of almost everything." She nodded back toward the room. "Who are your friends?"

"Dwight sent them."

She stiffened. "But Dwight's—"

"He's one of us, Rach. It's a long story, but Howie Stevens is the one who sold us out."

"Howie? I'll kill him."

"I'll help. As soon as we find him, that is."

"I need to get dressed and go—"

"The only place you're going is back home. With me." Elijah pressed a kiss to her mouth. "I love you, Rachel. When we're back in the States, we're heading somewhere private and we're not leaving until we've hashed out everything." He kissed her again. "And until you admit you love me too."

"I'll admit that now. I love you, Elijah. I want to go somewhere that we can be all alone, too. Just the two of us. We've got so much to make up for."

He kissed her again. "And this time we'll have all the time in the world."

EPILOGUE

Martinique, three weeks later

Rachel raced Elijah back to their bungalow. The loser had to cook breakfast. She hit the door before he did, but since she didn't have a key . . .

He pressed her against the door, kissing her.

She welcomed the onslaught, running her hands down the front of his swim trunks. He was hard. Again.

"If you think you're going to distract me with sex . . . that's fine. But you're still cooking breakfast when we're done."

He chuckled and opened the door. They both stopped in their tracks, realizing someone was inside.

"Perfect timing. Breakfast is almost ready," Dwight said.

Scowling, Rachel moved into the kitchen and grabbed a piece of bacon from the platter. "Damn it, Dwight! This is our honeymoon."

Elijah moved up behind her and filched his own

slice of bacon. "You heard my wife. Get out. After you're done cooking, that is."

"I brought you a wedding present." Dwight spooned scrambled eggs onto plates and divided the bacon between them. "Over there."

Elijah helped carry dishes while Rachel examined the suspicious box sitting on the table.

"Chase sends his regards, by the way," Dwight said.

"I was pleased to hear he entered rehab," Rachel admitted. "But the news he's going to work for you will take a little getting used to."

"Hey, you stole my man. I'm stealing yours. Fair's fair." Dwight sat down and grabbed the salt-shaker. "Now, are you going to open that present or not?"

Tearing the paper, Rachel opened the small box. She drew a sharp breath and withdrew the bundle of letters. She recognized her brother's bold cursive handwriting, her eyes flying to the unmarked stamp.

"Where?" Her voice cracked.

"We found them at Howie Stevens's place. Elijah said they'd all give their letters to Howie to mail."

Rachel looked at her husband. Elijah had told her about their mission five years ago. Howie had been their contact man, the go-between for the agents in the field and Dwight.

"I'm not exactly sure why he held them versus destroying them." Dwight took a bite of toast. "When we find the little bastard, I intend to find out."

She looked away, emotion threatening to over-come her. She had also learned the truth about where Nick had died and why Dwight's name had been in Kito's PDA.

Nick, Elijah, and the other agents had been in Syria at the time, not Afghanistan as the official records reflected. Kito had sold their location to a powerful warlord, who'd taken matters into his own hands and killed the agents while taking vengeance against the Syrian traitors who worked for the CIA. That same warlord had later captured Elijah.

Because the entire incident was sensitive, Dwight couldn't negotiate for Elijah's return through normal channels. Hence Dwight had bought information from Kito about the warlord's son's favorite hangouts.

Dwight had basically kidnapped the warlord's son and traded him for Elijah. Rachel understood that in certain parts of the world, those practices were common.

"I also thought you'd want to know Emily's been released from the hospital," Dwight continued. "She'll be in counseling, along with Alisa, for a long time, but they'll both recover."

Emily had been found in the basement of Kito's house. But the other Circle girls had died.

"Any word on Kito's extradition?" Elijah asked.

"He's fighting it. So are we. Kowicki, the man he sent to Shepherd's Cross, survived the contract hit Kito put on him. He's cooperating fully in exchange for immunity."

Elijah arched a brow. "He got immunity? Out of you? He must really have something."

Dwight nodded. "I'm going to keep him under tight wraps until Mason Wright's trial is over and we resolve the extradition issues with Kito."

Rachel pushed her plate back, her appetite disappearing at the mention of Mason Wright. He'd been arrested at the airport, preparing to flee the country. Knowing he would stand trial gave her a sense of justice. The women he'd victimized deserved no less.

In an effort to throw the spotlight off himself however, Mason had granted an interview from jail during which he disclosed the adoption scam and an even more startling revelation.

Shepherd's Cross used subliminal brainwashing techniques in their music and video products, as well as in their college class videos. It explained Hanson's ever-expanding popularity and exposed their seeming phenomenon of creating the perfect learning environment.

The scandal had rocked the church. The college had closed immediately as angry parents withdrew their children.

The one person Rachel felt wouldn't ever get any justice was Cindy Benjamin. Lenore Benjamin had succumbed to her illness while Rachel was in Thailand. The senator had committed suicide and was eulogized as a man overcome by grief after losing his wife and daughter. In death, he'd been lauded as a hero, which sickened Rachel.

Unfortunately, exposing the senator meant exposing Cindy, who had done nothing wrong.

Rachel held the packet of letters up. "I can't thank you enough for these, Dwight. It's the best wedding present anyone could have given me."

"Oh, that's not your wedding present. This is." Reaching into his pocket, Dwight withdrew a faded Polaroid picture and handed it to her.

Tears welled in her eyes. "Nick."

Elijah leaned in and narrowed his eyes. "Can I see this, sweetheart?"

She watched him take the picture and study it. "What's wrong?"

Elijah glanced at her, then pinned Dwight with a hard glare. "Does this mean what I think it does?"

At Dwight's nod, Elijah handed the photograph back to Rachel. "This picture was taken outside the prison where I was held. It was bombed shortly after I was released. They've since rebuilt it. This is the new prison, Rachel."

It took a minute for the significance of his words to register. This photograph of her brother had been taken *after* Elijah's release.

"Nick didn't die? He's . . . he's alive?"

"This is proof he was alive two years ago," Dwight cautioned. "Where he is now, or if he's even still alive, is unknown. I don't know about the two other men who died with him, either. But you have my word, I will not rest until I find him and we know what happened all those years ago."

Unable to speak, she clutched the picture to her heart as Elijah moved up behind her and wrapped his arms around her shoulders.

Dwight picked up his coffee cup and held it aloft. "Until then, Rachel, keep your hopes and dreams of your brother alive."